HERE'S WHAT CRITICS ARE SAYING ABOUT *TORN*:

"This ambitious, vividly detailed, sometimes dense novel demonstrates that Snodgrass knows his patch of America like Faulkner knew Yoknapatawpha or Donald Harrington knew Stay More." -- *Book Life Reviews Editor's Pick*

"Adding to an already impressive history of this fictional town, this latest intimate and enthralling tale is the best Furnass novel yet, bringing the town so sharply to life that readers easily forget it's fictional." -- *Self-Publishing Review*

"Richard Snodgrass's TORN is unquestionably noir, evoking a very specific industrial small-town America. . . Aspects of this America are so concretely human as to feel mythic.... Languid, evocative, and strangely relatable." -- *Indie Reader*

"This thoughtful and emotionally complex tale (one of many by Snodgrass set in the fictional town of Furnass). . .displays an impressive sensitivity to the profound ways in which a family's present is shaped by its past." -- *Kirkus Reviews*

Torn

Richard Snodgrass

A Novel

Calling Crow Press
Pittsburgh

Also by Richard Snodgrass

Fiction

There's Something in the Back Yard

The Books of Furnass

All That Will Remain

Across the River

Holding On

Book of Days

The Pattern Maker

Furrow and Slice

The Building

Some Rise

All Fall Down

Redding Up

Books of Photographs and Text

An Uncommon Field: The Flight 93 Temporary Memorial

Kitchen Things: An Album of Vintage Utensils

Memoir

The House with Round Windows

Moving the Hat

This book is a work of fiction. Names, characters, places, and incidents are the product of the author's imagination or are used fictitiously. Any resemblance to actual events, locales, businesses, companies, or persons, living or dead, is coincidental.

Copyright © 2025 by Richard Snodgrass

All rights reserved. In accordance with the U.S. Copyright Act of 1976, the scanning, uploading, and electronic sharing of any part of this book without the permission of the author constitute unlawful piracy and theft of the author's intellectual property.

Published by Calling Crow Press
Pittsburgh, Pennsylvania

Book design by Book Design Templates, LLC
Cover design by Jack Ritchie
Cover illustration by Joseph Daniel Fiedler

Printed in the United States of America
ISBN 978-1-7373824-6-1
Library of Congress Catalog Control Number: 2024919425

For Richard Cherney,

    who thought there might be

    more to the story;

And, of course, as with all things,

    for Marty.

The world revolves on misunderstanding,

fueled and generated by the endless search

to be loved.

. . . The time is 1935 . . . early November, which means the start of deep autumn . . . when the mornings are crisp, full of the bone-stiffening chill that won't leave now until April or perhaps even May, when the trees have gone through their displays of red and orange and yellow, the leaves now brown and wadded on the ground turning to mulch, all except the persistent oaks that keep their brown leaves like mementos of lost times through the winter months, dropping them later . . . when the days, already dark, darken further by midafternoon, turning to evening with lights coming on in store windows and streetlamps and in the houses layered up on the side of the hill as workers return to their homes for the night . . . it is the time of the Great Depression, the catastrophic economic downturn in the global economy that began with the stock market crash of 1929 and will continue until the start of World War II . . . it is a time of bank failures when otherwise respectable law-abiding citizens riot trying to get their money from behind locked doors . . . a time when unemployment nationwide reaches 25 percent at its worst in 1933, 15 million in America out of work . . . a time of breadlines and soup kitchens, tent cities and shantytowns, public works projects and the programs of the New Deal . . . Southwestern Pennsylvania, Pittsburgh and the surrounding mill towns up and down the rivers, hit particularly hard because of the predominance of and dependence on the steel industry . . . unemployment here hitting 40 percent and those workers who keep their jobs forced to take pay cuts of up to 60 percent . . . a time when, after decades of perpetual gloom, the killer smoke from the mills that previously blocked out the sun, creating night for day, all the lights of the city turned on at high noon, lifts, and people can actually see the sky . . . in all the mill towns of the area, that is, except in Furnass, a mill town of twenty thousand or so souls along the Allehela River

where it flows into the Ohio River, ten miles upstream from Pittsburgh or maybe it's downstream because the Ohio flows north here for twenty miles before making a left turn toward the West . . . the skies in Furnass during the Great Depression remain blackened, or let's say intensely grayed, heavy, by the smoke and steam from the main industry in town, the Allehela Works of Buchanan Steel, a mile-long steel mill that, though it did not thrive with the Depression, certainly did not suffer that much either . . . after an initial round of layoffs, work at the mill, perversely enough, picked up again in the early thirties, the result of the mill producing a particular grade of steel plate used for military vehicles and ships, a product for which the demand grew with the increased defense spending in response to the aggressions of Germany and Italy in Europe, the growing threat of Japan in the Pacific . . . the prosperousness of the mill affecting the other industries in town that either feed off or support the mill, so that the town never experiences the brutal economic conditions of the rest of the country, of neighboring towns up and down the rivers . . . life in Furnass goes on pretty much as it has for generations, few surprises disturb the life of every day in the town, some might describe as complacent, some might describe as boring, though on this particular day in early November of 1935, with the appearance of a passenger train rolling down the valley following the curves of the winding Allehela, one such surprise, one such anomaly, approaches. . . .

PART I

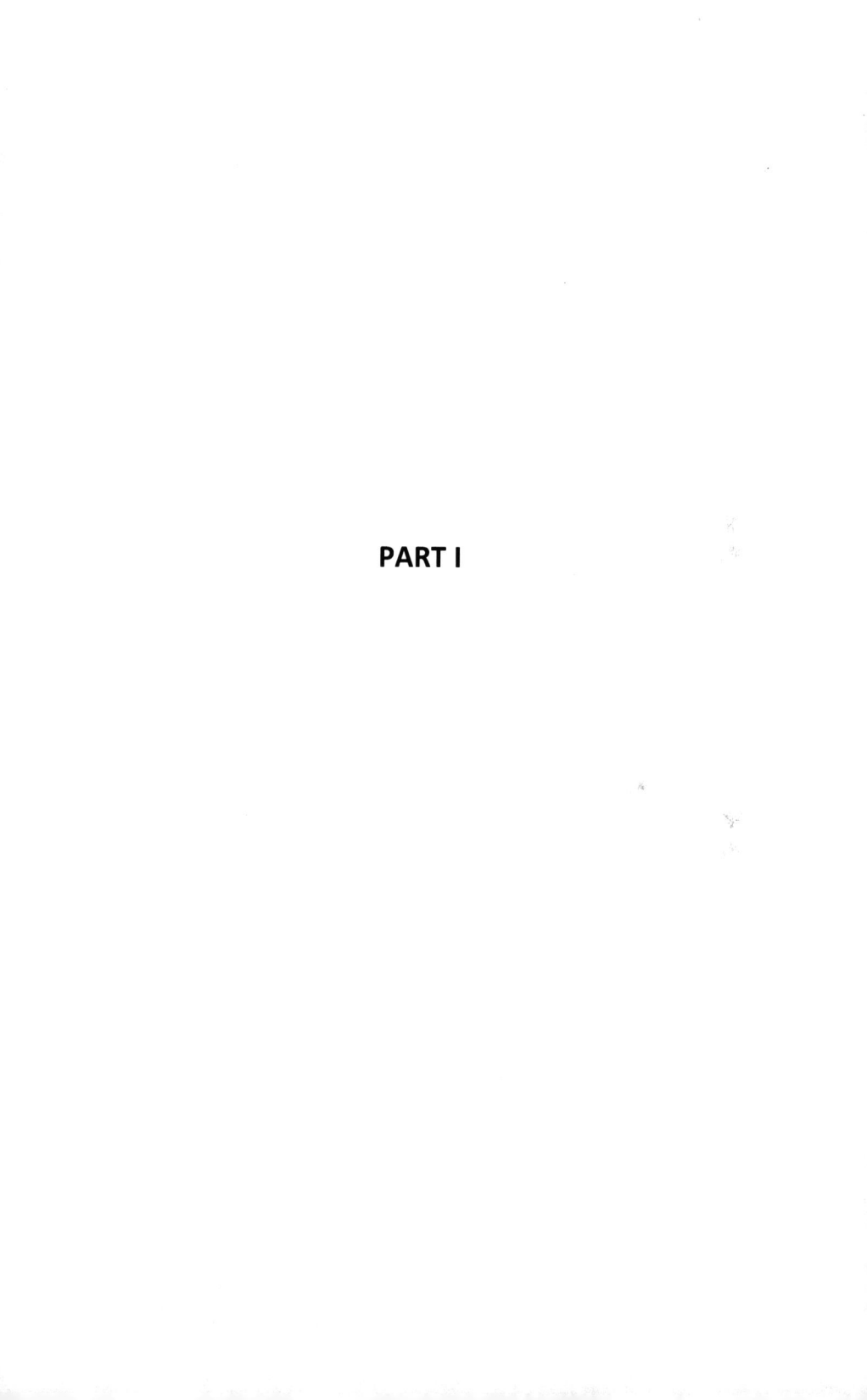

One

As he stepped down from the train and started to walk along the platform, even through the cloth mask that covered his face—all except the eyes, the left one partially collapsed, giving an indication of the turmoil beneath—even with what little was left of his nose and sinuses, John Lincoln recognized the smells. Smoke. Sulfur. Steam. Coal dust. Oil. Slag. Ash. Bringing it all back to him. His hometown. Home. He carried his suitcase, a man in a recently purchased blue wool topcoat, a recently purchased blue gabardine suit, and a gray felt hat, through the station and then across Third Avenue to the Grand Hotel sitting on the corner of Eleventh Street. All just as he remembered. The smoke and steam and fumes, an all-pervasive tinge of gray, at times drifting through the streets like fog, at times settling over the town, lowering between the valley's hills like a lid, dulling the colors, blurring the edges of the narrow peaked-roof houses stacked up the slope of the hillside, a defining presence even as it obscured the town. There was a satisfaction in a way that nothing had changed. An affront of a kind when so many other things were different for him now.

  The hotel was a large building of native stone, five stories tall, with upper-level towers at the corners bulging out over the sidewalk, stone arches over the windows and front door, and Gothic dormers along the high-pitched roof. Grand it was, or supposed to be, the first building that travelers saw when they came to Furnass, the vendors and drummers and executives who came to town primarily for business at the mill, or the Keystone Steam Works, an introduction to what were hopefully perceived as the genteel aspects of the town. Making a good impression. Always good for business. The lobby featured the tall arched windows. Rows of chandeliers, lit now in late afternoon on a

November day. Gothic columns amid groupings of comfortable leather chairs and sofas. His heels clicked along the tile floor as he approached the front desk. The clerk looked up, smiled glassily.

"I would like a room for a few days. Perhaps longer."

"Certainly, sir." The man spun the ledger book on the marble counter around so it was facing John Lincoln. The height of efficiency and impersonal service. Trying not to look at his mask. "Please enter your name while I check to see what we have available."

John Lincoln wrote his name and spun the book back around. The clerk looked at what he had written, looked at John Lincoln, then looked away quickly because of the mask, looked at the ledger again. "Mr. Lyle."

"That's correct."

The man's attitude changed abruptly, from impersonal to much too personal, though perplexed about how to address the man in front of him because of the mask.

"Well, sir, we're certainly glad to have you with us, heh heh. If we had known you were coming we could have certainly prepared something special for you. As it is, we have a very nice suite on the top floor at the corner, you can get a good view of the hills and the river from there."

"I don't need a suite, a room—"

"Absolutely not. We wouldn't hear of it, Mr. Lyle. We certainly hope you'll find it to your liking. Front!"

A middle-aged Black man appeared in full livery, suitably dressed for a coachman to a king's coronation coach.

"Edward, please take Mr. Lyle"—the emphasis on the name was noticeable—"to his room, 5B." Then to John Lincoln, no more able to look at his face now than when he started: "And if there's anything you need or any way that we can be of service to you, please don't hesitate to ask."

Edward took his bag and led the way to the elevator at the rear of the lobby. A wood-paneled, rickety affair—John Lincoln envisaged two trolls on the roof working a winch. On the top floor Edward unlocked the door to 5B—there were only a few doors on the floor—and entered, busily turning on the many floor and table lamps, pulling back the heavy drapes on the windows. If this was considered make-do accommodations, John Lincoln couldn't imagine what they would have given him with advance notice. Two rooms from the Gilded Age. Probably unchanged from the time the hotel was built. In the sitting room plush red upholstered chairs and a love seat. Busy, busy red velvet wallpaper, a dark red patterned carpet. Spindly bookcases with leather-bound books. An easel with a painting of the town on a good day. A chandelier like an explosion of white tulips. Through the doorway he caught a glimpse of a sleigh bed the size of a car. More busy wallpaper and carpet. The focal point of the suite being the circular tower area in the sitting room at the corner of the building.

Edward placed John Lincoln's suitcase on a rack in the bedroom, took a look around to make sure all was in order, then returned to him in the sitting room. The man didn't shy away from looking at him, unlike the desk clerk, but it seemed more like he was trying to see around the mask to discover what was behind it. John Lincoln tipped him—very well; he figured if they were making a big to-do about the Lyle connection, he would play along—which Edward accepted with practiced nonchalance.

"Let me ask you, Edward. Where would you recommend for dinner?"

"Call me Eddie. They like to be a little pretentious around here. And you can't do better than Anna's Parlour, right off the lobby. Best food in town."

"Good to know. Thank you."

Eddie started to leave, then looked back. "May I ask you a question, Mr. Lyle?'

John Lincoln nodded, curious.

"This," Eddie said, his hand circling in front of his face. "Was that from the Great War?"

"Yes."

"I thought it must be. A lot of that went on, back then. What happens when you have to poke your head up out of a trench to do anything. Does it hurt? If you don't mind me asking...."

"You were there?"

"Yes, sir. Ninety-Second Division, 184th Brigade, 351st Machine Gun Battalion."

"Machine gun battalion. Then you know as much as anything I could tell you."

"Deeds, not Words."

John Lincoln knitted his eyebrows, canted his head, looked at him questioningly. Was that directed at me?

"The division motto. Always seemed like a good idea to live by."

"Yes," John Lincoln said, and indicated the conversation was over.

When he was alone in his room, he took off his coat and hat, put them in the closet. Force of habit from years in the army, everything in its rightful place. He decided he'd unpack after he ate, he realized how hungry he was. In the bathroom he washed his hands, then slowly raised his head to look at himself in the mirror. To see what others saw. A man in a mask. It sounded glamorous in Dumas, Poe. The reality being something else. He was going to have to get used to the stares here; after years of being sheltered in army posts and military hospitals, he'd have to get used to people afraid to look at him, people unable to stop looking at him. He sighed. No help for it, they certainly didn't want to see him without it. That was hard enough for him at times.

He ran a check to make sure he had everything he'd need, wallet, room key, identifications, then left the room, pressed the button for the elevator. Another bellman he hadn't seen before arrived, though the same reluctance to look at him, the same peeks. As John Lincoln crossed the lobby, Eddie, at his bellhop stand, touched his forehead, a kind of salute. John Lincoln maintained his reserve, only a slight nod in recognition. Anna's Parlour was dark. Low ceiling. Dark wood paneling. Globes and sconces that seemed to glow more than give illumination. Dividers with etched-glass panels along the top. The room like an exclusive men's club, befitting the clientele mainly of business travelers and executives. There were only a few tables occupied, a few drinkers at the bar. A woman was at the maître d's podium making entries; when she saw him approaching, she smiled, put down her pen. Looked directly at him. Never flinched.

"Hello. Table for one?"

"Yes. Please."

"Certainly, Mr. Lyle." She gathered up the meal and beverage menus, then regarded him again. "You know, I'm thinking, eating with that mask is probably a bit of a challenge. How about if I put you in your own section. That way you could even take off the mask if that would be easier for you to eat."

"I'll keep it on, thank you. I wouldn't want to scare the server."

"I'll be serving you," she said matter-of-factly, not unfriendly, "and it would take a whole lot more than that to scare me. I'm Anna. Follow me, please."

She was in her early forties, sturdy not heavy. Attractive, not pretty. Her brown hair unfashionably long with brushed-out waves, a deep side part, curls bobbed at her shoulders. Spectator pumps. A light gray wraparound sheath dress, padded shoulders, a stripe of white piping down the front as if to say OPEN HERE, large white buttons all the way down. All business, no fluff. She led him to a small table in a rear section, away from the rest of the diners, facing away from the front, close to but not next to a window so he could see out but passersby wouldn't necessarily see in. She got him seated, arranged his place setting, handed him the menus. Still looking at him straight on. Unfazed.

"We'll call this your section and your table, as long as you're with us."

"I didn't mean to insult—"

"Good heavens, you're going to have to do better than that if you're going to insult me."

She listed off the specials; he decided to forgo the menus and chose the chicken marsala, fingerling potatoes, and green beans. A beer, whatever she thought best.

"I'll get this in right away, you must be hungry after traveling."

She returned in a few minutes with a stein of beer. And a straw. "I thought maybe this would make drinking easier."

"Actually, I've learned to carry my own." From his inside pocket he produced a stainless-steel straw, holding it up proudly for her to see."

"Good for you. I like a man who comes prepared. But I'll bet it's been a long time since that's been washed properly." Before he could stop her, Anna took the straw and disappeared with it into the kitchen. When she returned, he had to admit it had a noticeable shine.

After bringing his food, she left him alone. She was right, it certainly was easier to eat without the mask—regardless, his face was such that he always needed the straw to drink—and, after looking around to make sure no one could see him, he unhitched the strap from his right ear and let the mask dangle down his shoulder while he ate. As if she knew when he was done and masked up again, Anna appeared with a dessert menu. He said he was full and only ordered coffee.

She cleared the dishes, brought his coffee, asked if there was anything else he would like, if she should charge the meal to his room.

"That would be fine. Five...."

"Five-B. I'll bring you the bill."

When she returned with it and he had signed it, he asked, "How did you know my room number? And how did you know my name was Lyle?"

"I saw when you arrived and you looked interesting. So I checked you out after you registered. It's my job to know things around here, you know. And Eddie tells me you were a war hero."

"No. The furthest thing from it. And I wish you'd do anything you can to keep him from saying things like that."

"But you were injured in the war...."

Torn

John Lincoln sighed. "Early on my face was . . . damaged and the army used me in a new technique to treat such wounds. Then they carted me around to demonstrate the technique to battlefield surgeons. After the war they had me visiting veteran and army hospitals as an example that there was life after such a catastrophic injury."

"And is there? Life after such a catastrophic injury? Good life, I mean."

He looked at her. Surprised at the bluntness. And oddly put at ease by it. Liked that he didn't have to pretend. "There can be, I think."

"I'm sure you're working at it. I'll be leaving soon for a couple of hours. Is there anything else I can get you?"

And then she was gone again. He sat for a while longer, finished his coffee—with his freshly washed straw—and left. In the lobby he picked up copies of *The Pittsburgh Post-Gazette*, *The Pittsburgh Press*, and *The Furnass Chronicle* and took them up to his room—another bellman he didn't recognize operating the elevator, again calling him Mr. Lyle and giving his floor before John Lincoln could say it, again ducking away from looking at him. It was dark already in the November late afternoon, early evening at five o'clock, the lamps in his room creating areas of light against the shadows. He wondered what his view was from the tower and turned off the lights in that part of the room, standing in the half circle of windows. The view even with the curtains pulled back appeared as if seen through gauze because of the smoke. Across the street the lights on the train platform extended like a chain along the tracks, the lights of the station spilling out the windows. Somewhere in the darkness beyond were the buildings of the Keystone Steam Works, but he couldn't make them out specifically, the night in that direction dominated by the lights and the glow of the furnaces of Buchanan Steel, the mill extending a mile or so following the curve of the river. Without the lights on in his room, the walls and windows pulsed red and yellow with flare-ups of the Bessemers, the flames of the blast furnace and coke ovens reflecting off the clouds of smoke and steam. No, some things hadn't changed about his hometown. He didn't know whether he was assured or appalled.

Movement out of the corner of his eye. He looked down at the sidewalk in time to see Anna leave the restaurant and come along the front of the hotel, carrying a white food container with a wire handle; she disappeared briefly under the overhang of the tower, appeared again starting up the slope of the side street. She passed the alleyway, then disappeared again, turned into a house a few doors up from the hotel. Gone. Anna. Was she delivering food to someone? Did she make house calls? He was surprised at his curiosity about her. Her curiosity about him. *And is there life after such an injury? I'm sure you're working at it.* Interesting woman. Ah well. Not for the likes of him. If he leaned closer to the windows he could see farther up the hill, the lights of the little houses spaced across the darkness, the glow of the streetlights along the main street, the scene veiled with the smoke and steam. He wondered if one of the lights was hers, if she lived somewhere in town now or if she had moved away; for that matter he didn't know for certain that she was still alive. No, he was certain she was alive, he would know in his bones if she was gone. Mary Lydia. He wondered if she knew in her bones that he hadn't died when they said he did, wondered how she would take to seeing him again—he liked to think of her running into his open arms but he knew that was unrealistic, if for no other reason than his disfigurement; he had to expect shock, tears, disbelief, endless questions, before any joy of his homecoming; he could see her, her hands to her face, the sympathy in her eyes for what he had gone through, her great relief that he was alive, that he had come back. After all this time, he was this close to seeing her again. Sometimes he wondered if she was the only reason he had come back. He straightened up, stretched; it had been a long day. With the dancing flames all around him, the light flickering on the walls, he understood why the windows had such heavy drapes. He turned the lamps back on, closed the drapes on all the windows,

Torn

and settled down to read the news of the day.

Two

When Anna got home, she found Lois, the day nurse, in the living room, sitting beside Warren's hospital bed, the two of them listening to the radio, *Backstage Wife* or *Pepper Young's Family*, she never listened to the programs long enough to tell them apart. At least she thought Warren was listening, sometimes it was hard to tell if he was awake. She toodled her fingers to Lois, stopped in her bedroom to put on her slippers, then went on to the kitchen. When she bought the house soon after Warren's accident, when it was obvious he was going to need continual care, she remodeled the living room into his bedroom, converted the dining room into her own bedroom, and put in a downstairs bathroom, convenient for emptying his urine and colostomy bags. As she set about mashing up the food she brought from the restaurant—the day's special, chicken marsala—she heard Lois stirring about, getting Warren ready for the evening, talking to him about what she was doing. She was putting on her coat as she came into the kitchen.

"How is he today?"

"Seems good. Not a peep out of him. My, that smells delicious."

"If I had thought of it, I would have brought you some too."

"Thanks, but I've got my own dinner to fix. Harold's got bowling tonight, and the boys are off somewhere."

"Is Darla taking the shift tomorrow?"

"Yes. I'll be back the day after."

Anna put the finishing touches to her mashing, put down the fork, and dried her hands on a hand towel. "Thank you, as always, Lois. I don't know what I'd do without you." She accompanied her down the hallway to the front door.

"I'm happy to help, Anna." As they passed the doorway to the living room, Lois leaned in. "You be good, Warren. Stay out of mischief."

Richard Snodgrass

The man in the bed gave no indication that he heard her. Lois looked at Anna, gave her a tight-lipped smile, and left. Outside the night sky was roiling red and orange against clouds of steam and smoke, one of the Bessemers in blow several blocks away at the mill. After she watched Lois get in her car, Anna stopped back in the living room to make sure Warren knew someone was still with him. She straightened his covers, kissed him on the forehead, and went back to the kitchen. Ready to spend the next several hours with him until the night nurse arrived and she headed back to the restaurant to close out.

*

Anna O'Brien, née D'Angelis—she still went by Anna D'Angelis professionally; she found soon after she was married that no one sat up and took notice when they heard from Anna O'Brien, not the way they did when they heard from Anna D'Angelis—was born and raised in New York City. Grew up in Little Italy, her family—there was only the three of them, her father, mother, and herself—in a comfortable flat above a grocery store, her father the owner of a successful uptown upscale restaurant that went simply by the name D'Angelis. By her early twenties Anna had worked in every area of the restaurant—busing tables, dishwasher, server, line chef, sous chef, executive chef, maître d', bookkeeper, manager. She thought her life was pretty much lined out for her; she would continue working at the restaurant wherever she was needed, then, when her father retired, take it over as her own. It never occurred to her to question whether she was happy or not; she was content and settled and sure that her life was as it should be. God in His heaven and all right with the world.

Then one night she was cornered in the cloakroom by one of their regulars, a man known to her only as Frankie B. He grabbed her, pressed her back against the rack of coats, began feeling her up and reaching between her legs. Anna responded by kneeing him in the balls, and then for good measure while he was bent over, hitting him in the face with an uppercut, she learned later breaking his nose. When she went to tell her father what Frankie B had tried, her father was horrified.

"You kneed Frankie B? And then hit him in the face? Oh my God, what were you thinking?"

"I was thinking the son of a bitch had it coming. Trying a thing like that—"

"Don't you know who Frankie B is?"

"I know he's the guy who—"

"We know him as Frankie B. He's also known as Frankie Two-Eyes."

"So?"

"So he's Mafia. The mob. He's a made man. Don't you understand, that man kills people for a living?"

"I don't know anything about that. And why would we cater to people like that—?"

Her father sank back in his swivel chair, then leaned forward holding his head. Shaking his head. "I never talked to you about this because I thought you had figured it out. Yes, we got the bluestocking crowd coming here, but our bread and butter is people like Frankie B. Did you think all those Italian men come in here, meet in here all the time, because they like our tomato sauce? They're the mob, Anna. The mob is who financed this place to start with, and keep it going when other places are closing."

"Are you in the mob?"

"No, of course not. I run a restaurant, I run it good. But I know enough to keep on the good side of the people who help me pay my bills. Oh my Lord, I knew Frankie B was interested in you but I never thought he'd try something like this...."

"You knew it? And you didn't say anything?"

"I was going to . . . when I thought the time was right. I didn't know, I thought maybe you . . . might be interested in him . . . or become interested in him...."

"You were going to sell me off to that pig?"

"Not sell you off, I thought—"

She didn't wait to hear what else he thought, she had heard

enough, her faith in him once and for all shattered, never to see the world or people the same way again. She went home and packed a suitcase, took the savings she kept on hand under her bed—she could get the rest from her bank account wherever she ended up—and took a taxi to Penn Station. On the departure board she saw the next train leaving was headed to Chicago. Well, she had heard good things about Chicago, a good restaurant town; she bought a ticket and climbed aboard. The thing was, as she sat listening to the rails click through the night, if Frankie B was as dangerous and powerful as her father thought he was, there was a chance he might come after her, or get somebody there to get back at her. By the early morning, she had decided she was going to have to settle someplace else. Someplace out of the way, less known, easy to overlook. Someplace where she could get lost. After the train left Pittsburgh, she was attracted to the hills and the valleys of the area, Western Pennsylvania, the train heading north a ways then turning to follow the curves of a picturesque river. Before the tracks turned north again along the Ohio River they approached another mill town, the rails traveling along the length of the mill, a row of beehive ovens with glowing hearths, a huge ladle upturned shooting flames fifty feet in the air. She figured it must take hundreds, thousands to maintain a plant like that, men with families, plenty of stores and shops and, yes, restaurants, a place where a young woman with her skills could find opportunities to build a new life. She grabbed her suitcase from the overhead rack and hurried down the steps, the conductor helping her down onto the platform just as the train was starting to pull out. After the last car swung out of sight, she stood on the platform looking at the little town built up the hillside. In front of her across the street was a hotel called the Grand and she headed for it. Chiseled in the headstone above the doorway of the orange-brick train station, its tall swooping slate roof like the illustration for a fairy-tale cottage, was the town's name: Furnass.

 She spent the first couple of weeks exploring her new home.

Torn

The town enchanted her, the steep side streets leading up from the river, the rows of frame houses grappling for a foothold on the slope of the valley's hills, and trees, trees everywhere, lining the streets, filling the backyards, she had never seen so many trees. The life of the small town was entirely different from what she had known in New York, yet for all its strangeness—she loved the strangeness—it was familiar in a way too, the many Italians reminding her of Little Italy where she grew up, as well as the many Poles, Middle Europeans, Blacks. Her first thought was to open an Italian restaurant; there were a number of them already in town, of course, mostly tied to bars, and while the food was certainly good, she knew the recipes she brought with her would top anything available. But it occurred to her, returning to her room every evening, that the hotel lacked its own restaurant; all that was available was a coffee shop and its food, outside of breakfasts—and they weren't that special—was mainly in the way of snacks. There was certainly the clientele who would appreciate fine food—the hotel was always busy, to say nothing of the number of, if not well-to-do, at least better-off people in town, and there were a surprising number for a mill town, businessmen and professionals of one sort or another, plus those associated with the college—who would take advantage of a first-class dining room. Without such a restaurant, how could the hotel call itself Grand?

    The hotel's office was on the mezzanine overlooking the lobby. One morning, dressed in a blue wool suit she bought special for the occasion—and in the process made a new friend and business connection of Marie Wisniewski, the owner of Marie's Moderne Dress Shop on Seventh Avenue—she marched up the hotel's sweeping marble staircase to the manager's office and presented herself to the manager, a man named Harold Gilliman. He was a tall silver-haired gentleman who wore his pretentions of style on the sleeve of his European-tailored double-breasted suit. Anna recognized him as a man who liked men, though from her experience in New York she had found such men were often more open to a woman, identifying with them from their own proclivities. Anna spelled out her ideas, that the hotel needed an upscale restaurant to fulfill its image, that they had the clientele to support it, that such a restaurant would have the market in town all to itself, that there was no place in Furnass that could begin to compete with it.

"That's all very well and good—Miss D'Angelis, is it? And the owners, I must say, might very well go along with such an idea, you present a good case for it. But where would we find someone who could not only oversee the construction of such a facility, but manage it once it was up and running?"

Anna smiled. From the briefcase she also purchased specially for the presentation—making another new friend and business contact, Paul Murawski, owner of Murawski's Books and Stationery—she produced sketches she had made of what the interior would look like, an estimate of what it would cost to remodel the first floor of the hotel to accommodate it along with the necessary appliances and furniture, sample menus of the food they would serve—with the notation that she already had the recipes for such fare and had prepared such dishes herself—and estimates of the expenses and profits of the facility for the first five years, speculating that it would be self-sufficient in two years and turning a sizable profit in four. The name of the restaurant would be Anna's Parlour, giving a sense of intimacy that businessmen would appreciate, with the British spelling of *parlour* to telegraph to the general public that this was an upscale establishment. Harold Gilliman blinked. Beamed. After he took her proposal to the owners, the plan was approved after only a month's consideration. By the holiday season the following year, Anna's Parlour was attracting not only travelers and townsfolk; people were coming from nearby towns and even taking the train from Pittsburgh and back to dine at Anna's. It didn't hurt that Harold Gilliman's, let's say community, adopted the place and made it more than fashionable. In the era after the Great War that gave rise to the *bee's knees* and the *cat's meow*, Anna's Parlour was the place to be.

Torn

Over time the Parlour also became the place where everyday folk in town would celebrate special events—wedding dinners, baby showers, anniversary get-togethers. But it was obvious from its high prices and the usual clientele who could afford them that the establishment wasn't meant for everybody, meaning the working class in town. The thing was, Anna discovered she didn't enjoy that much being around the airs and pretensions of the very people for which she designed the Parlour. She missed being around the sort of plain folks she grew up with in Little Italy, she missed hearing all the gossip, the latest on Mrs. Mariani's baby, that Guido Mancini was arrested again for being drunk and beating his wife, that Bella Bodnar was seen dating Tony Mantucci. Fact was, she began to find the atmosphere of Anna's Parlour to be a bit stuffy and stifling. So when the weather was good she would take walks during the afternoons, just to get away, have some time for herself, sometimes climbing the hill up to the main street to do a little shopping, but more often walking along Third Avenue, past the orange-brick buildings of the Keystone Steam Works to the Allehela Works of Buchanan Steel, or simply *the mill* as it was known in town, following the wire fence that marked off the mill from the town, watching the goings-on inside.

She had long since recognized that the day she arrived in Furnass was the exception, not the norm; the blue skies and green hills and crystalline air were an anomaly, one of those rare days that occurred in May or June when the low humidity and prevailing winds swept the valley clean of the smoke—a sign she liked to think that was telling her, *This is your place, Anna, you belong here*—that most days in Furnass were like today, hazy and gray, the smoke and steam ghosting the streets, erasing the sky. She understood how people in town lamented the smoke, but to her, in love with her decision to settle here, it added mystery and drama, as enchanting in a way as the photographs she had seen of murky London. A place not meant for the likes of everyone, a curious pride in living where others wouldn't want to. In the same way she understood how those who had grown up in the town, who had lived around the mill all their lives, would take it for granted, might disdain and disparage the mill for the way it dominated the life of the town, the lives of the people who lived next to it, providing them with work and incomes while draining the strength from their bodies until there was little left of them, using them until were mere shells, old men and women standing on street corners and struggling home with shopping bags, living on savings and what was left of their lives. Yet if you asked one of them, chances are, man or woman, they would grip your hand and say, "God bless our Buchanan Steel!"

Yes, she understood the hold the mill had on the workers' lives, she found herself intoxicated with the strength and power of the place, the dominance of the soot-gray buildings, the Bessemers shooting flames into the air as they lolled in their berths, the ladle cars dumping molten slag down the banks of the river, exploding clouds of steam, the screams of the sirens as the blast furnace ladle was tapped, the rumble and clash of the machinery—it all fascinated her, it was like living next door to a dragon that might burst out of its containment at any time and destroy them all. She would walk along the fence watching the work going on inside for as long as she could—she rarely had time to reach the end before she had to turn back.

Then one afternoon in springtime when she was heading back to the hotel, past the block-long orange-brick Keystone Steam Works, a workman came out of one of the open roll-up doors, busy lighting a cigarette, and almost knocked her over.

"Aw shit, I'm sorry, ma'am!"

"You certainly should be," Anna said, righting herself. "The idea, calling me ma'am."

"No, I meant running into you—"

"And saying 'shit' to a lady, that isn't very nice either."

"No. Wait. What?"

Anna, thoroughly enjoying herself, burst out laughing.

The guy said, "Aw, to hell with it," tossed his cigarette away, and went back inside the shop.

Torn

She laughed to herself all the way back to the hotel, his frustration and his attempt to cover it over by hurrying back inside the shop, but she wondered if there wasn't a spark of interest on his part, she was aware that there was for her. She made a point of going for a walk the next day, made a point of walking on that side of the street past the Steam Works, past the open roll-up door, just in case he happened to be around, just in case he wanted to come out and see her. He didn't come out when she passed by, and it was too dark inside to see if he was there or not—she slowed down and glanced inside, but she couldn't very well stare, could she?—but on her way back, half an hour later, there he was, standing in the doorway as if waiting for her.

"You were laughing at me yesterday, weren't you?"
"Yes, I was. And I want to apologize."
"But I was trying to apologize to you."
"So it sounds like the apology ended up with an apology."
"You're doing it again, aren't you."
"Afraid so."
"You don't have to apologize."

They both laughed at that, and the connection between them was made.

His name was Warren O'Brien, he was a mechanic, a valve fitter he said, though she had no idea what that was. But it didn't much matter. Since she was a teenager she had been pursued, chatted up, hit upon, even nearly raped by Frankie Two-Eyes, but she had simply never been that much interested in men, their attentions were more of an annoyance than anything else, threatening to delay her in the things she wanted to accomplish. But Warren O'Brien was different. Standing there on the sidewalk, in his leather apron and work clothes, the backdrop of the work going on in the darkness behind him, she understood what all the fuss was about, understood the feelings behind all those soapy lyrics of all those soapy songs about *love* and *wanting you* and *will you be mine*. Talking to him there, chatting about the most mundane things, she felt a sense of security and release, feelings she was unacquainted with, certainly not since she felt her father betrayed her. In the presence of Warren O'Brien, despite all her accomplishments, she felt like herself; felt that she and Warren O'Brien went together like the ingredients of a good sauce, that they were supposed to be a couple, a done deal.

Fortunately, Warren O'Brien—stocky, solid, a ginger man the same age and height as Anna—had similar feelings, though his were more along the lines of *I want this woman*. Like Anna, he had put off entanglements with the opposite sex, though in his case he followed the customs of the old country, that a man didn't marry until the time was right—though playing around was okay, sowing his wild oats as the saying went, gaining experience as it were in the ways of sex and how to negotiate women, as long as he was careful not to get trapped—the right time being when he was settled in middle age with a steady income and ready to be a family man, whether it meant children or not. They dated briefly though she had one stipulation: they never went to Anna's Parlour. He knew of course what she did and who she was and where she worked, but Anna wanted him separate from the people she had to deal with professionally; that he was a working guy, without the pretensions of the business and privileged clientele she had to deal with daily, was one of his attractions. And they both knew where they were headed, why delay the inevitable? They were married within a few months at Holy Innocents, had the wedding reception to end all wedding receptions in her own River Room—she allowed him in the place this once—and were happily married as the saying goes for seven years. They bought a house on Ninth Avenue above the smoke belt—some people claimed the smoke belt, the area of town that was regularly enshrouded with smoke from the mill, stopped just below Seventh Avenue, though others insisted it ended right above it, noting the main street was as smoky at times as the streets below it stepped down to the river—close enough that they could walk together down the hill to work when the weather was good. At lunchtimes Anna walked over to the Steam Works and the two of them sat on a stack of sheet metal as he ate the hot lunch she brought from the restaurant. After work, they went home together for dinner, then Warren drove her back down to the restaurant and picked her up again after closing. Children weren't out of the question, though if they were truthful, they really liked their life as it was. By this time he had progressed at the Steam Works to senior valve fitter—she still wasn't sure what that meant, what it *really* meant, even though he explained it a dozen times, somehow it just didn't register—and was in line to be a supervisor. That she understood. It meant he was good at what he did and was respected for his abilities, she was so proud of him. Then the accident.

One afternoon, actually only an hour or so after they had lunch together there in the shop, a load of steel from an overhead crane fell on him, crushed him. They said afterward he was lucky to be alive, but Anna had to wonder. Yes, he lived through it, but it took the life out of him. The accident broke close to every major bone in his body; worse, the brain damage left him comatose, in a state not quite a coma but never fully conscious. She thought at times he blinked his eyes to give some meaning, but he never responded to setting up the signals of one blink for yes, two blinks for no. She wasn't even certain he understood what she was trying to do.

But so be it. The Lord giveth, and the Lord taketh away, even though she wasn't sure she believed in the Lord. She certainly had her doubts after this happened. But if this was what they were given, she was determined to make him comfortable all of his days. More important, she was going to make sure he knew he was still loved. She sold the house above the main street and bought one close to the hotel up the hill on Eleventh Street so she could visit him easily during the day. She arranged for nurses to come, one during the day, one overnight, and made it a stipulation among her waitresses that they might be asked to sit with Warren at times during the day if Anna had meetings or was otherwise detained at the restaurant. She remodeled the house to make it efficient for Warren's care, and people who knew her knew to ask about him whenever they saw her.

Her finances were such that she could afford to do all these things; the popularity of Anna's Parlour continued to grow over the years and Harold Gilliman knew to compensate her accordingly. Afford to do it, yes, but it was a stretch, and she was aware that if the restaurant ever started to lose its appeal, she would be in trouble. All of which made her work doubly, triply hard to guarantee its success. The disappointment—no, it was more than mere disappointment, it ran deep in her emotions, seethed there under the surface—was the reaction of the Steam Works. The Keystone Steam Works had always been known for the way it treated its employees; under its founder, Colin Lyle, and then his son, Malcolm, the company compensated its employees well, better than any other industry around, at a time when other companies worked employees like slaves or chattel. When the workers in other companies began to unionize to improve conditions and their standard of living, the Keystone Steam Works took pride that it already provided such benefits as medical care and even pensions—unheard-of at the time—and most of its employees were lifers, starting out as young apprentices and finishing up as journeymen well into their sixties and seventies. You were considered lucky indeed if you went to work at the Keystone Steam Works.

So Anna more or less took it for granted that the company would help her provide for Warren and his care. But not so. The present owner, Gus Lyle, refused to accept that the company was responsible in any way for what happened, even though other workmen bore witness that the load had been incorrectly secured, that the chains from which the load was suspended were worn beyond their safety. The spokesman for the company was a local attorney, David Laughlin, a nice enough individual; she knew him from the many lunches and dinners she served him over the years. He even indicated to her during the hearings and investigations that he was disappointed himself with the company's stance, that it opposed everything the company had stood for in the past. But that didn't change his fierceness in defending his client. The verdict came down that the accident was officially and for all intents and purposes "an act of God." Anna left the courthouse thinking if God not only let such things happen but apparently had a hand in setting them up, she was certain now she wanted no part of Him, would make her own determinations as to the nature of heaven and hell. The latter, incidentally, she thought a fit destination for hypocrites the likes of David Laughlin.

*

Back in the kitchen, Anna put the plate of food and silverware on a tray with collapsible legs, added a glass of water with a straw as well as a glass of wine for herself, and carried the tray into the living room.

"Here we are, sweetheart. Table for one, the best seat in the house. How was your day today, okay? Well, let me tell you about mine—let's do a bite of chicken first, open wide, that's the ticket—the delegation from the Commerce Department arrived to talk to Buchanan Steel, there's seven of them, from Washington, and I swear they not only all dress alike in their blue serge suits, they even look alike, all sort of plump and presumptuous—chew it up good, we don't want it coming back on us, do we?—but we're certainly happy to put up with it all for the money they bring in, unlimited expense accounts, our tax dollars at work—isn't that delicious? That's my father's recipe I brought with me from New York way back when I didn't even know you—and a couple from New Hampshire checked in, here to see some relative or other who's in Onagona Memorial, though I never heard who it was they were seeing. Oh, here's something you'll like—now how about some mashed potatoes and gravy?—Mr. and Mrs. Tortelli, you know from over there on Ninth Street, are having their sixtieth wedding anniversary dinner tonight in the River Room, Brian and Maurice spent most of the day preparing the food, the children—you remember Tony and Angela?—they kept going back and forth as to whether they wanted beef or pork but I settled the whole thing by suggesting chicken in tomato sauce to go along with the pasta—you ready for a drink of water? Here, let me turn the straw around—I'll need to check up when I go back to make sure everything went okay. But, and here's the real news of the day, guess who turned up today out of the blue: John Lincoln Lyle. Wearing a mask to hide his face—now let's try some green beans, I'll cut them small so they're easier to chew—it seems like he's suffered some really catastrophic injury along the way, you can tell from the glimpse of scar tissue underneath the mask, though I haven't got it out of him yet what it is, but don't worry, I will—you're doing really good tonight, darling, let's do some more chicken—you can imagine the chaos his arrival is going to cause, I get the idea nobody knew he was coming, just turned up on his own. I would love to see the look on Gus Lyle's face when he learns his younger brother is back in town, I wonder what effect that's going to have on the Steam Works and all their problems these days—here, let me wipe your chin—yes sirree, John Lincoln Lyle, for twenty years everybody just assumed he was dead...."

Three

When John Lincoln woke the next morning, the first thing he did, before anything else, still in his pajamas and bare feet, was to pull back the drapes from the tower windows. Rather than a wash of sunlight, the grayness of the morning seemed to ooze over the room, making it as gloomy indoors as it was out. Yes, it was just as he thought (as he was afraid of?), there was the river, the hills on the opposite side of the valley, the tracks and the railroad station across the street, the day shrouded in smoke, the colors muted as if seen through the sheers though he had pulled them back from the windows, with no trace of sky; and, if he leaned forward, looking up Third Avenue past the train station, the orange-brick Keystone Steam Works, and of course, farther on, the monstrous black buildings of the mill encased in steam and smoke and flame. He hadn't imagined it, hadn't dreamt it, no hallucination from the drugs, it was true, he was here. Furnass. Dare he say *home*? As he headed back to the bedroom, he turned on all the lamps as he went—they didn't add much in the way of illumination but they made a stab at adding a little cheeriness about the place.

In the bathroom after his basic ablutions, he began the daily necessary ritual of treating his face, using cotton swabs and hydrogen peroxide to clean the seams of scar tissue that covered the exposed sections of dermis and hypodermis. He hadn't told Anna the whole story of his injuries when she asked last evening, and why would he, he barely knew her, no use scaring the poor woman, or worse, eliciting her pity, he had devoted his life avoiding that in himself and others. He only told her that the army had used him in a new technique to treat such wounds, he didn't tell her what that treatment was. The army's idea was to treat severe facial trauma, wounds where the skin and muscle had been torn away, by leaving the layers of skin as well as the cavities and craters under the face mask exposed, sealing off the live skin by cauterization and burning to leave the exposed areas intact, as opposed to some British doctors like Gillies who had worked out ways to close the craters with skin grafts taken from other parts of the body. Initially the army had success with their treatments though they caused incredible amounts of pain in the burnings, hot waxes, and compounds painted on the areas. But the long-term results didn't hold up. In John Lincoln's case, his face eventually was wrenched to the left from the shrinkage of skin and muscle, the nose half-mutilated, only one nostril intact and it at an odd angle, with everything above the mouth, which amazingly was untouched, open, the cheek torn away leaving a gaping hole with exposed muscle tissue, hardened now after many years into a glossy sheen, as well as the openings to passageways leading deeper into the head, the tear looking fresh though in fact it had solidified years before, the eye above half-closed as if in a perpetual wink, caught in a never-ending cringe.

When he was discharged from the army and realized he had to deal with everyday life for the first time in twenty years, as well as get used to dealing with the stares of strangers, he bought himself a full wardrobe of clothes, including casual wear, though today he thought was another day for his suit, more businesslike attire, considering whom he needed to see. Dressed now, mask in place, he left his room and took the stairs down to the lobby, not ready yet this morning to deal with the possibility of confronting other people in a closed elevator, inquisitive bellhops. The lobby was busy and he was able to slip past without being noticed. Inside the restaurant Anna was again at her podium, talking to a trio of businessmen; when she saw him, she deftly passed off the trio to one of the waitresses and motioned John Lincoln to follow her. She led him again to the same table in the unoccupied section, seated him again facing away from the front, made sure that the single place setting was correct.

"Good morning, Mr. Lyle. I hope you had a good night's rest." She handed him the breakfast menu. "Coffee?"

"Oh yes, the stronger the better."

"I'll see what I can do. Are you one of those who like a light breakfast, or something hearty?"

"Remember, I'm coming from the army. . . . "

She laughed. "Then I suggest Number Five, the Railway. Two eggs, pancakes, sausage, ham, your choice of toast."

He agreed, and she went to get his coffee. When she returned she brought him his own carafe.

"So. What's on your agenda today? I imagine you're anxious to see your family and all. Excuse me, I don't mean to be nebby. . . . "

"*Nebby.* I haven't heard that word in twenty years. Now I know I'm home."

She laughed at herself, shook her head. "I guess I'm more acclimated to this place than I realized."

"Where are you from?"

She told him, sketched out how she came to be in Furnass without giving away any of her reasons or details.

"You're a ways from home."

"No, this is my home now. And I expect you're anxious to see your family again, you said they didn't know you were coming."

Torn

"Actually, before I do any of that, my first stop is to take care of some business. Do you happen to know if there's still a lawyer in town named David Laughlin? I remember he used to handle all my family's affairs as well as those of the Steam Works...."

She looked at him, her smile hard to read. Bitter? Ironic? He wasn't sure. She went on, "Yes, there's still a David Laughlin who's a lawyer in town. And he still handles the affairs of the Steam Works and I presume your family."

"Oh, so you know him."

"Yes, I know him."

He noticed she was choosing her words carefully. She thought of something, refilled his coffee.

"Have you had dealings with him? What sort of man is he?"

"He comes in occasionally, has lunch or dinner here with clients. I'm being nebby again, why would you go to see an attorney before going to see your family? Oh, your food is up, I'll be back."

She hurried off, he thought somewhat relieved to get away, returning in a few moments with a tray. She laid out the plates of food, made a mental inventory of the table. "I think you have everything. If you need anything else just let me know. I'll check back." And she was gone again.

He was curious. She raised the question of why he wanted to see David Laughlin before any of his family, then didn't stick around to hear the answer. Maybe she wasn't curious as much as she wanted to direct the conversation away from any connection she had with Laughlin. It was probably just as well, his were private matters, not things he wanted to talk about, especially with a woman he barely knew. He went ahead and ate his breakfast. He took off his mask as the day before, letting it dangle from his left ear down his front; when she returned, she made plenty of noise to let him know she was coming, to give him time to get the mask back in place.

She redd the table for him, leaving his coffee cup and his unfinished toast; she lifted the carafe, judged it was nearly empty, and took it away, coming back with it full again. Then regarded him.

"I didn't mean to imply anything negative about David Laughlin. He's a very fine attorney, and very well thought of in town. I've had some dealings with him, yes, and though the outcome wasn't in my favor I have to say I thought he was very fair and straightforward."

"Well, that's good to know," John Lincoln said. "That's what being around the army for twenty years does for you, you think about things like the territory you're about to enter, the lay of the land, to avoid an ambush."

"It sounds like you're expecting a fight."

"No, no, nothing like that. Well, I guess it's possible. Mainly I'm just on a fact-finding mission, I want to know how a number of things stand with the family before I make direct contact with them."

"I guess I can understand that, given the circumstances of your return and all, Still, I think you'd be anxious to see your mother."

"Missy's not my mother," he said solemnly, looking down at the tablecloth.

"She's not? But I thought—"

"I'm sorry, I shouldn't have said that. In that way. Of course she's my mother, my biological mother. But she never acted like a mother, I think she was absent the day they handed out the mothering instinct. My grandmother's attendant, Perpetual, was more of a mother to me than Missy ever was, she's the one who raised me for all intents and purposes, her and the family's cook at that time, Margaret. Two Black women. Missy made it very clear from the beginning she didn't want any part of taking care of children."

"I never knew Margaret, but I knew Perpetual. I think everybody in town did, though she never came in the restaurant. Some people would say she stayed away because she wasn't sure Blacks were welcome here, even though she was Caribbean. I think it was probably more the case that she wasn't sure that we'd measure up to her high standards."

"She was something," John Lincoln said, thinking for a moment. "You seem to know a lot about my family. I was wondering if you know anything about my sister, Mary Lydia."

"Oh my goodness, that's right, I had forgotten. You're a twin."

John Lincoln only blinked. Smiled though no one could see it.

"I'm afraid I can't tell you very much. I never knew her personally, she wasn't around much when I arrived. I did hear she was married, I believe she lives somewhere south of here, toward Little Washington."

"Ah yes, Little Washington. To distinguish it from Washington, D.C. And of course if you're from this area you say *Warshington*. As for Mary Lydia, you know more about her than I do. I haven't heard anything since I left, of course. She wouldn't very well write letters to a dead man. Nor would a dead man write to her. Something else I can ask David Laughlin about."

What was he doing? Bringing up all these things from his past, talking about them with a woman he barely knew. A woman who was in a position to hear things about everyone in town, know their business. How did he know she wouldn't blab all they talked about to anyone who came in the Parlour?

As if she could read his mind, she said, "I don't want you to worry. Anything we talk about, that's only between us, I won't go repeating anything you tell me."

"No, of course not, I know that."

"No, you don't know that, it would naturally be a concern for you. But I promise you, I don't spread gossip. Yes, I hear most of it around town, but it's only because I don't repeat things that people feel they can tell me things. What you say to me goes no further. Now, I have some other things to do, and you're on your way to scare the pants off David Laughlin. I would love to be a fly on the wall for that meeting. I hope you have a good day."

She smiled at him as if they shared some confidence, placed his bill on the corner of the table, and headed back into the main part of the restaurant. How did she know he was wondering if he could trust her with what they talked about? No matter. For reasons he didn't understand, he did trust her, as if he had known her a long time. How strange.

*

After breakfast, John Lincoln walked up the hill, the four blocks on Eleventh Street, to the main street. It took him a few moments to get his bearings, not from how much the town had changed but from the fact that it seemed not to have changed at all. Like stepping into a dream of what his hometown used to look like except that it looked like that now. The same stores; they could be the same people on the sidewalks. The cars were different, in 1914 they were all boxy, more like motorized carriages; in 1935 a number of the cars were more rounded, with curves and smooth surfaces, the concept of modern. Otherwise the town was the same. He might have never left.

    The attorney's office was where he remembered it, up the hill a block from the main street on Twelfth Street, one of the handful of storefronts along the base of the Masonic Temple, a marble-faced monolith that fronted Eighth Avenue. The plate-glass windows were painted three-quarters of the way up the color of pickled olives to keep passersby from seeing the goings-on inside while providing some light from the outside world. The reception area was all plush carpet, wood paneling, glass-front barrister bookcases loaded with law books; a secretary as gatekeeper sat in front of a door leading deeper into the offices. The older woman at the desk seemed vaguely familiar though John Lincoln thought it impossible that it could be the same woman twenty years later. She looked up as he came in, looked down, then her head snapped up again as he approached her desk. Wide-eyed at the mask. He wanted to tell her not to be afraid, that it wasn't a holdup.

    "I'd like to see David Laughlin, please."

    "Do you have an appointment?" she said, knowing full well that he didn't.

    "No, but I'm fairly certain he'll find time to see me. My name is

John Lincoln Lyle. Tell him that, please."

The woman left her desk, never fully turning her back on him, and disappeared behind the closed door. In a moment the door opened again and David Laughlin came out, the woman hanging back.

"And who do you say you are?"

"Hello, David." He had to smile at that, but of course no one could see it. "How strange to say that; it was always Mr. Laughlin when I used to come here with my father. Part of the business of getting older, I guess, the terms of address change."

Laughlin had aged well, tall, thin, a runner's build, all his hair though it was gray now, wire-rimmed glasses, a distinguished man even in his shirtsleeves without his suit coat; but then he had been as a young man, barely out of law school, when John Lincoln's father appointed him as the business and family attorney. He eyed John Lincoln, not unfriendly but definitely suspicious.

"Why do you think I would believe a man wearing a mask who appears out of nowhere and says he's someone who was known to have died twenty-some years earlier?"

"Obviously, *incorrectly* known to have died, I'm glad to say. No, I wouldn't expect you to necessarily believe it out of hand. Your natural wariness and attention to detail were some of the qualities my father saw in you when he took you under his wing and set you up in this practice." John Lincoln was proud of that, give the guy a little kick, remind him whom he owed for who he was. "I have some identification that will help clarify things, though I'd appreciate it if you looked at the papers in private, for reasons you'll understand when you see them."

Laughlin put the tip of his tongue against an upper canine as he considered it, then turned to his secretary. "Everything is okay, Betty, you can go back to your desk. I don't think you have to call the police." He looked at John Lincoln, half-jesting, half-serious. The woman squeezed by him in the doorway, still keeping an eye on John Lincoln, and regained her place at her desk. Settling herself again like a hen ruffling her feathers.

John Lincoln followed Laughlin into his office. More wood paneling, more barrister bookcases. The obligatory green-shaded lamps on his desk, the credenza, a conference table. As John Lincoln got seated in one of the curved wooden captain's chairs in front of the desk, he took a sheaf of documents from his inside coat pocket and handed them across the desk. Laughlin took them, opened them slowly: the army ID card, a passport, his discharge and separation papers.

"I think you can understand why I wanted you to look at these in private. I realize the photographs are . . ."

". . . Are disturbing," Laughlin said. Looking at John Lincoln, then back at the photograph on the ID card. The photograph taken without the mask.

"You want to ask me if it hurts, if I'm in pain. The answer is no, for the most part, it's a low-level pain, more like a continual pressure, an ache. Though the wounds are susceptible to changes of weather and the like. I can tell when it's going to rain a day ahead of time."

Laughlin nodded, continued to study the documents. Thinking carefully what he wanted to say. "Here's the thing: I see two problems with these documents. First of all they show you with these wounds, not as a young man before your injuries happened. Not as a young man I would recognize as John Lincoln Lyle. The photograph for the army ID card, for instance, would have been taken close to the time of induction, that would indicate you had these disfigurations at that time, and we know John Lincoln Lyle did not. But more to the point, all these documents are made out to someone named John Lincoln. Not John Lincoln Lyle. A man who we were told had fallen off a troopship on its way to Europe. The official designation from the government being that the body was lost at sea."

"Which was ironic at best. I didn't get any farther than New York Harbor." John Lincoln sighed. "There's an explanation—"

"As I'm sure there would be. I can't imagine you coming in here without one."

John Lincoln ignored the hint of sarcasm; Laughlin wasn't convinced as yet.

"When I went over the railing, all from my own foolishness for standing on it waving to the Statue of Liberty, I was carried under the ship, somehow missing the propellors of the troopship, they would have made mincemeat out of me. But I was caught by the propellors of a tugboat. The crew knew they hit something and pulled me out right away, saw what the propellors had done to my face, and, of all things, but fortunately, packed my face with towels and ice and got me ashore. The emergency room doctors knew they were out of their league, and after stabilizing my wounds as much as they could, transferred me to an army hospital outside of Poughkeepsie where they were aware the government was studying facial trauma in preparation for our troops being sent to Europe. The army doctors were actually delighted to see me, I was a real live case with half my face missing; before all they had were clay models to play around with. The thing was, they couldn't operate on me because I wasn't in the army. So they inducted me into the service, then and there. I vaguely remember them discussing it with me and me agreeing to it; I was drugged out of my mind at the time, but I would have agreed regardless, it seemed the only way I was going to survive the injuries. Later on, when they used me as a kind of goodwill ambassador to other facial trauma patients, they promoted me to captain. Which meant I was able to retire with a good pension along with twenty years of saved salary."

"That's all well and good, and certainly plausible. But it still doesn't answer why your papers are made out to a man named John Lincoln."

"Apparently, when the tugboat crew got me on board, they asked my name and I said John Lincoln. They didn't have anything else to go on, the troopship was hired by a private organization providing Americans who wanted to join the English or French armies, there was no passenger manifest or documentation, they just took anybody who wanted to go and were going to sort out the recruits when they got to England. As for me, I was passed out or drugged and didn't regain full consciousness until I was well in the hands of the army doctors, and learned they thought that was my name. I didn't have the energy, or maybe the will, to correct the error—after all, I had signed up to join a foreign army to get away from my old life as much as it was to fight the kaiser. I had had a new identity handed to me along with a new, if hideous, face. So John Lincoln I became."

Laughlin thought a moment. Took off his glasses, rubbed the bridge of his nose, put the glasses back on. "You'll understand if I remain, let us say, guarded."

"Of course, I would expect no less. There's another thing too, it's probably more decisive than any of those papers. I have a birthmark on the back of my neck, right underneath the hairline, I can show it to you if you like."

John Lincoln twisted around in the chair, pushed up the hair above his collar. Laughlin nodded.

"I would think there are records at the hospital, Onagona Memorial, that mention it, or with the doctor, I'm fairly certain it was Dr. McArtle who would verify it. And of course you could ask my family, though I would appreciate if you would hold off talking or discussing my return with them for a few days until I have time to talk to them first."

"You haven't made any contact with them yet?"

"No. And I would think my turning up like this is going to be quite a surprise."

"An understatement. I think it's going to be quite a shock. So why now? Why come back to Furnass now and announce that you're alive? And why am I the first one you're talking to?"

"While I was in the army I was pretty much sheltered from the outside world. I was mostly around military hospitals and medical facilities, so my injuries weren't that much out of the ordinary, I didn't have to deal with the general public's shock when they saw me. And I was, if not happy, at least satisfied with my new identity.

I was, after all, alive. But my usefulness to the army was coming to an end, they no longer needed or wanted me going around to visit the sick and wounded, now I wasn't so much an example of surviving a past war but a harbinger of the injuries and disfigurements a coming war might bring. When I thought about what becoming a civilian was going to mean to my way of life, I started to think how I was going to be fixed financially. Yes, I have a good pension and my savings, but I wondered if with the death of my father there had been any provision for his heirs that I might be entitled to. I'm not a gold digger, but I was wondering if there was any money that I was entitled to."

"You realize, I would think," Laughlin said, "that your father wouldn't very well make a provision for you in his will because he considered you dead."

John Lincoln just looked at him; it didn't warrant a reply.

Laughlin tilted back in his leather chair for a moment, gave a couple of short swivels, then leaned forward again, his hands folded on his blotter as if in a kind of prayer.

"There is no money. I can tell you that whether you are John Lincoln Lyle or not. There is no money."

"I don't mean just in the way of inheritance. I've followed the fortunes of the Steam Works as best I could over the years, and I know that the business has really slackened off, partially from the Depression but also on its own. But I was wondering if there was any provision in the will that would allow me to become involved with the company in some way—"

David Laughlin was shaking his head. "Your involvement with the company in any context would depend solely on the discretion of your older brother. And I doubt very much whether he would welcome such involvement, Gus keeps the workings of the company close to his vest. I actually know very little of the financial affairs of the company itself these days. One of the challenges of representing a family-owned business. I only see what Gus wants me to see. For example, I have no access to the company's books. In fact since he fired his bookkeeper a while back, Gus is the only one who sees the books. As for his personal finances, he still maintains the big house up on the hill, he still provides for the care of your mother. As for the rest, it's a mystery. He still, apparently, makes payroll, but he's reduced the company's workforce to a skeleton crew. There is still a limited market for the company's construction equipment, steam rollers and steam shovels and the perennial well drillers, but that market exists almost exclusively, as I understand it, overseas, particularly third world countries, where access to fossil fuels is limited. But otherwise. . . . " He trailed off, thinking of something. "As far as that goes, I haven't been paid my retainer in a year and a half, which Betty, my secretary, never fails to remind me of each month when we send out our billings." David Laughlin opened his prayerful hands on his blotter, palms up, as if to say, There it is.

"All because of the Lylemobile."

David Laughlin just looked at him for a moment. Blank. A good attorney, giving nothing away that he didn't want to. "I would think that is certainly a major drain on resources. Gus' commitment to it has been total from the beginning. But I suspect there may be other factors in play as well, though I don't know what they are, and I'm not sure that I want to know. Gus has never shown much skill as a manager, he's an engineer and that's a totally different way of thinking of problems and solutions, there are a lot of things he apparently doesn't grasp or understand about running a business. My first indication as to the severity of the company's financial situation was when there was an accident in the shop a while ago and Gus refused to fulfill the company's promise to help with the medical expenses and long-term care. That had always been the Steam Works' policy in the past, but Gus said he wasn't going to abide by it now."

"And you think the money just isn't coming in to cover the compensation?"

Laughlin shrugged. "I don't know. As I said, I have no access to the books."

"What was the accident?"

"Oh, a load of steel fell on one of the workmen. He survived but it left him pretty much a vegetable and needing continual care. It was difficult to defend the company in regard to responsibility, there were several workmen ready to testify for the plaintiff that the company was negligent, there was talk that one of the links of the chain suspending the load had broken but no one could produce it afterward. I made the case that the man should have known to get out of the way with a load traveling overhead, that he had a history of carelessness, it seemed he and his wife had sat on that very load of steel an hour or so earlier to eat lunch. It was certainly stretching a point, but it was enough to raise doubts and the company was declared free of legal responsibility. The fact is, there wouldn't have been any question if your father was alive, the company would have paid all the expenses and the man's ongoing salary regardless. But not so with Gus."

Your father. Laughlin said it as a matter of course, along with details of the case he wouldn't discuss with just anyone. John Lincoln was encouraged, Laughlin must be beginning to believe and accept his story. "I have to say I'm not surprised at my brother. Half brother."

"The whole business, I have to say, was distasteful to me, especially so because I knew the man's wife, she runs a restaurant in a hotel here in town and—"

"You mean Anna?"

David Laughlin blinked.

"Anna's Parlour? I don't know her last name. . . . "

"Anna D'Angelis, her professional name. Or Anna O'Brien, her husband's name. Yes, I guess you might have run into her since you're in town. You're probably staying at the Grand."

"I've talked to her a couple times. She's been very helpful with getting me situated with this mask and all."

"That would be Anna." Laughlin looked at his hands. It was obvious that the memory of the incident, his role in denying her the company's financial support, played on him.

"Regardless," Laughlin said, getting up, signifying the meeting

Richard Snodgrass

was over. "There was no help for it, your brother's mind was made up, for whatever reason, and that was that. If after you talk to your family and they confirm that you are who you say you are, let me know if there's anything I can do to help you." He smiled, not unfriendly. "Your story, if true, is quite compelling, you've been through quite a lot. I would like to help, both in honor of your service, and in memory of your father."

John Lincoln allowed himself to be escorted to the door before stopping. "There is one thing. I was wondering about my sister, Mary Lydia. I haven't heard anything of her, actually since I left."

"Yes. Mary Lydia. She's alive and well, as far as I know, though she has little contact with the rest of your family. She's married to a fellow she met at Covenant College, White I believe his name is, and they live on a farm in Hickory, south of here."

John Lincoln wanted to ask about children but he didn't dare. Afraid what he might hear.

*

Anna brought his dinner, the smoked pork chop with peach and cherry relish, herb-roasted fingerling potatoes, and green beans, made sure everything was as it should be, then took a seat at the empty table across the aisle from him, slightly behind him so he could take off his mask.

"So, how was your day today?" she asked. "Do you mind me talking to you while you eat?"

"Not at all." He didn't say, though he thought it: Matter of fact, I would like it. "I went for a long walk all over town, I even made it up to Orchard Hill. I wanted to see how things had changed, if they had changed."

They stopped talking as a passenger train pulled into the station across the street. The freight and coal trains took the tracks close to the river, but the passenger trains followed the tracks that ran along Third Avenue; though the trains slowed through the town, they were still enough to cause silverware to jingle against each other, knickknacks and pictures on the wall to quiver, glasses if filled too close to the brim to need a steadying

Torn

hand. As he sat there waiting, John Lincoln smiled to himself, thinking he had arrived in town with such a rumble.

"And had they? Changed?"

"Not in the least."

The way he said it made her laugh.

"I was a little surprised. You'd think after twenty years at least some things would be different, but nope, I don't think I even saw any new buildings. It was like they say, like stepping back in time. I was different, but the town wasn't. Which of course makes you wonder if you're basically the same too. Probably more than you'd like to admit."

"Did you find David Laughlin's office all right?"

Ah, there it is. John Lincoln had the feeling that was what she had been wanting to ask him all along.

"Yes, it was just as I remembered it too. I knew him when I lived here, I went with my father to his office a number of times, I have no idea what for. Maybe Father just wanted to introduce me to another aspect of the business, he was always doing that, subtle things, having me come down to the shop for one thing or another, hoping I guess to get me interested in the company. But it never really took for me. I guess I always felt the Steam Works was Gus' territory. And I wasn't mechanically inclined or anything, machines didn't hold any attraction for me like they did for Gus. So I had never talked to Laughlin on my own, held a conversation with him or anything. It seemed a bit odd, talking to him now."

Anna didn't say anything as John Lincoln continued to eat. After a few minutes, he said, "He told me about the accident with your husband."

Though he couldn't see her, he had the feeling she stiffened. "He did?"

"He told me about Gus not wanting to help you with the expenses."

"What else did he say? Did he describe his condition?"

"No, nothing like that. It was more of an example—"

"He shouldn't have told you anything about it. He had no right."

"He only brought it up as the first time he got an indication as to how bad the company's finances were when Gus wouldn't pay for the medical or long-term expenses after the accident. He was talking about how Gus keeps information from him—"

"He had no right to go around talking about it. Under any circumstances. I wonder who else in town he's talked about it with."

"I'm sure he didn't mean anything by it. . . . "

"You'll excuse me," she said, and he heard her leave. He finished his meal but she didn't return. Another waitress came, announcing herself by coughing so he could put on his mask again, to clear his dishes and leave his check. When he left, Anna wasn't at her usual place at the podium; nor was she there the next morning when he came down for breakfast, another waitress greeted him and took him back to his usual table, explaining that Anna had prepped her about him. When he asked where she was, that he hoped she wasn't ill, the waitress named Susan said that the chef hadn't shown up that morning and that Anna had taken over the kitchen. He wondered if the story were true.

Four

After John Lincoln left his office, David Laughlin went back to his desk and tried to pick up his work where he left off, reviewing some contracts for Furnass Screw and Bolt, tried to put the whole business of John Lincoln or whoever was behind that mask, the Lyle family, and the problems of the Keystone Steam Works out of his mind. But they wouldn't go. His thoughts kept returning to one or the other, regardless how he tried to concentrate on the documents in front of him. And then there was Anna. He kept at it as long as he could, sitting there until Betty had returned from her lunch, then gave up, gave in, put the contracts back in their folder, telling himself that he'd have to go through them all again when his mind was clearer, and left his office.

"Are there any appointments this afternoon?" he asked Betty, stopping at her desk.

"Mrs. Elliott, about her dog biting the paper boy."

"You'll have to call her and reschedule. I'm leaving now."

"Is everything all right, Mr. Laughlin?" Ah Betty, always worried about him. He knew she was in love with him, that he was undoubtedly the subject of middle-aged unmarried fantasies, that she would walk to the ends of the earth if he asked her to, would drown him in sugary concern and spiky solicitude if he let her.

"A personal emergency," he said, and left it at that, left the office. Wondering to himself why he ever said that to her, she'd be in turmoil the rest of the day worrying about him. He didn't like to think that was the reason he said it, just to wind her up a bit. But it probably was.

He got his car from the parking lot across the street and drove away from town, taking steep Eleventh Street up the side of the valley to Furnass Heights, then along the ridge to the Onagona County Country Club. He parked his car in his reserved spot, took his gym bag from the trunk, and walked around to the side entrance on the ground floor into the locker rooms. He changed into his tracksuit and running shoes, leaving his clothes in his locker, and started out across the golf course—there was no one playing today—running easily across the manicured greens and fairways to Seneca Road, following it along the berm to the Eleventh Street Extension, then down the backside of the valley to Colonel Berry Park, circling the lake, then resting at one of the wood tables in the empty picnic area, sitting on the tabletop with his feet on the bench, staring out at the lake in the afternoon light of late autumn. Thinking of Anna.

She came to him on a referral—he never knew who referred her to him; God bless them, whoever it was; God damn them—when she was first establishing her restaurant, needing help with the contracts to make sure she was treated fairly by the hotel. After the Parlour opened, he made a point of eating there at least once a week, a good place to take clients or have a business lunch; he told himself he needed to support a new business in town, needed to keep an eye on the place, after all he had a vested interest, he had been instrumental in its existence. But who was he kidding? After a couple of years he finally had to admit to himself that he went there as often as he did to see Anna.

David Laughlin was a man of the intellect, it was what made him a good attorney. He loved the intellectual challenge of being an attorney, of being able to take either side of an argument and reason it out to a conclusion—the subject didn't necessarily matter, it was the life of reasoning, that was all. So a life of emotions was foreign to him, the kind of emotions that Anna stirred in him. The fact was he had never experienced desire before, the desire for someone. Lust, if you will, though he hated the term, it seemed dirty. Which wasn't the case at all for his feelings toward Anna, they were elevated, on a different plane, he was on a different plane thinking about her. Yes, he had been attracted to his wife, Emma, he still was for that matter, but it seemed now on a mainly intellectual level. Emma seemed almost like a good business deal, they revolved in the same social circles at Penn State where they met, were both ambitious, were of the same tall slim body type, they could have been brother and sister, had the same goals toward a comfortable life, he was still comfortable around her, talking things over with her. But the feelings he had for Anna were different, much different. Because they were feelings.

He wanted Anna. There was no other way to put it. And as time went on he started thinking that she wanted him as well, though he couldn't be sure, being in unfamiliar territory. She welcomed him warmly every time he went to the restaurant, which was several days a week now, almost flirty but he noted not as flirty as she was with other men. Face it, she was an attraction at Anna's Parlour, men came because she was there. At first he took her reserve with him to mean she wasn't interested in him, which ate at him, depressed him, but didn't stop him from going to see her; then thought it meant that she was really interested in him, that she thought of him differently than she did other men. She took to sitting with him as he ate—he always went there alone now, never with clients or business associates—keeping him company as much as she could while tending to her other duties; accordingly he started going later in the afternoon, after the lunch crowd, so she had more time to be with him. What did they talk about? He couldn't have said after he left, this and that, he only knew that being with her he was happier—more at peace with himself, at the same time more excited, the world electric—than he could ever remember.

Then she met Warren, a workman at the Steam Works—she told David all about it, confided in him, what was that about? To make him jealous? To force his hand to get him to admit his own feelings for her? He didn't know. Soon enough she had married Warren and they were happy together, she told David all about that as well. He thought the marriage would set his feelings to rest, hoped it would, but it didn't, his feelings for her continued as before, as their relationship continued as before, Anna sitting with him as he ate his lunch, unburdening her heart as she made his own heart heavier.

Then the accident. To his credit there was never a trace, at least on any conscious level, that he thought this would give him an opportunity with Anna; all he felt was compassion for her, he wished he could do something, anything to comfort her. He thought his being the attorney for the Steam Works would help her, work in her favor, he could make sure that she got all the financial help she needed. But that was before Gus decided that the company was in no way responsible for the accident, and used that as his reason for denying all benefits and compensation to Anna and Warren. That left David with a choice. Anna or the Keystone Steam Works. His heart or his career. If he chose the latter, it was his job to defend Gus' position, in effect to destroy Anna's chances for financial help. And he chose, for whatever reasons, the Steam Works. The life of the mind kicked in: he reasoned that he was a professional, and his profession demanded that he must be the best attorney he could be; the Steam Works was his client, Gus' father had set him up in business, he owed the company his livelihood, his way of life. But Anna did not equivocate, it wasn't in her nature; she came to see him as the enemy, which in this matter he was. From that time on, any friendship between them came to an end. A hole in his life that ate at him all his days.

 David took off his glasses, cleaned the lenses with the tail of his T-shirt, put the glasses on again. The light was lowering, the day fading, the early evening of a November day, it was time to head back. Beyond the lake the creamy blue sky ended in a band of orange tracing the outline of the distant hills, a sky that, because of the smoke, you'd rarely see above the town of Furnass. Ripples chased each other across the water of the lake, but whether from fish feeding beneath the surface or a breeze he didn't feel, he couldn't tell. He got up, stretched, started off again at his easy, comfortable, never-to-be-deterred pace. With Anna he had experienced desire for the first time in his life; without Anna now in his life, even if only in the life of his dreams, his longings, for the first time he experienced loss.

Five

"John Lincoln."

"Hello, Mother."

What had he expected? The house was just as he remembered, unchanged from the time he left, sitting by itself on the slope of the valley wall above the town, away from the last block of houses as the town crept up the hillside. Sycamore House. A white frame structure among the surrounding trees, though he doubted that it had been painted in the time he was away, no doubt Gus' doing, or rather, his not-doing, neglect, he simply would never think of such a thing, think that it needed to be done. Carpenter Gothic, they called it, but with some distinctive touches: the veranda extending the width of the house; the twin high-peaked gabled windows on the second floor flanking the balcony over the double front doors and the wide front steps; the addition of the two wings, one on either side of the original structure, added by his father, Malcolm, to leave his mark on the place, to make the house more of his own and not just as he inherited it from his father, Colin. His father added the extra living spaces for his children when they got older, Gus and his wife Lily on the left side—always called the Farther Wing though it was no farther away from the main part of the house than the opposite wing—and his father and mother in the right wing, waiting until the time John Lincoln or Mary Lydia was ready to occupy it, leaving the upstairs center of the house for the twins' bedrooms as they were growing up along with those of their grandmother, Libby, and her personal assistant, Perpetual. All so very long ago.

A maid, an unfamiliar Black woman, had answered the door and led him into the front hallway, leaving him there as she disappeared into the rear of the downstairs. How strange, to be treated as a stranger in his own home; but that was who he was now, wasn't he, a stranger, he had to realize that, accept that. Particularly with his wound, his mask. He had borne the disfigurement for so long that he sometimes forgot that, although he might recognize someone from before, there was no way that person could recognize him now. As for Missy, his mother, the image he always had of her was a small fragile woman, less than five feet tall, her blond hair cut short like a skullcap, wearing one of her many white peignoirs, a cigarette in one hand and a martini glass in the other, lounging on the couch in the living room that she had taken over as her room, spending her days there reading movie magazines and eating bonbons. So he was taken by surprise when confronted with this trim if petite older woman coming down the hallway toward him, her hair fashionably bobbed, in a tailored casual shirtwaist dress and low heels, a nonplussed expression on her face. He was as surprised that she greeted him by name as he was to have called her Mother.

"I always told them that I fully expected one day for you to turn up, to walk in here as if nothing had happened," she said, appraising him while keeping her distance. "Though I can see by the mask that quite a lot has happened."

"Yes, a lot. I can tell you about it if you're interested."

"Of course I'm interested. Though I can understand why you might wonder about it. I certainly was never that interested in the things that went on with you in the past, one of my great regrets. But come in," she said, leading the way into the living room, motioning him to sit down across from her.

"Did David Laughlin tell you I was back?" He took off his topcoat and draped it over the chair arm, adding his hat on top of it, before sitting down. He remembered this big blue overstuffed chair, he sometimes hid behind it, for hours on occasions, tucked in between it and the radiator, to watch the woman they said was his mother but who never acted like it.

"The attorney? No, was he supposed to?"

So maybe she really did recognize me, he thought. Mask and all. After all this time. "He said he might call you to verify that I am who I say I am. I showed him the birthmark on the back of my neck."

"No, I haven't heard from him. But I will set his mind at ease if he calls." She smiled at some private thought. "David has been very good to me after your father died. I wondered when Malcolm passed how David would treat me, I'm sure he had some very strong opinions about me, I was quite insufferable in those days. But if he did harbor bad thoughts about me he never let them show. For which I'll be eternally grateful, In fact his attentions helped me to change my life around."

"You seem . . . different. . . . "

She let it slide. "But tell me, about the mask, about your injuries, about your life since you disappeared." She leaned forward where she sat on the couch, her hands clasped in her lap, the model of attentiveness.

He recounted for her all that had happened to him in the time since he left, the accident, the rescue, the treatments by the army and his enlistment and promotions, his life after the treatments failed. Surprised himself at the detail he went into, recounting his pain and disappointment and frustration, things he hadn't told, wouldn't tell, anyone else.

When he was done she asked, "Would you show me the wounds?"

"Why would you want to see them?"

"Because, despite how I've acted in the past, I am your mother. You are my son."

He thought a moment, then unhooked the cloth mask from one ear, then the other. She winced at first sight but then did her best to remain expressionless as she studied the layers of scar tissue, the gaping holes, the twisted flesh, before sitting back. Nodding as he put the mask back in place.

"Have you seen anyone else besides David Laughlin since you've been back?" She was trying hard to put the conversation back to where it was.

He thought of mentioning Anna O'Brien, Anna D'Angelis, but caught himself, why would he think of her? "No, I've only been back a couple of days."

Was she fishing as to how she ranked on his list of people he wanted to see? He couldn't blame her if she was, but he didn't think that was the case.

"I'd like to see Mary Lydia," he went on. "Laughlin said she lives in Hickory?"

"That's right. She married a fellow she met at college, Claire White, his family had a farm and she moved down there with him. The way of life seems to suit her, she seems very happy and content, though I've rarely seen her since she went there. I suspect one of the appeals of life on a farm is that it's away from here. Sad to say. Another regret."

"And the baby? Well, I guess it wouldn't be a baby now—"

She cocked her head. "No, of course, you wouldn't know."

"Know what?"

"There was no baby. If you're thinking of when she was pregnant before you left. Mary Lydia miscarried, actually right after we heard that you had drowned in New York Harbor. I've often wondered if the shock. . . . " She let it trail away.

"No, I didn't know...."

"The same way I've wondered if Mary Lydia's getting pregnant didn't have something to do with why you disappeared."

"It wasn't my baby, if that's what you're getting at."

"No, no, I never thought it was, though I have to say there were some who questioned it. No, I knew you would never let that happen. No matter how much you might have been tempted—"

"Mother!" Even in his indignation, he noticed the word came naturally to him now.

She laughed a little, looked at her hands in her lap before looking at him again. "I don't blame you for being repulsed at the idea, that's what I know about you. But I also know such things happen between siblings, and it was no secret the way you two looked at each other, clung to each other. Mary Lydia especially to you. It would almost be unnatural if there weren't such feelings floating around. But I also knew you, even if you didn't always know yourself. Still, the idea that somebody had relations with her, well, it might have been enough to send you off to a foreign land. She was never pregnant after that, I might add, though I never knew if it was by choice or some injury I wasn't aware of."

John Lincoln was taken aback. That this woman whom he barely knew growing up turned out to have known him so well, expressing thoughts about his motives that he could only consider about himself when he got much older, and then only vague suspicions, nothing concrete or determining, nothing he could hold on to or would want to.

"Do you think she'd want to see me?"

"I would think so, I would hope so, but you never know. She's spent the last twenty years living with the idea that her treasured brother and twin is dead. I'm sure it wasn't an easy adjustment for her to make. Now, suddenly, here you are, and in a much-altered state. But she's bound to hear that you're back and alive someway or other, it's undoubtedly better that such news comes from you directly and not from gossips. Among her first questions, I would think, is why didn't you let her, of all people, know that you had survived."

"And I don't have the answer to that."

Missy opened her hands on her lap, as if displaying the result: There you are.

They sat in silence, each digesting what the other had said. After a few moments, Missy said, "And what about Gus?"

"What *about* Gus?"

She gave him a pretend-annoyed expression. "You know very well what I mean."

"Actually, I don't."

"Are you going to go see him? I assume you haven't yet, from what you said."

"No. Yes. I mean, no, I haven't seen him yet. And, yes, I'm going to."

"You don't sound very sure. You were close to your older brother when you were growing up, you and Mary Lydia both, and then something seemed to happen as you got older."

"When we were younger I think we both idolized him, our big brother, he was always taking care of us, looking out for us. Showing us the ways of the world, what to watch out for. But as we got older, or at least for me, I realized he had his own agenda, his own reasons for everything. Including why he wanted to big brother us."

Missy shook her head, not comprehending.

"He was a bully, for one thing. A very subtle bully, to be sure, but a bully nonetheless. He was fine as long as you did everything Gus' way, the way he told you, but try to have a thought of your own and he bullied you back to seeing the world according to Gus."

"I know I never got along with him that well, but I thought it was understandable, I wasn't his mother, I was put in the position of replacing his mother, and he resented it."

"One of the main things he did was to try to turn me and Mary Lydia against Father."

Missy looked questioning.

"Gus blamed Father for killing his mother. When he watched her come home that evening and fall into the trench for the new gas lines and the kerosene from the lantern she was carrying spilled on her clothes and set her on fire—"

"And Malcolm thought there was a barrel of salt on the front porch and grabbed it and poured it over her to put out the flames, but it turned out to be flour and it only made things worse. Yes, I know that story very well."

"I guess it more or less baked her alive."

"And when he realized what had happened, Malcolm jumped into the flaming trench and beat out the flames with his bare hands. He bore those scars the rest of his life, his hands were never right after that, he was in constant pain."

"Well, to Gus' mind—six years old, watching the whole thing from the front window—he got the idea his father poured the flour on her on purpose. That he killed his mother on purpose, Lord knows why he thought his father would do such a thing but he did. And Gus spent most of my and Mary Lydia's childhood trying to convince us that Father was a monster and a killer and that he couldn't be trusted, that we had to fear him or he'd do something awful to us too."

Missy was shocked. She looked in disbelief at John Lincoln. "I had no idea."

John Lincoln nodded. "It's true. And for many years we bought into it. We did everything we could to stay out of Father's way, we avoided him any way we could, which wasn't that hard most of the time because he was always tied up with the company. But it meant we were never very nice to him when he was around. If Mary Lydia and I seemed like a closed society it was because we felt we could only depend on each other."

"I'm sorry that I—"

"You don't have to be. I guess we were all doing what we thought we had to do in order to survive. The thing was, I started to question Gus's view of Father about the time we started college. I was beginning to realize Gus might be terribly terribly wrong and that Mary Lydia and I were wrong to have ever believed it, but then Mary Lydia got pregnant and everything else went by the boards. But I had a lot of time to think about it while I was in the hospital recovering. And over the years since."

"I had no idea," Missy repeated. "No idea."

"So you can understand why I might have some mixed feelings about seeing Gus now."

"Yes . . . of course . . . ," Missy said, lost in other thoughts.

"So, how is the Steam Works doing under Gus' guidance? Laughlin said he didn't think it was doing very well at all. I got the idea he's afraid the company's on the verge of closing down completely."

"I don't really know anything about it. Gus never talks to me about the business, any more than your father did when he was alive. As far as I know, he's still paying his bills, at least as far as this house goes, though as you can see he hasn't made any repairs or maintenance to it in Lord knows when."

"Laughlin said his first real indication the company might be in real trouble was when there was an accident in the shop and Gus declared he wouldn't pay any compensation for the man's medical expenses or long-term care. Laughlin said it was always the company's policy to do so in the past."

"I heard about the accident and the company's later refusal to pay compensation, it was all in the papers. I was surprised and disappointed, your father was always very proud that the company would take care of its own. His father, your grandfather, even set up a special fund, the Mercy Fund, to take care of such compensations, totally separate from the finances of the rest of the company so the payments wouldn't be a drain on operations. But Gus must have his reasons for not wanting to pay the compensation now, maybe he's making a stand on some principle or other, that would be like Gus, nobody's going to take advantage of him. As you said, Gus always had reasons of his own. For everything."

His mother was thinking about something. Something

obviously difficult to talk about. "He came to me for money a while ago."

"Did he say what he wanted it for?"

"No. But I assume it had something to do with the Lylemobile, everything does for him it seems these days. He said it would be a loan. But I knew if he was asking me for it, there was no way he could pay it back. At least in the foreseeable future."

"You didn't give it to him, did you?"

She paused. "Sixty thousand dollars. I thought that was as much as I could afford to just . . . lose."

"Mother."

"It's okay. I'm still in good shape financially, your father made sure of that. I have plenty in trust to take care of me all of my days. I only told you—well, I'm not sure why I told you."

"Gus must have been in dire straits to—"

"You know, don't you, that all of Gus' talk about your father killing his first wife was crazy talk," Missy interrupted him. "She was the love of his life. I knew that when I married him, he never got over her or could live with what he did to her, but I thought I could still find some place in his heart. Though it turned out I couldn't. I found a place on his list of responsibilities instead, things he assigned himself to take care of, but not a place in his love. It was the reason I acted the way I did in those days, which I'll always regret because it had an effect on others, such as you and Mary Lydia. I wasn't there for you when you needed me, when a mother could have come in handy, if for no other reason than to let you know you were dearly loved. There was no excuse for that. As for Malcolm, I don't believe he even noticed."

They sat in silence for several minutes; there seemed nothing more to say. At last John Lincoln got to his feet. "Well, I guess I should be going. . . . " Putting on his topcoat again, taking his hat.

Missy rose to her feet, smoothing the wrinkles from her skirt, a reflex. "I'm so glad you came to see me." She laughed at herself. "I'm so glad that you're alive. I feel like I should give you a hug for your return, the conquering hero or something, but I guess we never did such things when you were growing up, did we? My lack."

"What the hell, let's do it anyway," John Lincoln said, crossing the room to her and embracing her, holding her to him; he could look down at the top of her white hair. When they separated she was tearing up.

"Silly me."

"Is something wrong?"

"Oh no, no. Not at all. It's just no one has hugged me in thirty, maybe forty years."

"Father . . . ?"

"At the beginning, of course. But then he got busy. As you know."

"Well, maybe we can do something about the hugs. Suppose I come back again. . . . "

"Oh, I would like that."

Six

After John Lincoln left, Missy stood at the front door watching him go, the figure in the dark blue topcoat and fashionable hat, the man who had announced to her that he was her son, walking across the drive to the road leading down the hill to the streets of the town, losing him eventually among the trees of the hillside, the branches mostly bare now in late autumn, only a scattering of brown leaves left from the abundant green of summer, thinking, If I could ever use a drink, I could use one now. Though she wouldn't do that to herself, she had fought too hard for sobriety after Malcolm died, realizing that with him gone there was no need to be tipsy, drunk, the alcohol had served its purpose, or rather it hadn't at all, it never made Malcolm notice her more than he ever did, which was never much beyond what was required to get through the everyday, never got him to say, Stop it, Missy, right now, enough! After he was gone, she stopped it on her own, just woke up one morning and stopped drinking, canceled her order with the bootleggers, poured the bottles she had on hand down the kitchen sink, never touched the stuff or even wanted to again. Didn't really want a drink now either, but if there ever was a good reason to want one, today would be the day.

Thinking, I was no more prepared to be a mother than I was to fly. One night of sex, one time fulfilling my duties as a wife, and that so unsatisfying to either me or Malcolm that we never tried it again, and I ended up pregnant. With twins, no less. What were the odds?

Missy closed the door and returned to the living room, sat down again in the same place on the couch where she sat when John Lincoln was here. After all this time. Back from the dead, as it were. And the suffering the man had gone through. She wondered why he had come back—oh, she was glad that he did, it would give her a chance to right another of her many wrongs, but why, what would bring him back now after all he had gone through here as a child, all the neglect from his preoccupied mother, all the bullying as it turned out from a domineering older brother. She was sure there must be something there, something eating at him on some level of his mind, something he needed to resolve, but what? She regretted that she didn't know him better, know him well enough that he might tell her what it was.

And then there was Gus. A revelation, not a happy one, at what John Lincoln and Mary Lydia had gone through because of their older brother's delusions. Certainly, Gus must have been hurting too, tormented by his perceptions of his father—and of her, no doubt. His father's coconspirator. No wonder the boy never took to her, not that there was anything of a mother to attach to; maybe he came to the conclusion that his father killed his mother, burned her alive in that trench, because of Missy, to get rid of his then wife and marry Missy. No matter that she and Malcolm hadn't even met until several years after his wife's death. Apparently Gus wasn't aware of that. Or if he was aware, it made no difference. How sad, how sad.

Something occurred to her. She left the living room and went upstairs to her bedroom. Sitting at her writing desk, she pulled

Torn

open the center drawer and leafed through the sheafs of paper, letters from family and friends she wanted to keep, Malcolm's obituary in the paper, flyers for one thing or another she had long forgotten why she thought she should save. She found what she was looking for at the back, under an envelope of family snapshots, pictures of her mother and father and herself on a picnic at Colonel Berry Park, pictures of her father in a graduation ceremony at the college when he was head of the History Department, pictures of her mother at some Easter time in a fancy bonnet. A sheet of paper, part of a letter, a number five at the bottom indicating there had originally been more pages, in Gus' handwriting, written many years before:

> P.P.S.
> I say this in all seriousness. This is a matter of the greatest importance. You are fighting for your soul, for your right to a future—it is possible that you are literally fighting for your life. See that you are not distracted and see that you are victorious.
> I'm with you,
> Gus

She had found it years before, when she cleaned out John Lincoln's room, at the bottom of his underwear drawer, when they thought he had died in New York Harbor. At the time she had no idea what it meant, what it could mean; Gus must have written it to John Lincoln when he was away at church camp, the only time she could recall Gus was away from home growing up; Gus would have been in his late teens, John Lincoln in his preteens, scary stuff to be writing to someone little more than a child. Now, after what John Lincoln told her today, she knew all too well what it meant. Just exactly what it said: that the boy had to fear his father, that he had to fear for his life.

Gus. Gus. Gus. Growing up so troubled, so much weight to carry. Not just in seeing his mother burn to death in a trench.

Knowing that his father had appointed him the heir apparent to taking over the company, when all he wanted to do was tinker with his machines, work with his designs, probably knowing already that he had no talent for management, that he had no desire to run the company. The weight of his successful father, not to mention his grandfather, Colin, the founder of the Keystone Steam Works and a local hero, designer of a war engine, an armor-plated steam engine mounted with Gatling guns that could have ended the Civil War then and there; but when it threatened to fall into Confederate hands, destroyed the machines, blew up the bridge on their way out of town, and suffered gunshot wounds in the process that pained him the rest of his life. So much for a troubled lonely insecure little boy to own up to, measure up to.

 She remembered after she and Malcolm were married, Gus following her around the house, not talking to her, not saying anything, just always there, at the end of a hallway, standing in a doorway, half-hidden behind a chair. She found him one time going through her underwear drawer; when she asked him what he was doing, he just walked away. After the twins were born, she would find him standing over their crib, watching them in their high chairs, sitting nearby when they played in the sandbox, she thought the boy too intimidated to join in, but now she suspected something else. Thinking of it now, his actions seemed sinister, forbidding, threatening. Was she just making this up? She didn't think so. And here she was now, living in this house with him, just the two of them, the maid and cook Nancy only coming through the days. Two people who never cared for each other, who rarely even spoke to each other, together in this big otherwise empty house. Though it didn't matter to her now if it was odd or threatening or just crazy. She was sick of the Lyles, sick of everything they stood for, everything about them. John Lincoln said he might come to see her in the future, but she didn't want him to have to come to this house, she wanted it to be someplace warm and welcoming, someplace where they could discover their relationship to each other again. Love.

Torn

She still owned her family's home on Orchard Hill, two blocks from Covenant College, which she occasionally rented to visiting professors and instructors, lecturers, held on to mainly because she couldn't bear the thought of giving up the place, couldn't bear the thought of letting it go; it was currently sitting unoccupied, though fully furnished, the same furniture and fixtures that were there when her parents were alive, when she was growing up and lived there after college. She went to the top of the stairs and called for Nancy to come up.

"I need you to go up in the attic and get the two trunks and my suitcases and bring them down, if they're too heavy call your husband and ask him to come over and help. Then help me pack my clothes—don't forget to check the downstairs hall closet—and help me get the suitcases to my car, the trunks can come later. Matter of fact, call your husband regardless, I'm sure we'll need him. Then tomorrow, go through the house and collect up all the knickknacks and personal items you can find and pack them up—you know which things are mine, most of the stuff around here came with Malcolm and the house but there are things like those two black ceramic panthers on the mantelpiece, those crystal candlesticks, the picture of the cabin by the lake, you know which ones. Pack them up and I'll send movers for the rest."

"Are you leaving us, Missus Missy?"

"Yes, Nancy, I'm moving back to my family's house on Orchard Hill, where I belong. You could probably stop coming every day if you want to. I'll make sure Gus pays you the same but there won't be that much for you to do without me around."

"That's kind of you, Missus Missy, but I'll keep coming every day until Mr. Gus tells me to stop. My place is here, you know, the dust won't stop gathering just because I'm not around. And somebody has to keep an eye on Mr. Gus, Lord knows he can't do it himself. But I am surely going to miss you. The place is spooky enough with you in it, I can't imagine who will float out of the woodwork without you."

Seven

John Lincoln walked away from his family's house, the house where he was raised, back down the road, down the hillside, into the streets of the town, wondering what just happened. He went to visit Missy—because that was the way he had always thought of her before, a woman with a relation to him in name only, certainly nothing more—visit her as a matter of courtesy, to let her know he was back—and more than that, to let her know he was alive, as if it would matter to her that much—so that she heard it from him before she heard it from someone else, some town gossip; went to see her with no expectations, no more intention than to say hello and get such formalities out of the way with a woman for whom he had no more feeling, no more affection or connection than he felt for the maid who opened the door. And what happened? He came away feeling that he had found his mother. After all this time. His mother. He was having trouble adjusting to the idea, before he went there today he hadn't even known he felt the lack of a mother, such a figure in his life, he had lived so long without one, without such feelings. Aware that most people his age weren't aware of such feelings, at least consciously, such feelings, either good or bad, were deep-rooted and beyond easy access, a groundwork for their lives—the feeling that there was someone who had an unconditional tie to them, flesh of my flesh—that in the best scenario it meant there was someone who felt an unconditional love toward him—someone who didn't care what he looked like now, who felt only sympathy, empathy, for all he had gone through. Who wanted to make it better for him now. While at the same time he felt an unconditional protectiveness and concern for her welfare, ready to defend her against whatever. Such a cacophony of emotions made him slightly giddy, light-headed, as much as a middle-aged man could after all he had seen and been through; he had no idea what to do with such emotions, had no idea what to do with himself.

He was too restless, too wound up to go back to the hotel now.

Torn

He roamed through the back streets for several hours, the streets above the main street, streets that he knew well at one time but on which he never spent much time growing up, hurrying along them to get home because he didn't feel safe on them—the rich kid from the big white house on the hillside, a sure target for the sons and even daughters of mill workers—all through grade school and even junior high, born with a target on his back or so it seemed, so much for being a child of so-called privilege, having your name be prominent in the town. He ended up in his wanderings this day at the high school, the block-long red-brick building with two Gothic cement towers flanking the front door, at the practice field behind the school, sitting midway up in the empty bleachers, the football field spread before him. Then when he was in high school, a funny thing happened. He was no longer the target of bullying by the tough kids. He had ascended, quite without intending to, into the ranks of the really smart kids, the kids the tough kids left alone, respected even, for unknown reasons—maybe because the smart kids tended to be wimpy and were no longer worth the trouble to hassle; maybe because the smart kids were actually smart and the tough kids respected them for abilities they didn't have (not likely); maybe because the tough kids thought the smart kids could help them with their assignments if the tough kids were nice to them (more likely)—becoming a favorite in school. Voted Best Liked three years running. Star of talent shows and the school plays, *Our Alma Mater*, *The Furnass Follies*, *Sweet Sixteen*. School mascot for the relatively new game of football, wearing a large papier-mâché head and dressed in too-large work clothes, carrying an oversized shovel as the embodiment of a Furnass Stoker, best known for climbing up the goalpost—he needed a ladder at the back—and waving his shovel at the opposing team. His most devoted fan was Mary Lydia; she basked in the reflected glory that he was her twin brother, as he basked in her adulation and pride in him.

Unfortunately, his glory years were short-lived. When he started at Covenant College he found himself surrounded by equally smart and talented students and he no longer stood out. The cruelest cut of all was that Mary Lydia no longer considered him as special as she had, she found other boys who were his equal, and at times, his betters. Was that when the distance started to grow between them? The distance that culminated with her becoming pregnant—no, he wasn't going to think about that. Behind him a switch engine was coming down a siding at a walking pace along the base of the valley wall, emerging from its own clouds of smoke and steam, its warning bell with a steady *ding-ding-ding-ding*, heading toward the factories along Walnut Bottom Run. Across the practice field he heard the buzzer at the high school signaling the change of classes. He got up and stepped down the bleachers, not wishing to confront hordes of inquisitive and not always friendly teenagers if school was letting out soon, continuing on down the hill, the stepped city blocks, to the shopping district along Seventh Avenue.

    He was glad to see Peluso Bros.—*Fine Men's Wear*—was still in business, not only the best men's shop in town but the only one unless you wanted work clothes. The salesman was an old man he remembered from the time he used to buy clothes here—John Lincoln thought he was an old man then—still with a yellow tape measure draped around his neck. The salesman was so bent over now that he had to cock his head to look at John Lincoln, though it was obvious he didn't want to, did everything possible not to look at John Lincoln's face as if whatever was behind the mask might be catching. John Lincoln paid no attention to him, bought himself a heavy wool jacket, more appropriate for casual wear than his topcoat, certainly if he was considering a trip to the country, three solid-color flannel shirts, a cable-knit sleeveless sweater, and a couple of pairs of corduroy pants. As he paid for them, he wondered what the man would think when he figured out from the town gossips who it was he waited on, and carried his purchases down the hill to the hotel.

    In the lobby he stopped at the bellhop station and asked Eddie, after tipping him well, to take his packages up to his room, then

Torn

continued into the dining room. Susan was again at the host's podium and he let her take him back to his table, thinking it was fruitless to ask about Anna again, he must have really offended her in some way when he mentioned David Laughlin talking about her husband's accident. Well, so much for that. He ordered the day's special, coq au vin, and was looking out the window, up the street at the houses stacked up the hill, as he waited, when he heard a commotion in the front of the restaurant, beyond the partitions and etched glass, raised voices, Eddie saying, "You can't barge in here like this," Susan saying, "Sir! Sir!" whatever was happening coming his direction. John Lincoln stood up and looked around as a gray-haired heavyset man in his early sixties, permanently rumpled, in his shirtsleeves and braces as if he had just come from his office—Gus, it could only be Gus—rushed toward him between the empty tables, with Eddie and Susan trailing in his wake. His older brother did not look friendly.

"Okay, what's going on here?" Gus demanded, confronting John Lincoln.

"Hello, Gus."

And Anna was there, coming from the kitchen, still in an apron. She glanced at John Lincoln—and in that split second, the intensity in her eyes, he felt as if there was a connection between them, a recognition of that connection, that flick of her eyes burning twin holes in his consciousness outside of time, beyond time—before she turned back to Gus. "What's this about?"

"Don't you 'Hello, Gus' me. Who the hell are you?"

"I'm sorry, Anna," Eddie was saying, "he came in the hotel and then barged in here before I could stop him."

"I think you should settle down, Mr. Lyle," Anna said, "and tell me what this is about."

"Who the hell are you?" Gus said, ignoring her. "My mother called me to say John Lincoln is back, but I know you're not John Lincoln, no matter what she thinks—"

"Mr. Lyle—"

"You stay out of this, Anna. It doesn't concern you—"

"It concerns me if you come barging in here causing a disturbance."

"Gus, I think you should settle down," John Lincoln said. "We can talk—"

"The hell we can talk. I want to know who you are." Without warning Gus reached out and snatched the mask from John Lincoln's face.

Gus gasped. Susan screamed, more like a *Yip!*, and turned away. "Holy Mother of God," Eddie said. Anna was nowhere in sight.

"Satisfied?" John Lincoln said, his face stinging from Gus's hand.

"But," Gus said, seemingly transfixed at the sight of John Lincoln's face.

Then Anna was back, with a baseball bat cocked on her shoulder; she swung it at Gus, purposefully missing him but purposefully not by much.

"Jesus, Anna! Watch it!"

"I'll watch it, all right. I'll watch you walk your sorry butt out of my restaurant and don't you ever come back. You hear me? Don't you ever come back!"

She was ready to swing again but Gus backed up, backed into Eddie, who pulled him back farther, turned him around, and pushed him toward the front door.

Anna rested the bat on her shoulder. "You go back to your station, Susan. I'll take care of things here. I don't think Gus Lyle will be giving us any more trouble."

The woman hurried back to the front of the restaurant.

"I'm so sorry about this," John Lincoln said.

"Oh, don't be silly," Anna said, putting the bat on an empty table and turning toward him. looking at the wounds on his face but never flinching, just interested, concerned. "Did he hurt you when he grabbed the mask? Can I get you something? Sit down, sit down. You might as well leave the mask off to eat, nobody else is going to see you and I've seen it now."

Torn

John Lincoln sat down, with Anna taking the seat across from him. "Would you have really hit him?"

"You know, I think I might have," she said. "At least I'd like to think so. He's had it coming for a long time."

John Lincoln thought a moment, then decided he should just come out with it. "When I didn't see you, I thought maybe you were mad at me."

"You didn't see me with a baseball bat, did you?" she said. "That would be a good way to tell if I was mad at you or not. And why would I be mad at you? Didn't Susan explain where I was? I told her to."

"Yes, she told me you were working in the kitchen, but I still wasn't sure. I was afraid I had offended you or something, when I said David Laughlin had talked about you and your husband's accident."

"It threw me a little off guard, I'll admit, but the more I thought about it, Laughlin had every right to say whatever to you about it, you being part of the family and all. I guess I was a little too sensitive." She considered what she wanted to say. "Actually, I think I was most upset because I would have liked to tell you about all that myself. Private things. Like you telling me about your wounds."

"Well, there's nothing much left to the imagination about those now, is there?"

"Nope. Nothing left to the imagination. They are what they are. Your dinner must be up, I'll go get it so we don't upset Susan any more today."

Anna went to the kitchen and got his meal, went to the bar and got his beer, and then settled herself across the table from him again, as naturally as could be. Just as John Lincoln hoped.

"What was Gus going on about your mother calling him?"

As he ate, John Lincoln told her about the visit to see Missy, and all the confusion of feelings afterward about discovering a relationship with his mother. He also told her about Mary Lydia, her pregnancy and how it drove him away, his unresolved feelings all these years about what had happened back then and his concern for his sister.

"So that's why you were on the troopship, and your accident happened."

John Lincoln nodded. "I'd like to see Mary Lydia, to maybe resolve some things."

"You said you thought she lived near Little Washington."

"Yes, Hickory, Mother said. Do you know if there are buses or trains that run there?"

"Not offhand, but let me take you. I have a car."

"Why would you do that?" he asked, and wished he hadn't, it sounded too leading.

"Well, it's going to be hard for you to get there otherwise. And I wouldn't mind an outing, a chance to get away for a day, breathe some air that you can't see. But can you wait till Saturday? That would be better for me. Getting someone to look after my husband and all."

"Of course. Thank you, I can't thank you enough, that's really nice. . . ."

"Nice for me, too." She got up and retrieved her baseball bat from the empty table. "Now, I've got things to do in the kitchen and I need to get this bat back to the bar." She stopped and looked at him intently for a moment and smiled. "I'm looking forward to Saturday."

It was as if she didn't even see his wounds. Then was gone. But she was just starting to live in his thoughts, his anticipation of seeing her again, at the meals between now and Saturday, glimpses of her from his tower window. And then Saturday itself. An entire day with her. How would that unfold? What would they talk about? He almost forgot the reason for the trip was to see Mary Lydia.

Eight

Gus Lyle was in his office, going through some changes for the redesign of the Lylemobile with the designer, Daniel Spalding, the

Torn

two of them hunched over the plan table, when Janet Santelli knocked and opened the door.

"I'm sorry to bother you, Mr. Lyle, but there's a man out here in a mask who says he's your brother."

I was afraid of this, Gus thought, straightening up. He told Daniel he'd talk to him later, and told Janet to show the man in.

"Hello again," John Lincoln said. He stood aside as Spalding left the room, the younger man making no attempt to hide his staring at the visitor. John Lincoln nodded thanks to the secretary, who was staying as far away from him as she could.

Gus moved across the room and stood in front of his desk. "I was wondering if you were going to come see me."

"I had planned to before, but thought I should see Missy first. Mother. You said she called you and told you I was back...."

"I didn't mean to create such a scene...."

"It certainly was that, a scene...."

"I was just surprised, is all. The whole business... you showing up and all. Do you really think Anna would have hit me with that bat?"

"I don't know her that well, of course, but I got the idea... yes, I think she would have."

"I guess it's understandable. Me causing a disturbance like that, she does care about her restaurant. And we've had some bad business dealings in the past—but why am I telling you all this? I'm not even sure you are John Lincoln."

"Yes, you are."

Gus sighed. "Yes, I guess I am. But what happened? Everybody thought you were dead. We were told you were dead. And, you know," Gus said, pointing vaguely to his own face. "Look, I'm really sorry about pulling off your mask, it just sort of happened, I never meant, you know, I hope I didn't hurt you."

John Lincoln had taken up a position standing behind the three wingback chairs circled in front of Gus' desk, fingertips resting on the chair backs. He shook his head at Gus' almost question.

"Would you like to sit down?" Gus said. "Can I get you

something? Coffee? Tea?"

"I'm fine, thanks."

Like he's staying behind a low wall, keeping those chairs between us. What's the matter, he afraid I'll attack him again? Oh, I get it, if I'm standing, he'll stand. "So, what happened to you, how did you get like this?"

"You always were a master of tact."

"You know what I mean. You disappear for twenty years and let everybody think you're dead, and you've obviously been through a lot. I'd like to know what happened."

John Lincoln told him the story of his accident, a quick gloss of the intervening years. Gus thought there were a number of holes in the story, things John Lincoln seemed to leave out for whatever reasons, but he didn't know enough to ask the right questions.

"So, what did you say to Missy when you were up at the house?"

"I didn't know I said anything."

"Well, you went to see her, and the next thing she moves out. Just like that. I went home last night and she was gone, packed her bags and left, just like that, back up to her family's house on Orchard Hill. She has movers coming to get her furniture. You must have said something."

"Not that I'm aware of. Actually I went there expecting the worst, more of a courtesy call than anything else, and it turned out very nice. I found we had a connection after all this time, something we never had before."

"Is that why you came back after all this time? To make connections?"

"You don't have to worry, Gus. I didn't come back to take over the business."

"I'm not worried, little brother. You couldn't if you wanted to." It was harsh but Gus thought John Lincoln deserved it, the nerve of him, bringing up such an idea. He couldn't take the company, could he?

"I was just joking, Gus. Laughlin already told me Father left it solely to you."

"You went to see Laughlin already?"

"I thought I should check things out before I made contact with anyone else. You never know, with people thinking you're dead...."

"Laughlin doesn't know very much at this point, about either the family or the business," Gus said.

"It sounds like you set that up that way on purpose."

"What does that mean?"

John Lincoln shrugged. "Nothing. Just an observation. Seems a bit odd, though, for a company's legal counsel to be kept in the dark about the company's affairs, that's all."

"Was Laughlin complaining about that to you? Because—"

"Not at all. Relax. It only came up when I asked him how the company was doing, and he said he didn't actually know that much about the company these days. He was the perfect legal counsel, blank-faced as a sphinx, butter wouldn't melt in his mouth."

What's he getting at? What's he want? No, he doesn't know anything, he's just throwing things out to see if he can get a rise out of me, like when he was a kid, poking at me to see my reaction.

"Actually, the company is doing very well, if you must know. Considering the Depression and all."

"I was surprised when I came through that there weren't more workers in the shop. Didn't seem like much was going on."

I won't let him get to me, I won't. "We've got a lot going on, as a matter of fact. Come over here, take a look at this."

Gus pushed himself off the edge of the desk and went back to the plan table, John Lincoln following reluctantly. Gus shuffled through the drawings till he found the one he was looking for and unrolled it.

"The redesigned Lylemobile. This is the schematic I use for investors, but it'll give you the idea."

Richard Snodgrass

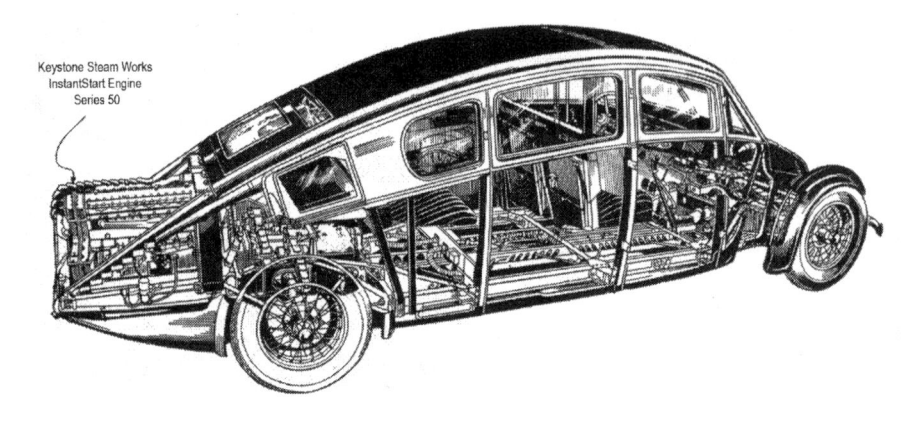

Keystone Steam Works
InstantStart Engine
Series 50

"Actually, I'm thinking of renaming it. Lylemobile could have negative connotations because it wasn't successful before. I'm thinking of calling it the Zephyr. Zephyr Motors. What do you think?"

John Lincoln shrugged, noncommittal. "I don't know. That's certainly a very different automobile than the way I remember it."

"I know, it's exciting, right? I realized the mistake I was making a couple years ago, well, more than a couple now, the design had barely changed from the time we introduced it, it was much too old-fashioned, like the Model T's looked too old-fashioned. So I hired a designer, he was the guy in here when you arrived, he really knows his stuff. This new design incorporates all the features you'll see in the latest Fords and Chevys and Dodges, except it's a steam vehicle. We've brought steam into the twentieth century."

"Do you think the twentieth century is ready? It hasn't been up to now."

"We're making sure it's ready. When the buying public sees this new design and hears of all the benefits, the Lylemobile—the Zephyr—is going to revolutionize the automobile industry, you mark my words."

"And this is where all the company's money has been going to?"

"Who said anything about that?"

Torn

John Lincoln shrugged again. What was he getting at? Gus could tell, even with the mask, that John Lincoln wasn't impressed. And what was this talk about spending all the company's money on the Zephyr? Who had he been talking to? Just forget it. What would he know about anything anyway. He's been stuck away in army hospitals for twenty years. John Lincoln wouldn't like it regardless because it's something I believe in, something I'm doing, he never liked anything I was involved with. To hell with him, I tried. . . . Gus walked back to his desk, this time taking his seat behind it.

"Have you seen Mary Lydia? Or are you planning to?"

"I'm going to this weekend," John Lincoln said, staying where he was. "From what Mother said, Mary Lydia hasn't been that welcoming to family."

"I went down to see her once, but no, it didn't go very well."

"I can't imagine why."

"Look, John Lincoln—"

He was interrupted by another knock on the door, this time with a young man sticking his head in.

"Dad, I was wondering if— Oh, you're busy. Oh!" the young man said, seeing the mask for the first time.

"Well, speak of the devil," John Lincoln said. "This must be Mal. I was just going to ask you about Lily, I didn't see her up at the house when I was there."

"You son of a bitch," Gus said.

"What?" John Lincoln said.

"If I'm interrupting something—"

"You're not interrupting at all," Gus said. "Say hello to your uncle, John Lincoln. He was just leaving."

"Hello," Mal said, thoroughly confused.

"I guess I am leaving, then," John Lincoln said, looking at them both and then heading for the door.

Gus was sure that behind the mask his younger brother was laughing at him.

When he was gone, Mal said, "I thought he was dead."

Gus thought, I have the feeling we're all going to wish he was. But said, "Evidently, he's not."

Nine

"What do you think he wants?" Janet says.

"I don't know what he wants, he didn't really say, though it's hard to believe he came back to town after all this time, and in the condition he's in—those hideous wounds—for no purpose."

Alone again, sitting at his desk after everyone had gone, Gus imagined, as he often did these days, talking to Janet, his secretary, explaining to her things that happened, what he thought about things that happened. They are sitting on a bench by the river, behind the Steam Works, a place he imagines they often go to for their little talks. He had often thought of putting a bench there, the place had a history, his father told him that his father, Gus' grandfather, Colin Lyle, often went there to think, to make decisions, to get away from the noise and activity of the shop and to look at the river, the Allehela, the hills on the other side of the valley. From here they, Gus and Janet, can see downstream, the bridge over the mouth of the river, at the end of the valley, before the Allehela flows into the Ohio, continuing on to join the Mississippi, the Mississippi into the Gulf of Mexico, and on and on, the mouth of the Allehela where the original bridge spanned the valley, the bridge that his grandfather destroyed single-handedly along with his war engines to keep his invention from falling into the wrong hands. So hard to find a hero these days.

"Did you get a look at his wounds, beneath the mask?"

"Yes, and I wish I hadn't. I saw them earlier, over at Anna's Parlour." He thinks to leave it there, he is ashamed of how he acted at the restaurant, what he did, he doesn't want to admit it to her. But his conscience gets the better of him. "I wish I had handled the situation better when I saw him at the restaurant. I . . . pulled the mask off his face."

"Gus!"

"I know, I know, I wish I hadn't but I did, and there's no way to change it now. I thought Anna was going to hit me with a baseball bat."

Janet thinks a moment. "Well, it's understandable and all. Him just turning up like this, without any warning beforehand. What did he expect?"

"I like to think I'm a better person than that. Not someone who would do such a thing."

"You're fine. You mustn't let it bother you. He must think it was okay as well or else he wouldn't have come to see you today."

Gus hopes that it's true. "I couldn't believe that it was really John Lincoln. I thought someone must be playing a terrible trick, or a scam or something. I wanted to get to the bottom of it."

"That's like you."

They sit on the bench for a while, not talking, looking at the day—it's warmer than it actually is today, she's wearing the gray fitted suit he likes so much, a kind of false spring, a last of autumn, the trees on the hillside across the river a hatchwork of sticks—the two of them not touching but close enough to do so if they wanted to, if, say, they wanted to hold hands, close enough, for that matter, if he wanted to put his arm around her, but he doesn't, he wouldn't, that is never a part of it.

"Were you and your brother close, growing up?"

"Hardly. Well, that's not true. When they were young, the twins, John Lincoln and his sister, Mary Lydia, we were very close for a time, they looked up to me, you know, the big brother. I tried to help them as much as I could, teach them from my experience, you know, guide them through all the pitfalls they might find themselves in. And I think they really appreciated it, for a while. But, you know, as they got older...."

"What were some of the pitfalls you thought they might fall into?"

Gus thinks for a moment, thinking how he wants to put this. "I wanted them to know, I thought it was important for them to know, that their father, our father, wasn't the nice man they thought he was. That there was a dark side to him that he tried to keep hidden from them, and it could hurt them if they weren't aware of it."

"It sounds sinister. He sounds sinister."

"He was, he was. That's what I tried to impress upon them, make them aware of. It sounds dramatic, I know, but I truly thought their lives could depend upon their being aware of what he was capable of, what he was really like."

"I can't imagine—"

"Their father, my father, killed my mother."

"Gus. . . ."

"I saw it with my own eyes, Janet. I saw it as clearly as I'm seeing you right now."

"You mean when she fell into the trench that night and caught on fire?"

"Fell? Or maybe was pushed."

"How can you say a thing like that?"

"Because it's what I saw. Okay, I couldn't tell if he pushed her or not, but from what I did see it could be possible. As they were crossing the boards over the trench, Mother was in the lead, she had the lantern, and the boards were shaky, they gave a little when they walked on them, springy, and I saw Father do something, people said he must have reached out to steady her but it could have been just as easily that he pushed her, I can't be sure of that, I admit. But I do know that when she fell into the trench and the lantern broke and the kerosene spilled over her and caught on fire, I saw my father run to the front porch, the provisions were there that had been delivered while they were away in Pittsburgh, I saw him grab the barrel of flour and run back and dump it on her. And of course it only made it worse, it covered the flames all right but it held in the heat, she never had a chance, he burned her alive. He said he thought it was salt that he poured on her, to put out the flames, but it wasn't. I saw him grab the barrel of flour."

"But couldn't it be just as he said? That he grabbed the flour by mistake?"

"That's what he wanted people to believe."

"But then he jumped in the trench and scraped the flour off her, beat out the flames with his bare hands, he bore those scars the rest of his life, I saw them when I first came to work here. He suffered all the rest of his life with them, I always felt so sorry for him, what he went through."

"I have no doubt he ate up your sympathy. Maybe after he did it that night he had a change of heart or something, I don't know what his intentions were. All I do know is that she was screaming and screaming, I can still hear her. My mother. . . ."

"That must have been awful for you."

"I wanted the twins to be aware of what their father was capable of. That he wasn't the benevolent paterfamilias they thought he was. I used to have to pretend to be the dutiful son because I had to if I wanted to be able to work on my own projects here like the Lylemobile. But I had to be on guard every minute."

"But why would he do such a thing, Gus? Why would he do that to his wife?"

"I've thought a lot about that over the years. And I think he was already attracted to Missy, that maybe he was already seeing her and in love with her. You know, a younger woman, and her family was prominent in town and at the college, it would certainly help his standing to be married to her."

"That's crazy talk."

"Is it? I know people say that when I've mentioned it in the past. But is it crazy? You tell me. Such things happen, you know, a man wants another woman, they fall in love, but there's a wife standing in their way."

"Gus, I hate to hear you talking like this. . . ." Janet thinks a moment. "How did the twins react when you would tell them these things?"

"Well, when they were younger, they believed it. They would tell me instances of when they'd see another side of Father, when his true colors would come out. When he'd get angry with somebody, if they made a wrong delivery, or if somebody messed up at the shop. We would sit around and compare notes, and they would spy on him, tell me things that he did. But then as they got older, I don't know, maybe they got tired of it, thought of it more as a game and lost interest. I think John Lincoln simply didn't believe it anymore. Believe what I had told him. But of course by that time his relationship to Father wasn't very good. One of his reactions to the things I told him about his father was to give him trouble any way he could. He was a real snot. People always thought John Lincoln was this golden boy, oh he was so smart and intelligent, he read all the time, didn't even like to go outside to play or be with other boys because he was so special, Missy and everyone thought it was so precious. Father would do everything he could to get him more outside with other boys, but John Lincoln just mocked him and Father would give up."

"I never heard that about John Lincoln. I always heard how smart he was. People talked about that after . . . when everybody thought he was dead."

"Oh, he was smart all right. But he was devious too. People didn't see that side of him, people didn't want to see that side of him. I caught him a number of times being mean to Mary Lydia, he once almost had her fall out a window to look at something he told her was there, if I hadn't come along and put a stop to it, heaven knows what would have happened. He just wanted to see what would happen if she did it. And yes, she would do it, because she adored him, worshipped him, John Lincoln could do no wrong."

"It doesn't sound healthy."

"It wasn't. They were much too close." He thinks a moment. "I've never told anybody about this, but of course, when he disappeared just at the time Mary Lydia turned up pregnant, there was speculation, well, you know, people wondered. I never heard anybody come right out and suggest the baby was John Lincoln's, but the thought was there. I had wondered a long time before that if they were, you know. They were that close, especially Mary Lydia. I could see her doing that, could see her allowing him, and could see him forcing himself on her. I guess we'll never know for sure."

"Those are terrible thoughts to have."

"I'm not proud of them." He wonders if that is true. Not pride, exactly, but vindication in some way, justification. "I will be interested to know how she reacts to seeing him again. He's going down to Hickory to see her."

"You sound resentful of him, I'm afraid. As if you have a lot of anger about him. Anger that you've kept hidden for a long time."

"Yes, I suppose there is. Because eventually John Lincoln resented me."

"Why would he resent you?"

"Because it was obvious Father started to groom me to take over the business. The fact is, if John Lincoln had been at all interested, Father would have preferred him. Simply for the fact that John Lincoln was smarter than I was."

"Oh now, don't put yourself down—"

"No, it's true, it was obvious in school and all, I had to struggle for mediocre grades but John Lincoln buzzed right through school, he never studied, I don't believe I ever saw him take a book home or do homework, and he got nothing but one hundreds in all his classes. So he would have been the obvious choice for Father to prepare to take over the company. And if truth be known, I really didn't want it. My talents are more mechanical, not intellectual. I love working with machines, I love tinkering with them, finding out how they work, finding out how to make them work better. That is my strength, and eventually Father hoped that he could teach me all the other skills I'd need to know to manage a company. But he was wrong."

"Gus, you've done a good job with what you have—"

"No, I know that's not true. Thank you for saying it, I truly appreciate it. But I know what my failings are. And the thing was, John Lincoln, before he disappeared, resented that Father was obviously grooming me to take things over."

"But you said John Lincoln wasn't interested."

"That didn't stop him from resenting that Father was preparing me. That's one of the things that got me most puzzled about John

Lincoln's return. He said he meant it as a joke, but he said that I shouldn't worry, that he hadn't come back to take over the company. Why would he make a joke like that if it hadn't occurred to him to try to do that? He couldn't, there is no way it could happen, but it still makes me wonder. . . ."

"You wonder too much." She smiles at him. His friend.

And the river flows on; they sit and watch it for a while. Over the surface a small flight of geese wing their way toward the end of the valley; they will be leaving soon, flying south for the winter, he will hear them in the early mornings, flights of them, great wavering Vs across the sky, coming from the far north, their voices calling to one another, encouraging perhaps, or simply saying I am here, where are you?

Gus shook himself out of his thoughts. "Well now, this is getting me nowhere." He got up, made a visual inventory of his office, turned off the lights, and made his way through the outer office, along the corridor and down the steps, turning off lights as he went, out into the November evening, the evening chill just starting after the unusually warm day, going to his car, a Lylemobile, and heading home to Sycamore House.

*

"So. Tell me. Was he surprised to see you, that you turned up there at his office unannounced?"

After she got John Lincoln his dinner and beer, Anna sat across from him at the table, keeping him company, as if it was as normal as could be. He was aware that, without his mask, at certain angles if she looked, she could see inside his mouth as he chewed his food. The thing was, she didn't seem to notice, or if she did, it didn't faze her.

"He didn't seem surprised. He said he sort of expected that I'd come visit him."

"Did he apologize for ripping off your mask?"

"More or less. He offered an apology, but I got the idea that he was more sorry that it happened than sorry he did it."

"Bastard."

Torn

"I think Gus is probably genetically incapable of feeling true remorse for something, any more than he could be surprised by something. The gene for feeling emotions seems to have been left out of his makeup."

Anna folded her hands on the tablecloth, shook her head. Waiting for him to go on.

"When I arrived there was a young designer with him. Daniel something."

"Spalding. Daniel Spalding. He's here at the hotel, you've probably seen him around but didn't know who he was."

"He's working with Gus on the redesign of the Lylemobile. Or the Zephyr, as he wants to call it now."

"Spalding eats in here sometimes, comes in for a drink occasionally, but I think he favors one or two of the places up on Seventh Avenue. More to his taste, whatever that is. Probably just cheaper. Personally, I don't trust the guy, there's something not right about him. He's weaselly, if you know what I mean. Did you see Gus' secretary, Janet?"

"Yes, she showed me in. I got the feeling, in the way Gus looked at her, that there could be something going on between them."

"That would be weird if there was."

"Why?"

"Because she has something going on with young Daniel."

"She's got to be in her forties or so, doesn't she? Isn't that a bit old for him?"

"Apparently not. She was married but her husband left her, before I got to town. No one's supposed to know, but she visits young Daniel in his room fairly regularly. According to Eddie. And Eddie knows everything that goes on around here."

"I figured he did. That's why I tip him well, extravagantly really, every time I can. I want him on my side."

"He is. He's told me."

"I guess that's good to know."

He ate without speaking for a few moments, caught up in his vegetable medley, the mashed potatoes. "That's interesting, though, about Janet. I really got the idea that there was some attraction there, at least on Gus' side, you know, how you get a feeling about things like that. You can sense the energy going on. And he was really touchy on the subject of his wife."

"Lily?"

"The only time I got a real glimpse of the famous Gus temper was when I inquired how she was doing, I didn't see her when I went up to the house to see Missy—What?"

Anna was laughing. "Oh, you pressed the right button, that's for sure."

"What? What did I do? She's not dead or something, is she?"

"Oh no, she's very much alive. But they haven't lived together for years. The separation was another thing that happened before I got here."

"When I left, she had taken their son and gone to Kansas to see her parents. I remember she was gone a long time, but there was so much else going on, Mary Lydia getting pregnant and my preparations to go overseas, that I never paid that much attention. And of course Gus and I weren't close at all, he wouldn't talk to me about it if the marriage was in trouble."

"I guess what happened is that she left him, or at least tried to, but her parents gave her a bad time about it, they were strict Covenanters, I think the father was even a minister—"

"That's right, I remember that part."

"Well, so she came back, but she wouldn't live with Gus at Sycamore House, she wouldn't divorce him but she wouldn't live with him either. So Gus bought her a place up on Orchard Hill near the college, and she eventually got a job there in the registrar's office, became the registrar when the other woman retired. Though Gus, I'm told, still pays her a stipend. A line item at the company."

"So that's why he called me a son of a bitch when I mentioned her."

"He probably thought you were digging at him about her. Bringing up a touchy subject."

"He was touchy on the subject of money too. It's a wonder he can afford to keep paying her, there seemed very little going on in the shop. He said they had plenty of orders, but I didn't see any evidence of it."

"According to the talk I hear at the bar, from the few guys who still come in from Keystone, it's like a ghost shop, very little going on, and Gus continues to lay people off, with no intention to bring them back."

"I had a bad feeling about the company, talking to him, something really seems to be off. And yet he continues to pursue this redesign of the Lylemobile, the Zephyr."

"Did he show you what he's working on?"

"I saw a schematic he said he uses for presentations to attract investors."

"I can tell you, from the people who come in here and stay at the hotel, there's very little interest from any investors. They generally come away from meeting with him wanting nothing to do with it."

"It's too bad, in a way. He really does have a good thing there, with the quick-starting steam engine, and the new design is very modern and up-to-date."

"Go figure what the buying public wants."

"I just have this bad feeling. . . ."

"Well, you think about it, and if you figure it out, let me know," she said, getting up. "I've got the Kiwanis coming in tonight for an awards dinner. I'll see you tomorrow morning, we'll leave right after you have your breakfast. We should be on the road sometime around nine, it'll take us some time to get down to Hickory."

"I can't thank you enough, are you sure you—"

"One thing you'll learn about me is that I don't do anything I'm not sure of. And yes, I'm sure I want to take you to Hickory, I wouldn't miss it for the world. I'll send Susan back in a while to redd your table and get your dessert. I know she wants to show you that she is okay having had a glimpse behind your mask."

"That's nice of her to be concerned, but I'll put the mask back on while she's here."

"Probably best," Anna said. "Incidentally, you've got quite a name for yourself around town, from all your walks. You're known as Johnny No-Face. People tell stories about when they've seen you. The guys at the bar try to one-up each other, claiming where they've seen you, some try to say they've talked to you. Johnny No-Face."

"I've been called worse things."

"And probably will again. See you tomorrow. John Lincoln."

"You can call me John. Less of a mouthful."

"I will, then." She smiled, more to herself than to him, nodded, and went to take care of whatever needed taken care of.

Ten

Saturday morning, in Anna's late-model Ford Touring Car—"What, you don't have a Lylemobile?" he asked her; "Another crack like that and you'll walk back," she replied—they followed the Ohio River as it headed north to Rochester, then when the river turned westward, crossed over at Monaca and followed Route 18 as it meandered through farm country, reaching Hickory late morning. On the outskirts of town they stopped at a service station to refuel, check the tires, and refill the radiator, as well as ask directions to the Claire White farm. The attendant, who looked like a farmer himself in his denim shirt and overalls, told them how to find it.

"But won't be nobody there today. Nobody home."

"How do you know?" Anna said, taking charge of things to spare the attendant from having to deal with John Lincoln's mask.

"Fall Festival. Mary White makes the best apple cobbler in the area. I'm closing up right after you folks to get some before it's all gone."

Hickory was strung out along the curves of Route 50—more a designation than an actual place—with a few necessary shops and a post office intermingled among residences. The festival was being held in a small fairgrounds beside the volunteer fire

Torn

department. They parked on the shoulder in the first space they came to and walked back to join the crowd. John Lincoln was concerned that his mask might draw undo attention, he pulled the collar of his jacket up around his face and tipped his hat low, but as they mingled among the booths—weavers and woodworkers, a tinsmith, a couple of potters, an apple press pressing apples, canned foods and baked goods for sale, carts selling funnel cakes and candy apples, along with displays of farm tools, a line of John Deere and Allis-Chalmers tractors, some of them idling, their exhaust flaps *pinging pinging pinging*, a thrasher and a plow for sale—most people didn't seem to notice, or if they did, paid no attention.

"How are you going to find her with all these people?" Anna said. She was wearing a stylish fitted wool suit, a tan and navy windowpane plaid, with a long jacket and culottes, a black archer's hat with a feather canted on her head; he wondered if she bought the outfit special for her outing in the country. "You're not even sure what she looks like these days."

"Let's look in the food tent. I'm sure I'll know her."

At the back of the fairgrounds was a long open tent with a cafeteria line serving hot dogs and hamburgers, potato salad, baked beans, pulled pork, buckets of salad, and toward the end near the cash register, desserts and coffee. The woman he recognized as Mary Lydia was standing behind the table close to what must be her pans of apple cobbler. The attendant at the service station was talking to her as she dished up his plate; when the man saw John Lincoln and Anna, he waved, pointed to Mary Lydia and grinned. Mary Lydia looked to where the man was pointing, stared for a moment without expression, then turned and walked away from the tables, out the rear of the tent.

"I'm going after her," John Lincoln said to Anna, heading back along the line.

She walked along the edge of the grounds, unhurried but apparently aware that he was following her, up the slope toward the fireman's hall, going to the back door and letting herself in.

John Lincoln followed, stepping into the dark hall; in the wedge of light coming from the door behind him he caught a glimpse of Mary Lydia as she swung a straight-armed blow aimed at his head, then apparently realized his damaged face, tried to pull it back and ended up hitting his shoulder, following that with a barrage of tight-fisted blows against his chest.

"You son of a bitch, you son of a bitch, you son of a bitch, you son of a bitch...."

The only way to stop her was to grab her and hold her tight against him, Mary Lydia struggling and pushing at him at first, then dissolving into tears with her face buried in his chest. In a few minutes she had regained her composure, pushed away from him, and went in search of a light switch. The switch she found was for a bank of lights along a side wall; they pulled a couple of wooden chairs from the nearby stack and sat down at right angles to each other. There were glimmers of the girl he once knew, though not many. An expression here and there, a tilt of the head, a sidelong look of her eyes. Otherwise she was a broader, thicker, stubbier, and of course older, version of Mary Lydia, her hair pulled back in a serviceable bun, wearing a green-and-black buffalo plaid wool shirt that looked like it must belong to her husband, baggy brown slacks, and shoes that would do well in mud. It occurred to him the years had brought the magnitude of changes to her that the mask had brought to him.

"I'm so very, very sorry, I didn't know how—"

"What has it been, twenty years now, and never a phone call, a letter—"

"When it first happened, I was either unconscious or drugged most of the time, and there was a lot of pain. And when I finally did get into my right mind again, so much time had elapsed, I realized I must have been declared dead a long time before, and I was going to have to deal not only with you but with Father and Gus and Missy, to say nothing of all the people in town...."

"But here you are now."

"Yes. And you recognized me... despite...."

"Of course I recognized you. We're twins, you're the other half of me. I knew you hadn't died, if you had I would have known it on a level beyond knowing, the same way I would know you now, no matter what happened to you. So, go on ahead and tell me, what did happen to you?"

He told the story once again of his accident, his treatment, and his life in the army, though he was surprised, he gave her only a gloss of what had happened, none of the details that he had gone into with Missy—it was closer to what he told Gus, though for a different reason. She was staring at him intensively, keeping her gaze focused on his eyes, or rather his good eye, avoiding the damaged one.

"Does it hurt?" she asked when he was finished.

"What is that old joke? 'Is your face hurting you, because it's killing me.'"

She looked at him blankly.

"Let's say I'm aware of it all the time. But what about yourself? I never would have expected that you'd end up living on a farm."

She looked away, laughed a little to herself. "I never would have thought so either. After you left and the baby and all—you do know about the baby, don't you??"

"Yes. I'm told that some people thought it was mine."

"The father's name was Dimitris."

"Papalas. Yeah, I remember him. An exchange student, from Greece, right?"

She nodded.

"Good-looking guy." As soon as he said it he wished he hadn't, not the type of thing to say.

Her eyes narrowed, but she went on.

"After that, when I went back to college I met Claire and he was very kind and gentle and accepted me for who I was, who I am. I was pretty shattered, but he seemed determined to put me back together. When it looked like we were going to become involved, I told him straight out what had happened to me, and that I really wasn't interested in a relationship with anyone, much less wanted to get married. You see, I was damaged in the miscarriage . . . and I could never bear children, and I told Claire I didn't even want to try, the whole idea . . . But he said that was okay, I guess maybe as a farmer he was used to taking care of things, he said he wanted to marry me anyway and so I did and we moved down here and it's my life now."

John Lincoln didn't know whether to be happy for her or distraught. She seemed contented enough but there was none of the liveliness, none of the excitement or fire of the girl he grew up with. But then he supposed he had no room to talk on the subject of being different. Johnny No-Face.

"Who is the woman you're with?"

John Lincoln was jarred back to the present. "Oh, that's Anna. She's a friend, from the hotel."

"She seems very nice."

He wondered how Mary Lydia could get such an impression from just looking at her. Even though her appraisal was correct. She went on.

"Who else have you seen since you've been back?"

"Mother, of course."

"Mother? Missy?"

"She said you've barely been in contact with her since you moved down here. And I know it's understandable, and she knows it's understandable, the way she acted while we were growing up. But she's genuinely changed her life—don't pooh-pooh it, she really has, people can change. She knows how badly she acted while Father was alive, but she's given up the drinking and truly wants to make amends. I found to my surprise that I really had a connection with her—well, she is our mother after all. You should consider reaching out to her, I think you'd be surprised. She really wants to get to know you, get to know both of us. Her children."

Mary Lydia gave him a noncommittal look. "Have you seen Gus?"

"Yes. Purely by accident, not by design, though before I stumbled onto him, or rather he stumbled onto me, I intended to let him know I was back."

"And alive. How did he take to that?"

"It was a strained reunion, let's put it that way."

"I can only imagine."

"It seems the Steam Works isn't doing very well since he's been running it. But I can't really be surprised at that, he was never going to be able to fill Father's shoes and he was always aware of that."

"I hadn't had any contact with him for years, he didn't even come to my wedding, it was here in Hickory and he said he couldn't travel that far, said he couldn't get away. Then a few years ago he turned up one day, said he thought it was high time for a visit, but what he really wanted was for me to take out a loan using our farm as collateral and give him the money."

"What? How big a loan?"

"As big as we could get. He said he needed the funds to save the Steam Works and was calling on my family loyalty to save the family business."

"He had already hit up Mother for sixty thousand a few years before that."

"The bastard. I'm glad I told him no."

"He must have really been desperate. Did he give any specifics at all?"

"When I asked him he said it was for the legal expenses to stop a suit involving long-term payouts that would sink the company. His words, 'sink the company.'"

Long-term payouts? Such as to pay the compensation for O'Brien's accident? The timing seemed right. . . . "That's all he said?"

"That was enough. Who did he think he was? Having no contact with me for all those years, and then waltzing in here with a harebrained scheme like that. Typical Gus. He must have tried to get a loan elsewhere and no one would touch it, so he thought he could manipulate me like he used to when I was younger. But I told him I wanted no part of it and he went away and I never heard from him since."

"I've thought a lot over the years about how Gus tried to manipulate both of us while we were growing up, all that business of trying to turn us against Father."

Mary Lydia shook her head. "I have nothing to do with that now. That's all in the past."

"Yes, I guess so."

They sat in silence several moments. Realizing there was nothing else to say, about anything.

"Well, I should be getting back," Mary Lydia said, standing up, looking away from him. "Are you home for good now or just here for a visit?"

"I'm not sure. It all depends. . . ."

"I'm sure it does."

He could tell she was anxious to be off. He thought of saying that they should stay in touch but the words never materialized. After she turned off the lights, he walked her back across the lot to the food tent, neither one saying anything. He found Anna sitting at one of the wooden tables in front of the tent, writing something for the attendant they had talked to at the service station.

"Say hello to Arnold," she said to John Lincoln as he walked up. "We got to talking and I'm writing out my recipe for tomato sauce for him."

John Lincoln started to introduce Mary Lydia to Anna but realized his sister was already headed inside the food tent, back to the dessert table. John Lincoln looked at Anna, apologetic. Anna shrugged and said, "She probably knows best." She added a line to her recipe and handed the festival program she had been writing on back to Arnold.

"I thank you, ma'am," Arnold said, glancing at the recipe and extricating himself from the bench. "Hope you folks have a safe trip back up to the city." Adding to John Lincoln, "And I hope your cold gets better real soon. Nice of you to wear that mask and all to protect other people."

As Arnold headed toward the line of tractors, Anna looked at John Lincoln. "It was easier than trying to explain otherwise. You ready to go?"

"Yes. I've seen enough."

John Lincoln tried to catch Mary Lydia's attention to wave good-bye, but she was busy talking to people in the food line. He and Anna walked back through the booths, up the slope to the highway, and started toward the car. In front of the fireman's hall was a small memorial garden with a bench.

"Let's sit down for a minute," he said.

"Are you okay?" Anna said, all concern.

"I'm fine, I'm fine. I just feel worn-out all of a sudden."

After a moment, Anna said, "Quite a shock."

"How do you mean?"

"You can't tell me you were ready for the girl of your dreams, the one you carried with you all those years, to turn out looking like a farm woman. In fact, turned out to *be* a farm woman."

They laughed a little. Then John Lincoln grew serious again.

"You know, I was aware rationally that she'd be older. But I guess I still must have had her pictured in my mind. . . ."

"The way she was when you saw her last. You couldn't help that, it's only human."

"It's terrible. When we were children growing up we talked about how we'd live together when we got older, just the two of us, together forever. And maybe I was still thinking that way, on some level of my mind. She was the love of my life, or so I thought, she was the only love I had ever known. I judged all girls, all women, in terms of her. And then with my accident and everything that came after it, getting to know other girls, other women, was out of the question. I guess all my knowledge of women came to a halt back then when I was a teenager, frozen in time with her."

"And the big thaw came today in the presence of a rather dowdy though pleasant-looking middle-aged woman dishing out food at a country festival."

"But the fact she looks different now isn't even the worst part. And as far as that goes I have no room to talk, I couldn't look more different. No, the worst part, the saddest part, is that she hasn't changed in her thinking at all. In some ways she's actually regressed over the years. Look at her, buried away down here in the boonies, surrounded by yokels whose thinking goes no further than wondering when it's going to rain so they can bring in the hay, her greatest accomplishment her ability to make apple cobbler. What kind of a life is that? It makes me want to cry. She's living the brother-and-sister life with this guy Claire. Never really knowing love, never knowing all the things the world has to offer, all her education, all her potential to really do something, to be somebody, thrown away. I was sitting there with her, this woman who at one time knew me better than anyone else in the world, who I knew better than anyone else in the world, and I had nothing to say to her. Not now, not ever. We were total strangers, and always would be now. The familiarity we once had only made the unfamiliarity now that much deeper, a chasm we could never bridge."

"So who wouldn't be worn-out after carrying the load you have for twenty years? You were not only keeping alive the image you had of yourself, you were carrying the image of who she was or who you wanted her to be as well. That's quite a load to be lifted all in one go. I would think you'd be worn-out. On the other hand, I wouldn't be surprised if you were also relieved."

"Why would I be relieved?"

"Because a part of you must have known that what you were carrying around was a lie. And there's nothing more exhausting than that."

"But if on some level of my mind I knew it was a lie, why did I come back here? If it wasn't for Mary Lydia, or if she was only part of the reason, to get her once and for all out of my fantasies, what am I doing here?"

"I'm afraid you're the only one who would know about that."

And who was this woman sitting with him who made all this good sense? What was she doing spending time with him anyway? Was he another charity case for her, another wounded person to take care of like her husband? The thought of her husband brought back what Mary Lydia said about Gus wanting her to take out a loan for him, the possibility that it was linked to Anna's husband's accident, but he decided not to mention it. This was supposed to be a getaway day for her, he didn't want to remind her of such unpleasantries as her husband, though John Lincoln also knew, and wasn't proud of it, that not bringing it up was as much for his sake as it was for hers.

*

Mary Lydia turned off the highway, past the embankment with the arrangement of whitewashed stones that spelled out,

THE WHITE FARM

and started down the lane, the late afternoon sunlight in the bare branches of the line of birch trees throwing shadows across the dirt drive in front her, closing like the two sides of a zipper as she passed, down the long hill toward the farmhouse and collection of farm buildings in the hollow at the bottom. On the hillside beyond the house she could see Claire plowing the field they called the Far Forty. The sound of her tires across the small wooden bridge over the creek brought their two border collies, Wolfer and Buzz, bounding off the front porch, dancing around the pickup with much tongue flapping and tail wagging. She parked the truck—it started out once upon a time as an old Model T coupe but Claire took a torch to it—beside the house and unloaded the several trays she had used for her apple cobbler from the front seat.

"Yes, yes, I'm glad to see you guys too. Now, watch out, settle down. . . ."

She carried the trays through the basement and upstairs to the kitchen, leaving them soaking in the sink to be washed later. After grabbing a couple of her home-baked dog treats, she went back down the narrow wooden stairs and through the dark unfinished cellar and out into the light.

"Good boys, good boys. One for you, and one for you."

She waited till the dogs finished their treats, then sent them off to the barn. And stopped. Took in the view, the bowl of the surrounding hills and the fields, the hardscrabble farm that she and Claire had devoted their lives to tending. Thinking, I'm sure it wouldn't mean much to anybody else, John Lincoln would hate it, and you can bet Gus never saw it before he wanted me to take out a loan on it, he'd know that in this market it must be worth next to nothing, but to me it's the most beautiful place on earth. Gus. What a fool. He always was. At least John Lincoln and I would agree on that. But as far as that goes, John Lincoln was never much better when it came to being foolish.

Everyone thought when the twins were growing up that John Lincoln was the dominant one, everyone considered him special—as did John Lincoln himself—everyone thought that Mary Lydia was the follower, enthralled by him, dazzled by his brilliance, oh how he shone. But she was the only one who understood how vulnerable he was, how he dangled emotionally by a thin thread; the truth was that it was Mary Lydia who held him together, her displays of supposed adoration in fact the only thing that kept him from crashing to pieces from his delicate constitution, his overwrought nature, his nerves that threatened at any time to shatter. How he got to that state, why he was in that condition, she never understood, she was only a child after all, she only knew that without her propping him up there would be nothing to him. Did he know it? Was he aware of his dependency? She thought he must be. There were times he did everything he could to dispel her influence, prove his strength and independence—no, it was more than that, his superiority, his dominance. The time when they were eight or nine and he told her there was something she had to see outside the attic window, that she had to lean out to see it, told her to lean our farther and farther when she said she didn't see anything, letting him direct her, wondering how far he would have let her go, wondering to what degree he would endanger her, wondering if he would really let her fall out the window just to prove to himself that she would

Torn

do anything for him, when Gus came along and put a stop to it before either she or John Lincoln could learn the result.

She closed the basement door behind her and stopped at the root cellar to pick up a couple of Granny apples and stuck them in her pants' pocket. Then she started up the continuation of the drive, curving up behind the house and past the barn. She opened the gate to the field known as the East Twenty and started across. Betsy lay in the grass at the top of the rise, along with the rest of Mary Lydia's Girls—Sally and Gerry and Floppsy—spent cows that could no longer produce milk but that Mary Lydia wouldn't allow to be slaughtered for ground beef; when Betsy saw her, the cow stood up and lumbered stiffly toward her, tail flapping.

"Hello, girl. Miss me today? I missed you too."

Mary Lydia rubbed her snout and the cow fell in behind her. The others joined the little parade to the opposite fence, watching as Mary Lydia unhooked the gate, hooked it again from the other side, and continued into the plowed field.

"Hold on, girls," she said over her shoulder. "I'll be back in a minute."

Claire was coming toward her behind the plow, the reins of the team draped around his shoulders. The horses, Dewey and Dowd, came up to her and lowered their heads for her to rub their foreheads; she took the apples from her pants pocket and gave one to each.

"How're you boys doing today? You helping him out okay?"

Then she walked back to Claire, who had his straw hat off and was wiping his head with a bandana.

"Wanted to let you know I'm home."

"How did it go?"

She nodded. "Quite a good turnout. Bigger than last year." She had some news for him but it would keep till later.

"I'll finish this little section before the milking."

"They're already in the barn waiting for you."

"I figured."

"I was going to do the rest of that stew tonight."

"Sounds good. And biscuits?"

"Yes. And biscuits."

She touched the flat of her hand against his upper arm; they smiled to each other and he flapped the reins to get the team's attention. "Walk on."

The team started off again and she fell in behind her husband to the end of the row, then headed back through the gate and her waiting girls. She led the cows across the field, holding the gate open for them, then took them down the hill to the feed lot beside the barn, loosening the hay in the bale for them with a pitchfork. She watched them eat for a few minutes, made sure there was water in the trough, then headed back to the house. Thinking of seeing John Lincoln today. The mask. The twisted flesh behind it, thinking of the pain he must have gone through, probably still went through. She would have thought it would weaken him but it seemed just the opposite, he seemed stronger now than she had ever known him. More his own person, secure in himself. Curious, he lost his face and found who he was.

She had been glad he was dead. When she first heard he was dead. There, she could finally say it. Admit it to herself. Her first thought when she heard the news. Her first reaction. Not dead as in death, but dead as in gone. She was free of him. She could breathe for once. On her own. No, she hadn't felt he was still alive as she had told him. She wondered if she would feel such a thing if he had died as they said twins did, but she didn't, she only felt the relief that he was no longer in her life. And the guilt, the sadness that she would feel such a thing. The shock of the news had caused her to miscarry, but she knew it was more the awareness of what she was feeling than the word of his death. The shock that she could feel such a thing about someone she thought she loved. Well, she did love him, but that didn't mean she wanted him in her life. Wanted her life lived through him. And it didn't mean that she wasn't glad he was alive now. It only meant she no more wanted to be around him now than she did then.

No, Claire wasn't the man of her dreams. Thank heavens. He

Torn

was real, he was exactly what he appeared to be. Nothing more, nothing less. And this was her reality now. Her world. The old farmhouse. The hills and the trees and the sound of her girls behind her chewing, the swish of their tails, the smells of their shit and piss. Beyond the line of hills, the sky at the end of the day glowed blood red, the wind stirred in the bare branches of the sycamores and birch trees. In the distance the crows called to one another. She ducked her head and smiled to herself and headed inside the house to heat up the stew. Make Claire his biscuits.

. . . So, it is night now, and all our characters are in place . . . all the relevant themes introduced . . . all the groundwork laid for future developments, entanglements, conflicts . . . John Lincoln has been back in Furnass for one week, and already his presence is causing rifts in the established patterns of the town, tears in time-honored assumptions, though life goes on as life insists on doing, despite all attempts to thwart it . . . as in her house on Eleventh Street behind the Grand Hotel, Anna O'Brien, Anna D'Angelis, sits beside the bed of her bedridden husband, Warren, feeding him spoonfuls of apple cobbler, mashed in a bowl and soaked with milk, that she brought home with her from her day in Hickory, telling him what all she did that day (though omitting any mention of her traveling companion), the trip down and back, the people she met at the festival and the various displays and booths, thinking she saw a different side of the Lyle family today, she knew that she liked John Lincoln but she credited that to the fact that he had spent so much time away from the rest of the family, and that his traumatic experiences with his wounds must have purged the derogatory Lyle traits out of him, but saw today that there was more to the Lyles than she ever gave them credit for, more hurt and pain and desperation than her passing contact with Gus and Missy and Lily would have ever prepared her for, thinking maybe the Lyles are human after all . . . in his office on Twelfth Street a block above the main street, David Laughlin, sitting at his desk in

the circle of light from his green-glass-shaded lamp, puts down his pen from the brief he is writing, takes off his glasses, and with his elbows propped on his desk blotter buries his eyes against the palms of his hands, rubbing them until he's afraid he'll press them back into his skull, then stares into the darkness of the room around him, and as he usually does anytime he has a moment's respite, thinks of Anna, wonders how she's doing, tries to picture what she could be doing at this very moment, and wishes the world was such that he could see her in person but knows that that's impossible, as much from his situation as hers, to say nothing that she now considers him the enemy from his representing the Keystone Steam Works against her suit for compensation for her husband's accident, wonders if there will ever be a way to bridge that separation with her and change her feelings toward him, thinks the only way would be to somehow discredit the company and its management, cast doubt regarding the evidence the company used to counteract her suit, then wonders what kind of an attorney would think that way about a client and thinks the kind of attorney who hasn't been paid his retainer for the last two years and one who feels that his client is shitting on him, that's who, or one who's desperate to reach his love who is as unattainable as the stars ... as in Sycamore House, the large white frame house halfway up the slope of the valley above the town, after Nancy, the maid/housekeeper/cook/cleaner, fixed his dinner and left for the evening—walking back across the hill to the section of Furnass called Blacktown, just as her mother did before her, though Blacktown these days of the Depression is as much poor White as it is poor Black—Gus Lyle walks through the rooms, first downstairs then upstairs, on one side of the house and then the other, amazed at how empty it all seems without Missy in it, never for a moment thinking he would miss her if she weren't here, and now she's not here and he's missing her indeed, wondering what it was that made her move out though he knows he's hardly been friendly or even civil to her over the years, barely tolerating the presence of his stepmother in the house and letting her know it—but no, that's not true either; he wasn't intentionally unfriendly or mean to her, he simply ignored her because he didn't care, considered her another burden to take care of, his father's second wife, certainly not his mother in any way, shape, or form—realizes now, despite whatever feelings he had about her, or lack of feelings, he should have been better to her, treated her with more consideration and respect, and thinks it must have been something John Lincoln said to her that made her leave, that turned her against him, wonders for that matter all over again why John Lincoln decided to come back to town, what his younger brother is up to, is it to try to horn in on the company, or does he feel that he's owed some inheritance from the death of their father, maybe he wants this house, John Lincoln wouldn't just show up this way after all this time without some reason, some intention, his younger brother always was devious, couldn't be trusted, a born liar, up to something, Gus tells himself he's going to have to be careful, watchful at every step, keep his eyes open, be prepared for anything . . . as in her family's house on Orchard Hill, in the gray stone house built in the style of an English country cottage, two blocks from Covenant College where her father was a longtime professor and chairman of the History Department, Missy Lyle stands in her father's study, shifting his books around on the wall of shelves to make room for her own books, the books she brought with her when she moved from Sycamore House that the movers delivered today, then sits down at his desk, turns in the swivel chair to look out the French doors behind her, the room on the first floor at the back of the house, the doors now in the nighttime only looking out into darkness though at the rear of the backyard the bushes are silhouetted by the lights below the hillside from the mills and factories along Walnut Bottom Run, the backyard where she played as a child, where her father built her a sandbox, where her family would have picnics on the grass, and where she sat on the bench with Malcolm when he came to court her—of all the improbable romances, he so much older than she was, Missy in her early thirties at the time already given up on any *possibility of finding love much less a husband, and here he was, a prominent businessman in town, with all the tales about the accident that he burned alive his first wife, his hands hideously scarred from the flames, and yet here he was, interested in her, wanting her, before they were married and it all turned wrong—turning back to the room, thinking no matter now, it was all over and done with, so glad to be back in a place she can call her own, away from the Lyle house, away from the fear every day even in daytime of looking in the shadows, around a door, down a corridor, having seen a few times the spirits that inhabited the house, the pale woman as transparent as fog, a column of smoke, the fetus covered in blood, and most disturbing of all, the time she saw her stepson Gus still very much alive transformed into an apparition standing in flames, reaching out to her, for what she didn't know, she only knows now she's grateful to be away, happy that John Lincoln came to see her and, dare she say it, that perhaps Mary Lydia will come visit her, her own children, any ghosts in her life the living kind that she can embrace and cherish and love . . . as elsewhere on Orchard Hill, in another house within easy walking distance to the college, Lily Lyle—an attractive middle-aged woman, lean and trim, still wearing the skirt and blouse she wore to her office today, a light blue cardigan draped around her shoulders—sits in her living room in the house that her estranged husband, Gus Lyle, bought for her close to twenty years ago when she came back to Furnass, after she left with their young son Mal to go live with her parents in Kansas, except her father, a hellfire Presbyterian minister, wouldn't let her stay, told her to go back to her husband, which she did though told Gus on her return that she couldn't/wouldn't live with him, so he bought the house for her and Mal as well as provided her with a generous monthly living allowance, though in time she didn't actually need the money, she took a job in the registrar's office at the college, in time becoming the registrar herself, sits now in her living room in front of the fire in the fireplace that she doesn't really need, the evening not that chilly, but loves the comfort of it, the hominess,* curls on the sofa reading through the applications to attend or transfer to the college for the spring semester, the piles of Yes, No, and Maybe on the cushions around her, when she hears Mal come in the front door and her grown son joins her in the living room, the first time their paths have crossed in several days, Mal, after giving his mother a kiss on the forehead—she hates that, so patronizing, just kiss me on the mouth and be done with it—goes into the kitchen and gets a bottle of beer and comes back and sits across from her, at an angle to the fireplace, leaning forward in his chair as he is wont to do, rarely sitting back as if he has trouble relaxing, ever, his elbows resting on his thighs, looks at his mother, looks at the fire, looks at his mother again, and says,

"So, what's new?"

Lily holds up her stack of applications and says, "What's new with you?"

"Did you hear that John Lincoln, Dad's younger brother, is alive and back in town? The walking dead."

"I heard a couple people talking about it, but didn't know it was true."

"Oh, it's true, all right. I actually saw him, met him briefly at Dad's office, but I didn't have a chance to speak to him." Mal takes a drink of his beer, checks the fire again, and looks back at his mother. "His face is all mangled, or at least it appears that it is, he wears a mask, one of those white surgical masks people wore during the pandemic. You can't really see that much of him."

"Then how do people know it's John Lincoln?"

Mal shrugs. "I don't know. But Dad I guess accepts that that's who he is."

"And how is your father doing with the return of his younger brother? I can't imagine that went over very well."

"No, you're right. He certainly doesn't seem happy about it. He was more or less throwing him out of his office when I went in."

"I'm sure Gus is imagining all sorts of dire things, plots against him, everyone out to do him in."

"I don't think it's John Lincoln that Dad should be worrying about," Mal says, turning away to look at the fire.

"Do you want to explain that?"

Mal considers something for a moment before turning back to her, though not looking at her, studying the pattern in the carpet on the floor in front of his feet. "It's that guy Dad pulled in to help with the design of the car. Daniel Spalding. I think he's up to something, I've seen some invoices that don't add up, some expenses that . . . I don't know, just don't seem right."

"If you suspect something, you should tell your father."

"I've tried, a couple of times, but Dad just brushes anything I say aside, he thinks Spalding is doing a great job and won't consider otherwise, and I don't have any hard evidence to show him, it's more like a feeling. And you know Dad, once he's got his mind made up, that's the end of that."

"Yes, I know your father."

Mal finishes his beer and stands up. "And maybe he's right. Maybe I'm just imagining things. Jealous because he pays more attention to Spalding's ideas than to mine." He tries to laugh it off. "Whatever, I'm going to bed."

He goes across the room and he and his mother clasp hands as he passes; Lily listens to him go into the kitchen, the clink of the beer bottle in the trash, then his heavy steps upstairs and down the hall. She knows Mal is right to feel as he does, Gus always did ignore any ideas that Mal had about things, some reservation he has about a son of his having thoughts worth listening to—why is that? Some doubting of himself, no doubt, but she doesn't care enough to take her thoughts very far, or rather, she has learned that trying to figure out the man who is still her husband leads nowhere. Gus Gus Gus. The man never got over seeing his mother burned alive in the trench in their front yard, never got over wondering about the role of his father in her death; never got over watching it all unfold and being only six years old and unable to do anything to stop it from happening, blaming his father for his own inadequacies, his own inabilities to control the world. Ah well, there was nothing she could do to change it during the time they lived together, there's certainly nothing she can do removed now from his presence; she adjusts her legs up under her on the couch, picks up the next application in her stack, and prepares to make a determination about a total stranger's education, future, in many ways life and death . . . as at the Grand Hotel, Daniel Spalding, having just returned from working late at the Keystone Steam Works on a Saturday, is starting to get ready for bed, has pulled off his tie and, his suit coat already thrown over the back of a straight chair—Daniel having never learned the first principles of keeping his clothes or his living space tidy, much less keeping himself clean and presentable besides splashing cold water occasionally on his face, washing his hands when there are visible traces of foreign substances on them, a bath maybe once a week if the world is lucky—is starting to unbutton his shirt when there is a knock on the door and his heart sinks, a queasy feeling in his stomach, waiting, hoping if he's quiet whoever knocked will go away, but they don't, the knock comes again, along with a woman's voice, "You might as well open up, Daniel, I know you're in there, I heard you," and he sighs, steels himself, and goes across the room and opens the door.

"Hello, sweetheart," Janet says. "Are you going to leave me standing here in the hall?"

"I told you, Janet, I don't want to see you anymore. I . . . it's over," and he starts to close the door.

Except Janet reaches out and stops it. Smiling. Her deadly little smile that he's learned to dread. Even fear.

"I don't think so, Daniel. And I don't think you want us to have this conversation out here in the hall where anybody can hear us. Especially with the information I came across at the office today when nobody else was around."

Daniel looks at her and realizes she's probably right, he doesn't want people hearing whatever it is she has to say. He lets go of the door and turns and goes back across the room, hears her come into the room and close the door behind her.

"There's really nothing to talk about, Janet," he says, turning to her, keeping the bed between them. "I told you, it was great, what we had together for a while, but these things run their course, I think we both have to realize we need to move on and. . . ."

Janet stands there, shaking her head, the deadly little smile never leaving her face as she removes the long hairpin and takes off her red felt fascinator hat with its encircling veil like a blood cloud and places it for safekeeping on top of the dresser, as she always does when she's getting ready to stay a while.

"Daniel, my dear. I know very well what you said and why you said it. You want to end it between us, I understand that. The thing is, I don't want to end it, I'm not ready to end it."

"What are you talking about? You can't make me have an affair with you, I told you—"

"Oh, Daniel, you're so young. But that's what I like about you. As a matter of fact I can make you have an affair with me, or if not an affair, at least, let's say, you can service me. Yes, I like the sound of that. You will service me, to my pleasure."

Daniel stares at her, as she calmly takes off her topcoat, begins to unbutton the jacket of her fitted gray suit. She stops and looks at him. "You need to continue getting undressed, darling."

"What makes you think—"

"Because I finally got a look at the company's books today, and took some photographs of what I found. I'd been trying to get a look at them for a couple of weeks, but Gus was always around, but today he was gone for a while and I had my look. Now, I'm no accountant or bookkeeper, but I know enough to see instances where you requisitioned certain materials and such, and the discrepancies between the actual cost of those items and what you billed the company. You've had yourself a tidy little moneymaker going on, haven't you? Especially since Gus got rid of the bookkeeper and he's supposedly been looking after things in that department himself, though he never has time to really look at things to see what's going on, right under his nose."

Daniel feels himself sinking. "What are you going to do?"

"Me?" Janet says, and goes back to removing her blouse, steps out of her skirt, her slip. Smiling. "Not a thing, sweetheart. That is, as long as you service me. When I want it. How I want it. Now, as I said, get the rest of your clothes off and come over here to Mama" . . . as in the office of Anna's Parlour, Susan MacKinnon sits at the desk making the last entries in the ledger for the day, closes the ledger book and sits for a moment, her elbows braced on the desk, rubbing her eyes, then gets a new shot of energy, sighs and stands up, looks around the office to make sure everything is in order and the safe is closed, then turns out the light and walks out into the dark restaurant, past the tables already set for tomorrow's breakfast service, and approaches Eddie the bellman sitting at the bar—though not in his uniform now, dressed in a stylish brown broad-shouldered double-breasted suit, wide striped tie, and cognac-and-white wing-tip shoes—waiting for her, having escorted the last of the other waitresses to their cars, slides off the stool and follows her to the front door where he waits as she locks up, pulling on the handle several times just to make sure, then he follows her at a respectful distance through the lobby where she says good night to the night clerk at the desk and continues on to the service entrance and out into the alley, Eddie still behind her, walking down the ill-lit alley to the small parking lot where Eddie waits as she unlocks her car, says good night and thanks him, then starts her car and drives slowly up the hill to the main street, the town for all intents and purposes deserted at this hour, the streetlights along Seventh Avenue haloed with the smoke from the mill, follows Seventh Avenue down to the Lower End and then across the bridge onto Ohio River Boulevard, in a short distance turning across the bridge over the Ohio River to Alum Rock and into the shabbier section of town, seeing the headlights now behind her, following her, drives to a small concrete building surrounded by empty lots in a poor section of town with a neon sign over the door, Jazzy's Place, parks up the street and waits till the car following her parks behind her and Eddie gets out, the two of them kissing and then going inside the club, greeted by the sounds of a small combo and a *bald-headed Black woman singing "Smoke Gets in Your Eyes," Susan in fact the only White woman in the club, the only White person for that matter, but she and Eddie are greeted with* Heys and How you doin's *and hand slaps and kisses on the cheek, regulars, a table at the front reserved for them, and the two of them sit there, holding hands, knowing they are safe here, safe in their love here, aware that some people would consider this place threatening but knowing, for them at least, it is the world outside that is dangerous . . . as a few hours earlier on a small farm outside of Hickory, Mary Lydia White sits in bed propped up on pillows, her husband Claire propped up beside her, Claire going through the latest copy of* Farm Journal, *Mary Lydia with Agatha Christie's latest mystery that she got from the library,* Death in the Clouds, *open on her lap, going through her mental checklist to make sure everything she was supposed to do is done—the dishes washed and put away, the pans for her apple cobbler soaking in the sink, all the appliances turned off, the dogs fed and watered, the chickens in their coop, the goats in their pen, all the lights turned off downstairs, the alarm set for four a.m.—and thinking about her day, the friends she saw at the festival, pleased that her cobbler was again the star of the desserts, and thinking about John Lincoln, how she knew him the second she saw him standing across the tables, even with the mask, knew it was him in her bones, thinking that it should have been a source of jubilation, a cause for celebration—her long-lost brother was alive!—but it wasn't, beyond any control her first emotion was a sense of dread, a sinking feeling in her soul, then the other emotions kicked in, relief, glad that he was okay, curiosity as to how he was still alive when everything pointed to his being dead, and then the anger, when he followed her into the fireman's hall, the rage that he would simply turn up one day after all this time without warning or letting her know beforehand, the presumptuousness of it, the inconsideration, regardless of what changes to his physical appearance his arrogance and self-centeredness unchanged; yes, it was good to see him, in a way, yes, she was glad that*

Torn

despite his obvious pains and tribulations he was alive and doing okay, though it was still unanswered as to what he was doing back in Furnass, why did he feel he wanted to come back to this place where he would no longer feel at home, and wondering how she should tell Claire, not that he would be upset in any way but aware that he would be concerned how it might affect her, upset her, aware that she somehow had to tell her husband that the return of her brother meant absolutely nothing to her, changed nothing in her life, and decides the best way is just to tell him, blurt it out, waits till he's finishes the article he's reading on early planting of corn and says as breezy as she can muster, "Been waiting to tell you, guess who turned up at the festival today?" . . . and now it's close to midnight and in the sitting room of his suite at the Grand Hotel in Furnass, John Lincoln sits in the easy chair, the drapes pulled closed to shut out the outside world, his mask taken off and sitting on the table beside his chair like a sail billowed before the wind, the imprint of his face, or what is left of it, left in the folds of the cloth, listening to the radio, a large walnut-finished consul that Eddie the bellman found somewhere and had brought up to his rooms, on the air a symphony music concert being broadcast from San Francisco that he found dialing around, the result of a quirk in atmospheric conditions, Mozart's Symphony No. 41, the Jupiter, singing along with the finale, molto allegro, caught up momentarily in its sense of triumph and jubilation until the station crackles into the distance, replaced briefly by a country station out of Denver, Gene Autry singing "Tumbling Tumbleweeds" until it too dissolves into static, John Lincoln reaching over and turning off the radio and sitting in silence, thinking over his day, thinking how he had waited for years to see Mary Lydia again, fantasized being with her again, the two of them together like they were growing up, their own little world, imagining at times, times he had to admit when he was at his lowest point, the two of them living together, brother and sister, it wasn't unheard-of, that closeness that he had with her never felt with another person, what they said about twins being two halves of a whole, and then seeing her today and feeling nothing but disappointment and sadness at who she had become, somebody he didn't know at all, surprised and amazed that in fact he felt closer to Anna now than to his sister, remembers snapshots of Anna through the day, looking over at him as she drove, her little smile, the two of them walking down the shoulder of the road, her look of concern for him when he spotted Mary Lydia, her taking charge of him as they sat on the bench as he told her of his feelings about his sister, the look of almost sadness when she told him she wouldn't see him on Sunday, that she needed to spend some extra time with Warren to make up for her absence today, never saying directly but implying that she'd miss seeing him, knows that romance isn't possible with her—it can't be, what with her obligations and his, well, deformities, there is no other word for it—but at least it is nice to think about. . . .

PART II

Eleven

On Monday, after he didn't see Anna at all on Sunday because she stayed home to spend time with her husband, John Lincoln was looking forward to seeing her when he went down to breakfast. But it turned out she was swamped with something called a Commemorative Breakfast, a large affair being held in the River Room, and it was Susan who took care of him. Every time Anna hurried past with a tray or carafe of coffee, she waved to him, a little toodle of her fingers, gave him a little look of regret, but it was small compensation. What the hell was a Commemorative Breakfast anyway? Then he remembered: Armistice Day. He knew it was coming, saw articles about it in the papers, but it hadn't registered that it was today. When it was apparent that she wasn't going to have any time to talk to him this morning, he finished his breakfast and headed back out to the lobby. Eddie was at his bellhop stand; when he saw John Lincoln, he pointed to his wrist. Of course: it was nearing eleven o'clock on the eleventh day of the eleventh month. Eddie gave a nod for John Lincoln to follow him. John Lincoln couldn't imagine what Eddie had in mind, but he had learned to trust him, Eddie always had good reasons, and followed him through the lobby, through the coatroom and a storeroom, out the back door into the alley.

"I thought you might like a good place to hear the cannon when they fire it off at the VFW," Eddie said. "Sometimes it's hard to hear inside there, and this is a little more private."

"Yes, thank you. It doesn't seem like the town makes much of a fuss over Armistice Day."

"You're right, but it's better than most of the towns around here. There's a bit of a parade upstreet, though it's mainly just the high school band and a couple of fire trucks. The college shut down I'm told, part of some kind of student protest about the U.S.

entering a war in Europe. Stupid bastards, if they only knew." He spit to the side, looked at the garbage bins along the back of the restaurant, the barrels of whisky and beer bottles. "And I guess the city ain't collecting garbage today. Someday maybe the government will make it a national holiday so it'll get the respect it deserves."

"You a member of the VFW?"

Eddie snickered. "Not hardly. I tried it a couple times, and nobody said anything directly, but you can tell when you're not wanted, when you don't belong. Not for Buffalo Soldiers."

John Lincoln looked at him questioningly.

"You don't know the term."

"No, I—"

"The 92nd and 93rd Divisions were made up of what the government called 'colored troops,' Buffalo Soldiers, get it? Even had our own shoulder patch, though by the end they could have called us Blue Hats like the 93rd. The high command didn't want us sharing trenches with White troops, so they farmed us out to the French. But that was okay, I even learned some French along the way, *Oui, oui, parles-tu anglais? Est-ce que mademoiselle aimerait coucher avec moi?* Enough to get by. We were in the final Hundred Days Offensive, Meuse River and the Argonne."

"I'm sorry, I didn't know."

"No need for you to be sorry. Though I'm getting the idea those wounds weren't the price of going up over the top."

John Lincoln told him the story, how he got the wounds, how the army picked him up and he traveled around to hospitals and recovery centers.

They were interrupted by the sound of the cannon firing off at eleven o'clock. They waited until all eleven rounds were fired, the explosions echoing off the valley hills, the birds taking flight from the trees and rooftops. Eddie with his head bowed. John Lincoln wondered what the man would say to him, he felt a total fraud next to him, he couldn't blame Eddie for despising him, thinking John Lincoln misrepresented himself though he was fairly certain

Torn

he had been careful not to, wouldn't be surprised if Eddie wanted nothing more to do with him. When the last explosion sounded and the echo died away, the silence was terrible.

Before John Lincoln could say anything, Eddie said, "Okay then, another year passed. I need to get back to work." He started in the door, then stopped and took John Lincoln by the arm.

Here it comes, I deserve this, John Lincoln thought.

"And don't you think another thing about it. Those wounds and how you got them and then what you did for the other guys in those hospitals, you're one of us, don't let nobody ever try to tell you different. Sir. Besides, Anna thinks you're all right, and that's all that matters around here." Eddie gave him a sideways grin and disappeared back inside the hotel.

*

Something Eddie said got John Lincoln to thinking: if the college was closed on account of Armistice Day, maybe Lily, Gus' estranged wife—if that was what she was—would be at home today. He didn't want to delay any longer seeing her, both as a matter of courtesy and because he owed her that, at one time when he was growing up she had been very important to him, an older friend in the family, a confidant, when he didn't know whom to trust, whom he could trust. He hadn't looked forward to seeing her at her office at the college, all the students looking at him, maybe embarrassing her with his presence, who could say? Now on his way through the hotel lobby he stopped at the front desk and asked to use their telephone directory; there was a listing for an L. Lyle on Orchard Hill. He went up to his room to get his hat and coat and left the hotel, sticking to the back streets to avoid any of the crowds left over from the parade, up through the town to Orchard Hill.

The house sat across from the college on a small terrace, gray brick with white trim, flower boxes at the windows. He rang the bell and held his breath. An attractive, dignified woman answered, cocked her head, and didn't seem at all surprised to see him.

"John Lincoln."

"Hello, Lily."

"I was wondering how far down the list I was of people you were going to see."

"I'm sorry, I—"

"No explanation needed. I'm just glad you're here now, it's good to see you again. Come in, come in."

As he followed her, hat in hand, through the hall and into the living room, he said, "I was hoping to catch you at home, I heard the college was closed today...."

The room was tidy and homey, very feminine, all flowery prints and frills, not at all the house of an academic, the few low bookcases displaying pictures and knickknacks and mementos, the only sign of the college a few books and a lot of papers spread across the sofa, obviously her place in the room.

"Take off your coat," she said, motioning for him to sit down in an overstuffed chair across from her on the sofa. "Yes, I was rather surprised the administration decided to close today, the college is generally not known for its activism or political sympathies. But a delegation of students brought to the president's attention that there was to be a nationwide student mobilization for peace, organized, I believe, from the University of Minnesota and supported by the Young Men's and Women's Christian Associations. I guess the academic council decided it was better to be seen to be *for* rather than *against* such a thing. So, a day off from the office, though, as you can see, the work continues."

"I hope I'm not interrupting...."

"Of course not. I'm glad to be taken away, and I'm doubly glad to see you."

"I was afraid you wouldn't recognize me, with the mask ... and all."

"I have to admit I might not have. But your reputation precedes you. You were a topic of conversation at last Friday's staff meeting."

"I was afraid of such things."

Torn

"You can't blame them, I suppose. But it's not really about your mask and your condition. It's big news in this town that a Lyle who was thought to be dead is back among us. The family certainly isn't as prominent as it was, but it's still prominent enough. I'm sure a subtext of any administration discussion was wondering if a Lyle brother might have a positive influence on future donations from the family or Keystone Steam Works. Gus, as I understand it, has been particularly tight-fisted when it comes to donating to the college."

"My brother tight-fisted. Imagine. Some things have certainly stayed the same."

Lily didn't respond. She moved some of the papers on the sofa, toed off her loafers, and tucked her legs up beside her, smoothing her camel skirt down over her knees. He was beginning to wonder if his concept of women and girls—and femininity—came less from being around his sister, Mary Lydia, as he had always supposed, and more from the time he spent with Lily when he was in his late teens.

*

He wasn't sure now how it started, but sometime during the summer after he graduated from high school he would spend hours at a time in Gus' wing of the house but not with Gus, with Lily as she worked in the kitchen, washing dishes, preparing meals, and when she did her other chores around their wing of the house, washing and folding clothes, the ironing, dusting, and sweeping, John Lincoln sitting in a chair nearby or spread out on the bed or even lying on the floor, talking about this and that. It may have started with his talking of his confusion about his future, what he was going to do with his life, where he was going to go to college, how he was going to find a girlfriend, and then things closer to home, why his family did the things they did, why Gus acted the way he did, which led to Lily telling John Lincoln more of her own situation and concerns and worries, the problems in her marriage, what was going to become of her. She had met Gus at Covenant College, a farm girl from Kansas, sent here because it was one of the few Covenanter colleges in the country, her father a strict Presbyterian minister. At first Gus seemed the answer for her, how she could get away from the stifling atmosphere of her father's doctrines, marrying into the Lyle family seemed a way to freedom that would allow her to become herself at last. But she found her marriage was just as crippling in its way as the church-heavy atmosphere she grew up in, here the doctrines based on social position, the family's supposed prestige in town, though it was more than that too, it was Gus' neglect and at the same time his overbearing attention, his insistence that the smallest thing be done his way and his way only. It meshed perfectly with John Lincoln's own growing disenchantment with the world according to Gus, his half brother's subversive hatred of their father, Gus' crippling viewpoints and accusations of their father.

Then things got ugly. John Lincoln had started college though he still spent as much time as his classes would allow with Lily. One night she had invited him to stay for dinner; when Gus arrived home from the shop he was full of his latest story of his father's duplicity and maneuvering: Malcolm had been in negotiations with a vendor over some piping and the rep had made a mistake in his calculations, shorting his company on the invoice, but Malcolm held him to the quoted price even though the mistake was obvious.

"Father had it all in the paperwork, he had him right where he wanted him, the poor guy couldn't move," Gus said gleefully from his position at the head of the table, helping himself to the tureen of vegetable soup, ladling spoonfuls into his bowl, looking first to John Lincoln sitting on the side of the table then to Lily at the opposite end and then back to John Lincoln. "In a way it was just like what he did with Mother, I don't know whether he planned to push her into that trench or not, maybe it just happened and she fell in, but once she was there and the flames of the broken lamp had broken out he had her right where he wanted her, he knew if he dumped the flour on her there would be no way to save her—"

"Oh, come on, Gus," John Lincoln said. "Let it go. You know

Torn

you don't believe that."

Gus, in the process of passing the tureen down the table to Lily, froze. "What are you talking about?"

"I mean, really. Come on. You're always saying that about Father, that he dumped the flour on your mother on purpose, but I don't believe it, and I don't see how you can after all this time."

"How dare you speak to me like that," Gus sputtered, still holding the tureen in midair.

John Lincoln tried to lighten the situation, laughing a little at the preposterousness of the situation. "I think Father tried to do what he thought was right to try to save her. That he got the flour instead of the salt was a terrible and tragic mistake that he's had to live with all the rest of his life."

Gus stared at him for a moment, then threw the tureen across the room, smashing it against the wall.

Lily screamed. "Gus! What are you doing!"

Gus stood up, glaring at John Lincoln. "You, blind, stupid fool. Who do you think you are, talking to me like that? You blind stupid fool!"

Gus tried to leave the table but his chair blocked him in; he tried to move it aside, but it snagged on the rug and he threw it backward, the chair flipping over and slamming into the bureau. Gus stormed out of the room, clenching his fists in front of him, his face wrenched in tears. "You blind stupid fool, you blind stupid fool. . . ."

John Lincoln and Lily heard him slam out the back door. After a moment, John Lincoln said, "Well, I guess I better be going—" but Lily held up her hand, telling him to stop as she listened. In a moment there was the sound of chopping wood coming from outside.

"I wanted to make sure he was using his axe on his woodpile, and not headed back in here with it."

"Are you serious?"

Lily thought a moment. "Gus is a sweet man and normally wouldn't hurt a flea. But sometimes his temper gets the better of him and he can't control himself, it's like someone else takes over, he's like an entirely different person."

"They have names for people like that. Jekyll and Hyde for starters."

"He's not like that at all. He just has a temper, that's all." She looked at the remains of the soup splattered on the wall, the shards of crockery on the floor. "That's hardly the worst thing about living with Gus."

"What can be worse than living with guy you think might come in brandishing an axe?"

"It's the hypocrisy. He talks all the time, to me, to you and your sister, about what a terrible man your father is, blames him endlessly for everything from the death of his mother to the bank failures and the state of the economy. But that doesn't stop him from letting Malcolm groom him to take over the company when he's dead, and while he's alive, using all of the company's money and resources to play with his machines, like his plans for a steam automobile."

"The infamous Lylemobile."

"But it's not just Gus, it's your whole family. You act like you're so very important to the town, like you're royalty or something, and maybe you were at one time, but you're not now. Yes, you own the Keystone Steam Works, but in terms of employers you can't even start to compare with Buchanan Steel and half a dozen other companies. The thing is, your family knows it, they know they're less important to the town than they once were, but that doesn't stop the way the family acts and treats other people, the way you all basically look down on everybody else, the way you all think you're better than everybody else. I'm sorry, John Lincoln, but I'm afraid it's the truth. And it's true about you, too."

So it didn't surprise him when, a few weeks later, Lily took Mal to visit her parents in Wichita, Kansas, a visit that was supposed to be for only a few weeks but then extended a few weeks longer, and there seemed to be some question as to whether or not she would return at all. But any concerns he had about Lily's return took a back seat to other things going on in his life. There was Mary Lydia's announcement that she was pregnant and all his confusion of emotions about it: the idea of some guy fucking his treasured sister (there could be no other name for it); the jealousy that there was somebody else that important in her life that she would do such a thing, that she would let such a thing happen to her; the suspicions some people had that the baby was actually his (he quickly put such an idea away, far away, buried it, any time it raised its appalling head). But there was something else too. Lily's condemnation of the family for its hypocrisy and pretensions struck a chord, a very dissonant but resonant chord. A moment of terrible realization and recognition. He was embarrassed and ashamed to admit that he was as guilty of such faults as anyone in the family, to his mind more than most. The embodiment of a fake and a phony. As a result, when he heard there was a call for able-bodied American young men to join the war effort in Europe to beat back the invading Germans, he decided he had to enlist because it was the right thing to do, because he believed the cause was just and for him not to enlist would be more hypocrisy, this was a chance for him to prove to himself if no one else that he wasn't a fake and a phony. That he was genuine. Real.

*

"And Mal said he saw you at Gus' office, though he said he didn't have a chance to talk to you."

John Lincoln grinned. "No, at the time Gus was busy throwing me out."

"I gathered that, from what Mal said."

"And Mal lives with you?"

"Yes. He seems content with the arrangement for the time being, and I haven't the heart to throw him out, at least not yet. I'm sure it's easier for him this way, he has enough to contend with, what with Gus and finding his place in the company, or what's left of it."

"I got the idea that things aren't going well for the Steam Works, irrespective of the Depression."

"I'm afraid, as always, Gus has found ways to achieve failure against all guarantees of success. It's quite an art, actually."

"As I said, some things have stayed the same." John Lincoln smiled, brushing his hands together as if clearing away some grit. "He was particularly touchy when I brought up the subject of expenses involved with the Lylemobile, or Zephyr as it's called now."

"It is? I hadn't heard. But that certainly sounds like a better name. I know Mal is concerned about the expense of it and all. But he seems to think the problems go deeper than overspending, or misspending as the case may be."

"What could be worse than Gus' mismanagement? I've had some questions about that myself."

"Mal thinks it could be a lot worse. Some kind of fraud going on."

"I've wondered if Gus has been—"

"No. Not Gus. Mal's got some suspicions about a designer Gus hired."

"You mean Spalding? He was there in the office while I was talking to Gus."

"Mal doesn't have any proof, but he's seen some things that don't add up. And Mal's not the kind to raise an issue like that without good reason. He's pretty levelheaded and astute. Unlike his father."

"I don't know how you'd prove a thing like that without access to the books. And Laughlin, the attorney, told me that Gus keeps them under lock and key. He doesn't even have a bookkeeper anymore, he fired her, and even Laughlin can't get access to them."

Lily looked at him. "You talked to Laughlin? What about?"

"I wanted to know what I was dealing with before I talked to anyone. I knew that me turning up this way after all this time was bound to raise some issues."

"Which certainly raises the question: Why did you come back?"

Torn

"You're not the first person to raise it."

"I'm interested to know how you answered it."

"To tell you the truth, the longer I'm here the less I know why I came back." He laughed a little, trying to make light of what he said, but Lily wasn't buying it.

"I wondered if it was to get some sort of revenge on your brother."

"Really?"

"It would be understandable. He wasn't the best brother to you while you were growing up. I wouldn't be surprised if there was some unfinished business on your part."

John Lincoln smiled. "No, he wasn't the best brother, especially as I got older and got ideas of my own."

"And now, here he is, the lord of the manor, as it were. I can see how that might cause some lingering hard feelings. And the first person you go to see when you're back in town is the family attorney."

"As I said, I only went to see Laughlin to find out how things stood, what I might face being back in town. Though I do want to talk to him again about why the company didn't pay the compensation with an accident that occurred a few years ago."

"Why would that be any concern of yours?"

"I've gotten to know the family involved since I've been back, and something's not right about it. The company always prided itself on taking care of its employees. I remember Father talking about it."

"Curiouser and curiouser. You say you're not concerned with the family business, but then here you are, poking your nose into its finances, discussing affairs with its legal counsel. One might note a certain inconsistency." She shrugged, raised her eyebrows.

"In regard to inconsistencies, I might ask you the same thing: Why did *you* come back? From everything you told me at the time, Gus was hardly the best husband. When I left to enlist you had been gone for a number of weeks and everyone was starting to get the idea that you weren't coming back, even thickheaded Gus. But here you are, you did come back, though you're living apart. Are you two still married?"

She turned pensive. "Yes, we're still married, if you can call it that. There is still an official piece of paper in the county courthouse that states we are husband and wife, and I still go by Mrs. Lyle at the college. It's an interesting phenomenon, you may run into it yourself. They say you can't go home again. Well, suppose you try to go home and your home won't have you? My father, the fire-and-brimstone minister, declared my duty as a good Christian wife was to my husband, and he wouldn't be part of something he considered a sin and sent me back. As it turned out, Gus, in his sweet mode, welcomed me back, would have been happy to have me living again in Sycamore House with him, but I wanted no part of that, and he set me up here in this house and paid all my expenses. A gesture that I'm sure appeared to all as Gus being generous, but I knew him well enough to know what was behind it. Gus needs an enemy to fight against, to blame for all his injustices, because it makes him the victim. And the fact is, when he has such a figure in his life he does his best work, gets his best ideas and comes up with his best solutions when he's fighting someone in his mind. For much of his life it was his father; then when I came back I was assigned that role. He was quite upset when I got the job at the college and eventually became registrar, because it meant I was no longer dependent on him, he couldn't count me as much of an oppressor, somebody making demands of him even when they were of his own devising, though of course I was still his estranged wife, that counted for something. I'm actually very glad to see you back in town—besides the fact that you're alive—because now I'm sure he'll put you in the role of his mortal enemy."

"A dubious honor."

"It's unbearably sad in many ways. I came to suspect that he actually relished the fact that the Lylemobile wasn't successful because he wouldn't know what to do with himself if it was successful, if *he* was successful. I don't think he could stand it. I wouldn't be surprised if he knows that Spalding is stealing from him and lets it go on even so, something else, someone else to feel bad about."

"That's a pretty jaded view of human nature," John Lincoln said.

She held up a stack of applications. "Going through these all day, seeing the ideals people have for themselves and then how they turn out, will do that to you. I always hope that I'm wrong, but it rarely turns out that I am."

Twelve

"So, who was the dinner for tonight?"

"The American Legion, for Armistice Day. Same cause as this morning, different group tonight. How was your pork roast?"

"It was amazing. It had a sweet back taste to it, so many of your sauces have that, it's like nothing I've ever tasted before."

"Want to know my secret? It's prunes. My father taught me that back in his restaurant. Prunes."

"Who would have guessed? The world is full of wonders."

They were sitting at his usual table in the dark restaurant, after hours, only a few night-lights on. John Lincoln had been hoping to spend time with Anna at dinner, they hadn't had a chance to talk since their trip on Saturday, but she was busy again, running back and forth between the kitchen and the River Room. But on one of her trips past, she stopped and suggested he come back later after the restaurant closed, he could have his dessert then, she'd leave the door from the lobby unlocked for him. Now that he was here, however, they forgot about dessert.

"Did you go see your sister-in-law today like you said you were going to, if she *is* still your sister-in-law?"

John Lincoln told her about his visit with Lily, described where she lived, how the house was decorated, something of their talk about her marriage and feelings about Gus, why she came back to Furnass after she fled to Kansas, her impressions of the family and its hypocrisy and pretensions. He thought of telling her of

Lily's theory that he came back to town to get some sort of revenge on Gus, thought it might make an amusing story for its absurdity, but decided it was probably better not to, for one thing it made Lily look foolish, that she could even come up with such an idea. He also told her that Mal had told Lily that he thought there was some sort of fraud going on at the Steam Works that involved Daniel Spalding.

"Spalding?" Anna said. "The guy who is living here in the hotel? Well, I guess that doesn't surprise me, there always seemed something not right about him, something shifty. Eddie says Spalding gets regular visits up in his room from Janet Santelli, Gus' secretary, so that could be tied into it somehow."

"The problem is I don't know how you could prove a thing like fraud without access to the books, and Gus keeps them under lock and key these days."

Anna cocked her head. "Well, if we can't get access to the books, I can do the next best thing." She looked toward the divider between them and the bar. "Hey Eddie, is Susan still in the office?"

"Yes, ma'am."

"Would you go back, please, and tell her that I need to ask her something?"

"Yes, ma'am." The sound of a barstool shifting, footsteps toward the kitchen.

"We may not have access to the books," Anna said to John Lincoln, "but we do have access to the bookkeeper."

While they were waiting, John Lincoln put his mask back into place. In a few minutes Susan came from the kitchen. Anna motioned her to pull over a chair and join them. She explained to John Lincoln that Susan had been the bookkeeper at the Keystone Steam Works but that Gus had suddenly let her go a year or so earlier. When Anna heard about it, she hired Susan both as her own bookkeeper and as a fill-in waitress.

"Tell John Lincoln what you told me," Anna said. "Why you think Gus fired you."

Torn

Susan, in the half-light, looked uncomfortable but didn't hesitate. "I had recently found some discrepancies in what we were being invoiced from some vendors and what we were paying them. It was very clever and hard to catch on to at first, but then I saw some of the original invoices and compared them to the requests for payments that Spalding had submitted. Spalding wasn't one of our own employees, he was an outside contractor, and when I traced a couple of the payments we made to him, they included the exact difference between what a contractor invoiced us and what we paid them. So I took it to Gus and started to tell him what I had found, but he brushed it aside, said I had to be mistaken, and then said he had been thinking about it for a while and he had decided that he had to let me go, that it was a salary he couldn't afford what with the downturn with the Depression and all, he had decided to take over doing the books himself. I thought of telling the police or someone, but to tell you the truth if there was that kind of thing going on I didn't want any part of it. I wasn't involved with it, but I know how these things go, everybody's a suspect, particularly a bookkeeper, and I didn't need that kind of grief in my life."

"What would you think," John Lincoln asked her, "if such discrepancies came out now?"

Susan smiled. "That would be fine with me. In fact, I'd like to see that son of a bitch get what he deserves. I had a good job there and he took it away for no other reason than to cover his flabby ass, pardon my Dutch. Enough time has gone by now, and if there was fraud then, there's fraud now, and it would be apparent I didn't have anything to do with it, I'd be in the clear from the start. Yes, I hope you do pursue it. I'd even testify if it came to that."

John Lincoln and Anna looked at each other. When Susan had returned to the office, Anna said, "So, there we are. But we'd still need access to the books to get things started."

John Lincoln removed his mask and said, "I think I need to go see David Laughlin again."

Thirteen

It was late the following evening, after seven o'clock, when David Laughlin got home from the office. Often on his way home he stopped in at the country club across the street for a drink, especially if he had been out for a run, but tonight it was late enough that he thought he should get right home, Emma would be holding dinner for him, there was no sense asking for trouble. He ran the car into the garage at the rear of the backyard and headed down the flagstone walk to the house; in the darkness of the November evening, Emma was at the sink in the light of the kitchen window, a tableau of sorts. Home is the sailor, home from the sea. And the hunter home from the hill. Robert Louis Stevenson, he thought. From a time when he knew such things, when such things, literature, mattered to him. It seemed a long time ago now. A long ways away.

He crossed the concrete slab that served as a patio in the summer and let himself in the back door. It was a compact red-brick colonial house, a small house that nonetheless felt a little too large for a childless couple; but they, or rather, Emma, wouldn't think of leaving it because of its proximity to the country club, a selling point to her even more than to him. She must have seen his headlights turning into the garage from the alley, she was busy warming up their dinner in the oven, one of her many casseroles. She was still wearing the outfit she wore when she golfed, plaid plus fours and a white blouse, a white sweater draped around her shoulders—why did she do that, wear such an outfit that she knew was controversial, racy even, did she like the idea that she gave the men at the club a little thrill seeing that much bare ankle and calf, or was it just to flaunt convention, throw it up in the faces of all the fuddy-duddies on the standards committee? For that matter, why didn't she change when she got home, why did she need to have him see her wearing it, was it to flaunt it in *his* face, that she was an independent woman and could do things, such as play a round of golf in an afternoon, without his permission or for that matter without even telling him beforehand? Or was it her idea to give him a bit of a thrill, the sight of the unconventional dress, the glimpse of the ankle and lower calf? He couldn't imagine it, she knew he was more than willing, or maybe had been, once upon a time, it had been her idea—what? twenty years ago now?—to take the sex out of their marriage. Now after they said their hellos as she moved about the kitchen, he started to give her a kiss on the cheek but she moved aside, saying, "You go ahead and get your clothes changed, dinner's almost ready." He smiled and went on through the kitchen and upstairs to do as she said; it was okay, it was more of a convention, he didn't matter to him whether he kissed her or not.

Dinner was in the dining room, a formal room with imitation cherry French Provincial furniture that Emma kept sacred for the evening meal, though David, if the truth be known, would have been just as happy, maybe happier, in the kitchen's breakfast nook. They sat at opposite ends of the spindly-legged oval table, looking at each other through the flames of the twin candles Emma always lit. After toasting each other with their long-stemmed gin martinis, and taking the first bites of tonight's chicken Divan casserole, David knew it was his turn to begin the nightly ritual.

"Well, so how was your day today?"

"Wait till I tell you. I got in two full rounds today. With winter coming I won't be able to play very often so I took a chance and went over to the club this morning and met two men who were visiting in town, some meeting or other at Buchanan, and they let me join them; and then this afternoon, I had arranged to meet some of the girls and...." There was more, ten minutes more, but David's attention flagged; he put in an occasional "Oh, really?" and "Hmm" to appear interested and following along, but his mind was far away, or rather, nowhere, on hold, waiting. When she began discussing Edna Ripley's lack of a decent play wardrobe and he sensed her own attention was drifting, he broke in.

"Well, I had another visit today from John Lincoln Lyle. You remember I told you when he came to see me when he first got back to town—"

"Is he still wearing that mask? You said he was wearing one of those surgical masks or something."

"Yes, he's still wearing the mask—"

"That's so weird. But then he always was weird, I remember him before he went missing or drowned or whatever it was."

"The word came that he had drowned but—"

"That sounds like something he'd do, go around wearing a mask like that just to get people's attention."

"I'm pretty sure you wouldn't want to see his face without it. You get glimpses of what it's like around the edges and—"

"Even so, that sounds like John Lincoln Lyle, going around wearing a mask like that."

"Let me tell you—"

"Well, go ahead, tell me, I'm listening."

David sighed. Tried to get his thoughts in order. "He's got the idea that there's some kind of fraud going on at the Steam Works, something to do with this designer, Daniel Spalding, that Gus hired to help him redesign the steam automobile that he's been working on for years—"

"Nobody wants a steam car. I could have told him that. They're too hard to start and they take forever to get going and they're dangerous with that fire for the boiler and all. . . ." He waited as she continued with her observations on the marketability of a steam vehicle as opposed to a gasoline-powered car, he figured it was easier than trying to interrupt.

When she was finished, he said, "Be that as it may, in order to prove there's fraud going on, he needs access to the company's books, evidently he's talked to the woman who used to be the bookkeeper there at the Steam Works and she confirmed that, yes, there appeared to be some kind of fraud going on—"

"Why did she leave?"

"Gus let her go."

"In other words, she was fired. Why was she fired? There must have been a good reason. I mean, that could have some bearing—"

It was his turn to interrupt. "The point is, in order to prove the fraud and other possible discrepancies, he needs access to the books or some of the records, and he wanted me to approach the bank, First Seneca, to see if there's some way we can see some of the company's records."

"The bank isn't going to go along with that, are they? I mean—"

"I thought they might make an exception in this case because the request was being made on behalf of a member of the Lyle family, in my role as the family's attorney. I hoped that could sway them into bending the rules for once. But no, Harold MacArthur, the president, told me he couldn't do it, as much as it might be in everyone's best interests."

"Well, I could have told you that. MacArthur's got enough on his hands just keeping his doors open these days. Besides, I don't know why you'd want to get involved with such a crazy idea anyway, and one brought up by a crazy person like John Lincoln Lyle. The idea, him just disappearing like that and then coming back here and stirring up all this trouble. You need to be careful, David, this is really none of your business, you're going to poke around and lose one of your important clients. You need to stay out of it, whatever it is."

Emma crossed her folk and knife on her plate, took a finishing swallow of her martini, and got up from the table, taking her plate and glass to the kitchen, conversation over.

David sighed. Crossed his own fork and knife on his plate, as he knew she wanted him to do, but he stayed seated. He had never told Emma that the Keystone Steam Works was hardly a good client anymore, that they hadn't paid their retainer in a year and a half, it would only worry her, make her concerned that she couldn't maintain her—her, not their—standard of living, all the new clothes, the membership at the country club, all the lunches and parties. But he had to admit she was right in a way, he really should stay out of it; even if such allegations were true it would be next to impossible to prove, even with access to the bank records, they would need the company's records and Gus had them under lock and key. For that matter, he also knew it wasn't the idea of possible fraud that had interested him, that got him involved, it was John Lincoln's idea that there were other improprieties going on within the company, with Gus' management, particularly the idea that Gus had been dipping into accounts that were meant for other purposes to support his work on the Zephyr. David still had hopes that somehow he might get the compensation for Anna that she had coming to her because of her husband's accident. The look on her face when he told her that yes, he had been able to secure that the company would pay to help with the medical bills, her husband's long-term care. "Oh, David, is it true? How did you do it, it's a miracle! How can I ever thank you? My hero!" She springs out of her chair and hurries around the desk as he stands to meet her, she throws her arms around his neck, they kiss. . . .

Fourteen

The next day, Janet Santelli was in her office at the Keystone Steam Works when the switchboard rang her with a call for her boss.

"Hello, Janet. This is Harold MacArthur at First Seneca. How are you this afternoon?"

"I'm fine, Mr. MacArthur. And yourself?"

"Just fine, just fine, thank you. I take it Gus is not available."

"I'm afraid not. He's out of the office this afternoon, he said he had some personal business to take care of."

"Oh."

"Is there anything I can help you with?"

MacArthur was silent for a moment. "Well, perhaps so. Gus has designated you his agent in the past, so I see no reason why I can't discuss this with you now. And this is more of a courtesy call than anything else, to inform you of a recent situation that came up."

"We certainly appreciate you letting us know if there's a problem of some kind."

"It isn't really a problem, it's only . . . well, we had a request from a Lyle family member, through the family's attorney, David Laughlin, to have access to the company's financial records. That's very unusual, of course, and of course we denied such access out of hand—"

"We thank you, of course." A Lyle family member, Janet thought, that could only be John Lincoln. Why do you suppose he's sniffing around? "Did this family member give any reason why they wanted to see the company's bank records?"

"No, and frankly I didn't ask. I didn't want to know. I have no idea what someone would hope to find in the bank records, they wouldn't mean much if they were looking for some sort of billing irregularity without the vendor's original invoices, and Laughlin would know that. Regardless, it's nobody's business, so to speak, except the company's, unless there's a regulatory agency involved and then it's a whole new ballgame. Though it did occur to me afterwards that perhaps Gus was aware of the inquiry and that there was a perfectly good reason for such a request, that Gus might actually want me to release such information."

"I can assure you that you did absolutely right by not releasing it. As you say, the company's business is its own business. Family member or no."

"Well, it's good to know that I was right in my assumptions. I can assure you that we will continue to deny such requests if they occur in the future, unless, of course, there is a court order or some such thing to release them. And I certainly don't expect anything like that occurring." MacArthur chuckled a little at the idea.

Janet chuckled in return. "No, I certainly wouldn't think anything like that would happen."

"Well, I'm glad I checked with you, just in case. And you will tell Gus that I called, will you?"

"Of course. And on behalf of Mr. Lyle I extend the Steam Works' gratitude for your watchfulness and attention to our interests."

"Certainly, Janet. Well, that just about takes care of it. I hope you have a good day. This weather is remarkable, isn't it, to be this warm in the middle of November."

"It certainly is. Thank you again for calling."

As Janet put down the receiver, a chill ran through her. Just relax, you're okay, you haven't done anything wrong, it's all on Daniel, you didn't have a thing to do with it. There's nothing he can say that could implicate you, and if he tried to say you knew about it, you can deny it, his word against yours, he has no proof of anything, in fact you're the one with the proof of his transactions. Though just in case I better destroy those photographs tonight when I get home.

She double-checked her calendar to make sure there was nothing else on the schedule for the few hours left of the afternoon, then went into Gus' office to check his calendar to make sure there wasn't something scheduled that he hadn't told her about—she was fairly sure there wouldn't be, Gus depended on her for such things, he got so caught up in his work she thought at times she was going to have to schedule bathroom breaks for him; thought of turning off his lights but decided he'd probably come back after he was done with whatever he left to take care of this afternoon, that would be like him, no matter how late, he would come back here, for that matter where else would he go, he certainly avoided Sycamore House as much as he could these days, it was a wonder he didn't get a cot and sleep here in the office—went back to her own office, got her coat and hat, and to avoid any question as to why she was leaving early, took the back stairs down to the production floor.

The area set off for work on the Zephyr was at the rear of the shop, the area closed off behind curtains hung from the roof trusses. She parted the curtains and stepped inside, at first not seeing anyone, then noticed the two feet sticking out from underneath the side of the car. She went over and gave the left foot a kick. Daniel, in a coverall, slid out from underneath.

"Hey, what's that for?"

She looked around to make sure no one else was working in the area. "I wanted to get your attention."

"Well, you got it," Daniel said, wiping his hands on a rag but making no effort to get to his feet. "What's so important that you have to assault me?"

She thought, You'll know it when I assault you. "I'll be coming over tonight to see you."

"That's not going to work."

"And why not?"

"I've got other plans. I'm not going to be there this evening."

"Well, then change your plans."

"Can't do."

She looked at him lying there on the wood creeper at her feet. It occurred to her to stick her high heel right in his solar plexus. Or his balls. "I just got a call. Or rather, Gus did. From the bank. Somebody wants to take a look at the bank records. Somebody's got the idea that there might be something irregular going on."

That got his attention. He hurried to his feet, stood in front of her. "Who? Who's snooping around?"

Janet had to smile. She had him. "All the bank would say was that it was a family member. But it has to be John Lincoln, Gus' brother who's returned from the dead. There's nobody else who would give two hoots."

"Son of a bitch! What are we going to do?"

We? Hah! "I don't know what *you're* going to do. But that's what we need to talk about, but not here. And that's why you need to cancel whatever little plans you had for this evening so you'll be there when I come over. Capiche?"

She patted him twice on the cheek; she thought of giving him a kiss on the cheek, sweet boy, but decided no, it was better to keep him off-balance. Wondering. Scared. She turned on her heel and started back through the curtains, then looked over her shoulder. "It'll be around seven, seven thirty, so you can get your dinner first. And don't drink too much. You don't want to impair your thinking. Or your performance."

*

Janet lived in the house she grew up in, beyond the downtown on the main street, a yellow-brick house set back on a small terrace where the street split in two, the inbound and outbound lanes separated by grassy traffic islands for half a dozen blocks before it started the climb to Orchard Hill. She parked her late-model Dodge four-door on the street—she had wanted a coupe, they were much snazzier, but there wouldn't have been room for her mother and aunt, and there always had to be room for her mother and aunt; the only satisfaction in the car being that it grated on Gus that she wouldn't drive a Lylemobile, nope, not on a bet—and hurried up the steps from the sidewalk and along the walk to the front porch. It was one of the few houses on the block, all originally midsized family dwellings, that was still a residence, that hadn't been converted into a funeral parlor or photography studio, insurance agency or beauty salon. She noticed the lawn needed cut again before winter set in. Always something.

    A dozen years earlier, single, in her early thirties, when she realized it was left up to her to take care of her aging mother and aunt, then both in their early seventies, her sister and brother having lit out early on to get as far away as possible, Janet had resigned herself to make the best of it that she could, had taken out a bank loan—from the same Harold MacArthur she talked to on the phone today—and completely remodeled the house, making the downstairs and upstairs into two separate living spaces, the downstairs for her mother and Aunt Rita, the upstairs, after walling off the interior central staircase, complete with its own separate entrance with outdoor stairs, for her. Now she leaned against the heavy wood door with its oval-leaded window with a rose pattern and matching sidelights, let herself into the downstairs of the house. As always, the first thing she noticed, no matter how hard she worked to prevent it, was the smell—a mixture of old women, dried urine, escaping farts, talcum powder. Of slow death. She hung up her coat and hat on the coat tree, braced herself, took a deep breath through her open mouth, and went into the living room.

Torn

Her mother was a thin frail woman in her late eighties whose strength belied her physical appearance, a former second-grade schoolteacher, her white hair fluffed around her head like a cloud. She was in the same exact place where Janet left her when she checked in on them this morning before going to work—could she have been there all day? it seemed possible somehow, if her mother willed it to be so—sitting at a card table in the middle of the living room working on a jigsaw puzzle, the picture of a musty landscape somewhere in France with a shepherdess and swain and dozens of sheep. Her mother had made no progress on it from what Janet could tell.

"Well, you're home early," her mother said, not looking up from the puzzle, poking at the pieces with a pointed shaky middle finger. "To what do we owe the honor?"

"I wanted to get Aunt Rita her shower before dinner instead of after."

"Do you think your aunt Rita will want her shower before dinner? I suppose you have plans this evening. . . ."

"I don't really care if Aunt Rita wants her shower before dinner or not. That's when she's going to get it. Lord knows she needs it."

"Don't be blasphemous."

Janet wondered if the blasphemy she referred to was toward God or Aunt Rita. "Where is she?"

"In the bathroom."

"How long has she been there?"

"Oh, an hour. Maybe an hour and a half."

"Great. She's fallen asleep in there again. Someday she's going to topple over and bang her head and kill herself."

"Don't sound so happy about it."

Her mother raised her head then, looked at her, and smiled. A shark pretending to be a goldfish. Janet went out of the room and down the hall to the bathroom. She knocked on the closed door, then went in. Sure enough, her aunt was sitting on the toilet, her head resting on her chest, sound asleep. She startled awake, looked at Janet as if she'd never seen her before. "Oh. Yes. What time is it?"

"It's time for you to get your shower before dinner."

Her aunt was also in her eighties, the younger sister by a couple of years though the larger of the two, a rotund blimpy woman, a former gym teacher whose body, once muscular, had turned to mush, her gray hair as if cut with a bowl. She glared at her niece, a look that at one time had sent chills of fear through the members of the family, enough to get her own way with things, but now just looked silly.

"No, it's not. I always take my shower after supper, before going to bed."

"Not today. Now, come on, stand up and get your clothes off. We don't have all day."

"But I don't want to take my shower now. I'll just get dirty again before bed."

"And I don't want to help you take your shower at all but we're going to do it anyway. You haven't had a shower in over a week, and your sheets haven't been washed in over a month, do you really think taking your shower a few hours earlier is going to make any difference? Now get your clothes off, I'm no more looking forward to this than you are. Undoubtedly a lot less."

The older woman, braced on her two canes, got to her feet after a struggle, letting the wool men's pajama pants she wore all the time fall down around her ankles, guaranteeing that she couldn't move. Janet got down on her knees, barely able to stand the smell, and took off the woman's moccasins, her white sweat socks, and then braced her aunt as she stepped out of the puddle of pants. Janet didn't bother unbuttoning the pajama top, she pulled it up over her aunt's head. There. Her aunt stood before her in rolls and wrinkles of fat. Terrifying, Janet thought. I would have never believed skin could do that.

After standing her in the bathtub, she wetted her, scrubbed her down with a long-handled brush, got her out of the tub again, and dried her off. She led her naked aunt into her bedroom and got her seated on the bed, laid out a clean set of pajamas beside her, a clean pair of white sweat socks, retrieved her moccasins from the bathroom. She knew she should scrub the bathroom down as long as she was at it, but she didn't have time.

"Get dressed and come on out as soon as you can. We're eating as soon as I can warm it up."

"What's the big hurry?" Aunt Rita said.

Janet ignored her and went to the kitchen. She had expected some flak, it was the third night in a row that they were having meatloaf, but she always made enough for several nights, it was nothing new, they shouldn't be surprised. She took the pan from the refrigerator and put it in the oven, quickly peeled some potatoes and put them in water to boil, opened a can of peas and dumped the contents in a small saucepan. She set the table in the dining room, got each of them a glass of water, moved her mother from the living room to her place at the dining room table despite her protest about leaving her puzzle—it wasn't worth the battle to get her to wash her hands before eating; Janet made a note to be carefully handling any food bowls or plates after her mother. In the kitchen again, when the potatoes were ready, she put milk in the pan with them, mashed the contents, sliced the meatloaf, taking the end piece for herself—she didn't particularly like the end either, but she knew neither her mother nor her aunt would touch it—divided the peas between the three of them, and carried the plates to the table. Her aunt was standing braced on her two canes in the doorway, as if waiting for Janet to appear so she could show her, wearing the same pair of dirty pajamas Janet had taken off her and put in the laundry basket. *Don't say a word, it's not worth it, let her rot in them for all I care, that's what the smell indicates she's doing anyway, I don't care at this point.*

Dinner conversation, when anything was said at all, consisted of comments as to why they were eating earlier than usual, which Janet deftly dodged being well experienced in evasive tactics, and why they were having meatloaf, potatoes, and peas again, didn't she know how to cook anything else? When the ordeal was over, she redd the table as her mother and aunt gathered around the radio console in the living room to listen to the evening news, *Slim Bryant and the Jersey Wildcats*, and *One Man's Family*. Janet washed the dishes, put everything away in the cupboards, laid out their late evening snacks of shortbread cookies and glasses for milk, put on her coat and hat, and stood in the doorway to tell them she was leaving. Neither one raised her head as if she heard her or cared. Thus another night was done.

As she left the house and retraced her steps down the walk across the wide lawn, the light now gone from the day, cataloging the evening—the streetlights on defining the street; the sweep of the headlights along the traffic islands; the trees and leafless bushes all sticks, black on black—she remembered she was going to destroy the photographs she had taken of the company's books; well, she wasn't going to go back now, she'd do it later tonight when she got home from the hotel. Which got her thinking: How in heaven's name did John Lincoln Lyle find out about Daniel's little scheme? Daniel. The fool, the young fool, he pushed a good thing he had going for him too far and now he's liable to get caught. What a pity, I really do enjoy these evenings with him, he's actually quite good at it, for somebody so young. And all things considered, it was worth it. Energy instead of experience. Exuberance instead of expertise. Excitement instead of passion. A semblance of love, of a life, even if it was only that. A semblance. A resemblance. It seemed enough to get by on. As long as she didn't think about it too much.

Fifteen

"Mrs. Lyle. There's a gentleman in the lobby who says he's Mr. Lyle."

Lily sighed. Thought, What is that old vaudeville routine: That's no lady, that's my wife. That's no gentleman, that's my husband. Well, she had suspected this day would come, eventually, but she didn't expect he'd show up here at the college. Expected him some Sunday morning, just as she was settling down with her coffee and crossword. So be it.

"Yes. Show him in, please, Marilyn."

Her secretary left the doorway, to be replaced with Gus, looking rumpled as always, a little pudgier, definitely paler, undeniably sheepish. They had lived in the same town now, how many years was it, close to twenty, had corresponded through third-party agents and occasionally family members, once in a long while a phone call if something needed to be discussed, kept track of each other's movements mainly through guesswork, innuendo, and rumor, but had never been face-to-face since the time she returned from Kansas. But here he was.

"Hello, Lily."

"Gus. Come in, sit down." She motioned him to the chair beside her desk, the one that prospective students sat in for their admittance interview. She gave him credit, at least he took his hat off, he used to keep it on indoors, simply forgetting it was there. "I'm surprised to see you here."

"I'm surprised to see myself here. I was thinking, the last time I was here at the college was twenty years or so, to see the dean."

"That must have been Elizabeth Quigley. I think she was still dean then."

"Quigley. Yes, that was it. I couldn't quite remember." He laughed a little at himself. "It was certainly a memorable visit otherwise. She more or less threw me out of her office. But I don't blame her, it was a fool's errand."

"Why on earth were you here to see the dean? You weren't a student, were you, I mean that was after your time. . . ?"

"Yes. No. I mean, no, I wasn't a student, in fact, I don't suppose you could ever call me a student here. No, I was here to inquire about Mary Lydia."

Lily folded her hands on her blotter, tilted her head, listening. Gus sighed, obviously kicking himself for ever bringing it up, but continued. As she knew he would if she gave any indication at all that she was curious.

"It was during that time when you were away, when you went to Kansas. We had just learned that Mary Lydia was pregnant, and

Father sent me here to find out who Mary Lydia's friends were, wondering who her secret boyfriend was who got her pregnant, if there was a secret boyfriend."

"Elizabeth Quigley wouldn't tell you a thing like that, even if she knew."

"Which Elizabeth Quigley made quite clear to me. I tried to tell her that I knew that, that I was only there because my father sent me, but the more I talked the more foolish I appeared. I certainly didn't have a good relationship with the college to begin with. Do you remember?"

"Yes, I remember." But he went on to recount the story anyway. As she knew he would.

"I had been around the college all my life, the Steam Works made some important donations over the years, so I had a hard time taking it seriously. Besides, I didn't want to go to college in the first place, it was all Father's idea, I wanted to work in the shop, be an apprentice to a machinist, learn the business that way, but no, Father wouldn't hear of it. I only lasted a few weeks here until one morning in the required religion class the professor drew a big lumpy circle on the blackboard and flecked it with chalk marks and said, 'Maybe it will help if we think of God as a great tapioca pudding floating in the void.' I gathered my books, stood up, and said, 'Okay, that's it, I've had it,' and left the class, left the college, never to return as a student. Apparently Elizabeth Quigley knew all about it, and wouldn't let me forget it."

Of course, I knew all about it, Lily thought, everybody in the college knew about it, it was a story that lives on in the collective memory of the school to this day, that's retold in the faculty lounge or administrative meetings every time the subject of difficult students or bad behavior comes up. The thing is, I could remind you that it was during those few weeks when you were a student here that you and I met, that we wouldn't have met otherwise, for better or for worse, but apparently that story has slipped your mind....

"Well, you're here now, aren't you? What did you want to see me about, Gus?"

"Yes," Gus said, a bit discombobulated, called back from his reveries, trying to get his thoughts in order. "This is a little hard to talk about, I never thought it would come to this, I thought the Steam Works would . . . I would be able . . . but there's no way around it. I hate to tell you this but I'm unable to continue to pay the mortgage for your house . . . and your monthly living expenses. I'm really sorry . . . What? Why are you smiling?"

"Oh, Gus. It's just not in your nature to listen to anyone, is it?"

"What do you mean? I don't see what's amusing about—"

"You never heard me, years ago when I told you. I remember writing you a letter about it after we talked on the phone because I was afraid something like this would happen."

"Like what?"

Lily sighed. "I told you six years ago that I no longer needed for you to pay the mortgage or the monthly expenses. I never needed the amount you were sending me anyway, except at the very beginning, and then I needed it even less after I got the job here at the college. But when I was promoted to be the registrar, I was, am making more than enough to cover all my obligations. I told you that, I know it was six years ago because it was at the start of the bank failures, when it looked like the country was going into the Depression. I was sure you'd need all the money you could get your hands on for the business, that you couldn't afford to keep paying me and that you didn't need to, I could make it on my own."

"And you told me?"

"Yes, I told you. I even sent you a follow-up letter when the checks continued to come."

"I know you said something of the sort, but I didn't think you meant it, I thought you were just trying to be nice."

"Of course I meant it. You didn't want to hear that I didn't need the money because you wanted to think I still needed your help."

"Well, you did."

"No, that was the point. I didn't need it and I didn't want it. When it was apparent that you weren't going to listen to me, I started buying bonds with the money. Actually they've done amazingly well even though stocks generally have fallen through the floorboards, it's built up into quite a tidy sum. I'd be happy to turn it all over to you, you say the company is really hurting."

The information was gradually sinking in. "No, no, of course not, I meant the money for you and Mal, you keep it, give it to Mal, it would be a nice nest egg for him to start on. . . ." Gus thought about something for a moment. She felt sorry for him, he looked totally lost, but it didn't change her feelings.

After a few moments he shifted in the chair, studied his hands chasing each other around the brim of his hat. "Well, that makes what else I was going to say certainly superfluous."

"What else were you going to say?"

"Seeing as how I couldn't make the payments, I was going to propose . . . that you and Mal consider moving back into Sycamore House."

She looked at him in disbelief.

"There's only me there now, since Missy left, you could have the place more or less to yourselves, you know me, I'm gone most of the time, down at the shop."

"You're serious, aren't you?"

"Well, yes. We had some good times back then, with the family and all. I was thinking the other day about that time we got a croquet set and put it up in the backyard, do you remember? The whole family played, Father and Missy, you and me and Mal. . . ."

"The only thing I remember of that day is that you were out to do everything you could to show up your father. Mal was only six or so and could barely handle the mallet, so your father was helping him, they were playing together. And you hit your ball so it hit their ball and Mal was so happy and thrilled, his ball was beside his daddy's, and then you went over and put your foot on your ball and shot their ball off into the weeds. You were so proud of yourself for doing that to your father that you never even noticed Mal was heartbroken, his daddy shot his ball away, and broke out crying and that was the end of that. No, Gus, I don't want to come back to live with you at Sycamore House."

"I guess I was pretty insensitive to Mal back then."

"Back then? From what he tells me you still don't listen to him any better than you ever did. He's been trying to tell you for months that he thinks there's fraud going on in the company, but you won't listen to him."

"Fraud?"

"With that designer you hired."

"Daniel? Spalding."

"I guess that's his name."

"I know Mal said something about some irregularities he thought he found in the billings, but I didn't get the idea that it was serious or anything."

"Because you don't take anything Mal says to you seriously. You don't take seriously anything anyone says to you unless it's something you want to hear. That's what fraud is, Gus, irregularities in billing."

Lily found herself furious with him as much as she felt sorry for him. Gus Gus Gus. When will you ever learn? The man looked lost, totally bewildered as he tried to process what she was telling him. Gus stood up, slowly, as if he couldn't quite remember where he was, what he was doing there. Lily came around her desk, offered her hand. "Can I get you something? A glass of water?"

"No, no, thank you, I'll be . . . It was good to see you. . . ."

He wandered out the door and through the outer office. She wondered if she should go after him, send someone to look after him, but decided no. She'd only get herself involved again, and he would mistake her concern for interest, she would find herself back where she was, sucked into his problems and messes and foolishness. And she had vowed never to let that happen to her again.

Sixteen

"You're worried about something."

"Does it show that badly?" Anna said, sitting across from him as he had his breakfast. "I'm sorry."

"You certainly don't have anything to be sorry about," John Lincoln said. "I'm only wondering if it's something I can help you with. I don't know much about the restaurant business, but I'd be willing to give it a try if there's anything I can do to help."

Anna smiled. "That's sweet of you, but it's nothing to do with the restaurant. I have to get Warren to the hospital this morning for some X-rays, the doctors are concerned that there might be fluid building up in his lungs, and now that Onagona Memorial has their new equipment they want to make sure it's not pneumonia. Susan was going to help me, she's letting me use her car, it's a four-door so it'll be easier to get him in and out. But now she's going to have to stay here at the restaurant and I don't know if I can manage him on my own. Maybe the hotel will let me borrow Eddie for the day, but they've never let me do that in the past. . . ."

"Well, I have a solution. Let me help you."

"Oh no, I wouldn't think of it. That isn't what I meant at all." Anna looked horrified that he got the wrong idea, that she gave him the wrong impression.

"Don't be silly. I may look like the walking dead or something, but I assure you I'm an able-bodied man underneath it all." He held up his arm, pretending to flex his muscle.

"Oh, I couldn't let you do that. I feel awful that you think I was hinting. . . ."

"I don't think anything of the sort. We are two friends and you were telling me your problem, and it so happens it's something I can help you with."

"It really would be wonderful, but you're sure I'm not taking you away from something?"

John Lincoln laughed. "Oh sure, you've seen how busy I am, all I have going on. Let me go up to my room and get my coat and hat, and we'll be off."

She met him in the lobby and they went out the back door, down the alley to get Susan's car, driving it around to Anna's house. John Lincoln waited in the hall while Anna went into the

Torn

living room and bundled up Warren in several blankets.

"Sweetheart, this is John Lincoln, remember I told you he came to town? He's going to help get you to the hospital today."

"Hi, Warren." John Lincoln was well practiced in dealing with wounded and traumatized patients, speaking in everyday tones, his manner offhand, as if it was the most ordinary thing in the world for a guy in a mask and a shattered face to be talking to a semiconscious guy wrapped up in blankets like a mummy. After his experience in war zones and army hospitals, there wasn't much that could surprise or disturb him.

"I thought if you could pick him up under the arms, I could take his feet," Anna said.

"I've got a better idea," John Lincoln said, hoping he could make good on it. He positioned himself beside the bed, got his arms under Warren, and lifted him in his arms. Thank goodness, there was nothing to the man, he must have weighed well under a hundred pounds. A wisp. Warren stared into the side of his head, only blinking a couple of times.

"Oh my goodness," Anna said. "Can you do that?"

I sure as hell hope so, John Lincoln thought. "Yep. Looks like it. Now, if you could get the doors. . . ."

Anna helped steady John Lincoln through the hall, out the front door and down the steps, then skipped ahead to get the car door open, John Lincoln easing his bundle into the back seat. After arranging Warren's blankets, John Lincoln straightened up, gave a sigh of relief, and said a silent prayer. Thank you, Lord, it would have been terrible to drop him.

Anna went around the car to sit in the back seat beside Warren while John Lincoln drove. Onagona Memorial Hospital was at the far end of Orchard Hill, tucked back against the valley's hills. At the entrance John Lincoln went on inside and got a wheelchair and lifted Warren into it, then Anna wheeled Warren inside while John Lincoln parked the car. He caught up with her in the X-ray department's waiting room.

"Is he doing okay?"

"He seems to be, as much as you can tell about anything with him. They took him in right away though they said it could be several hours. Are *you* okay?"

"I'm fine. I'll tell you, it's kind of nice being back in a hospital setting again. No one stares at the mask." He meant it as a joke but Anna seemed to take it seriously.

They sat for a while, looking at magazines, people-watching, staring into space, until the waiting room emptied out a bit and they could talk without being overheard.

She asked, "Have you heard anything more from Laughlin?"

"No, only what I told you. He wasn't hopeful of getting a look at the accounts, but thought it worth a shot to use the family connection. He said when he talked to the bank, MacArthur raised the point that just looking at the bank records probably wouldn't give any indication of fraud without more of the company's records, vendor invoices and such."

"I thought of that...."

"So had I. So had David. At least for showing any fraud going on with the billing. But I was hoping to see the activity of the Mercy Fund, and find some proof that Gus had been dipping into it for the company's expenses."

"We talked about that. It wouldn't be a crime even if he did. A privately owned company could do what it wants without regulation."

"Maybe not a crime, but morally reprehensible."

"No law against that," she smiled.

"No. And I thought it was my private crusade. But it turns out David was looking for such misuse of funds as well."

"Really?"

"Really."

Anna smiled to herself. "Maybe I've been a little hard on David Laughlin. I know, or at least suspected, he always had a crush on me before the accident, but I supposed that was long gone."

"I got the impression when I went to ask him about all this, that he was disappointed you weren't with me."

Torn

"Li'l ole irresistible me," she said, pretending to prim a little.

John Lincoln smiled though of course she couldn't, wouldn't see it behind the mask. She wouldn't see the pain in his eyes either, but he looked away just in case. Well, what could he expect, he had no hold on her, couldn't, wouldn't, she was a married woman. And why would she ever be interested in the town freak, anyway? Maybe that was it, maybe it was only pity, maybe he was only another wounded soul to her, like her husband, maybe she collected them, some people did. No, he knew that wasn't the case, nothing of the sort, that would diminish her, make her less of a person, and he knew in his depths that she was better than that. That she was as fine a person as he had ever known. No, he was lucky she was his friend, beyond lucky: blessed. He treasured that. Treasured her. He would never do anything to ruin it, such as thinking she might care for him as more than a friend.

When Warren's tests were done, they bundled him back in the car and started for home. It was Anna's idea to take him for a little ride, as long as they were out, Warren never got to see things these days, she thought it might be a real treat for him. Instead of heading downtown, John Lincoln drove them up Stephen's Hill to the top of the valley and then down the other side to Colonel Berry Park. They drove slowly along the meandering roads, past the picnic grounds and playing fields, in summertime crowded with picnickers and family outings, but now deserted, the tables and benches sitting empty, the pavilions hollow shells. He pulled into the parking lot at the lake and they sat for a while looking at the water, the trees bare and waiting for winter. John Lincoln, looking in the rearview mirror, couldn't tell if Warren was interested or even awake.

After several moments, Anna said, "Warren, did I tell you that John Lincoln was a captain in the army, and served in the Great War?"

"Anna, please don't—"

"No, Warren was always interested in the military, he liked to read about the war and all, didn't you, Warren? Maybe John Lincoln can tell you a story about things he saw."

"I told you, I wasn't in the war, I only came along after the fighting was done to help those who were. . . ."

"That sounds like being in the war to me, doesn't it to you, sweetheart? I'm sure we'd both like to hear about some of your adventures."

He moved his head to look at her in the mirror. What was she doing, trying to embarrass him or something? But she met his eyes; she smiled at him, nodded a couple of times toward her husband, asking him to do it for Warren's sake. John Lincoln decided he needed to lighten up, not take himself so seriously.

"Well, okay. There was one guy who sticks out in my mind, he had a lot of facial injuries like mine so maybe that's why I remember him so well. I asked him one day how he got his injuries and he said it was during the second battle of the Marne, from an artillery shell that was close to a direct hit on their trench; there was talk afterward that it was actually one of ours, but it didn't matter at that point, the damage was done. The explosion sent him flying, a piece of shrapnel tore into his face, and he was obviously in shock. The thing was that as he lay there on the duckboards, when his ears stopped ringing, he kept hearing a horse whinnying somewhere out in no-man's-land. Whinnying and whinnying, it wouldn't stop. All he could think was the animal must be in pain and that somebody had to do something to help it. As I said, he was in shock, and he knew he was in shock, there was blood all over his face and down the front of him, he could only see out of one eye, but his adrenaline was pumping and he got to his feet and before anyone could stop him he took his pistol and climbed up the ladder and went over the top. Now, as soon as he did that the bullets started flying, he heard them whizzing all around him, but that didn't stop him, he said it was as if he knew none of them would hit him, for those few minutes he was invincible, and he ran out across the battlefield listening for the sound of the horse. He finally found the animal in a shell hole, a

Torn

white horse, the animal was stuck, it couldn't climb up the sides of the crater, it was too steep and slippery, but he could tell otherwise the animal was unharmed. So this guy, Sergeant Riley his name was, he jumped into the hole and slid down to the bottom. There was a foot or so of water in the shell hole and him and the horse stood there in it looking at each other for a couple of minutes, and then the horse tried again to climb up the side but it was muddy and slick to begin with and the horse's attempts only made it muddier and slicker, but Sergeant Riley decided there was no help for it, he'd come this far, risked his life this far, he had to do something to help it. So he did the only thing he could think to do, he got behind the horse, got his shoulder up under its haunches and lifted, pushed, slipping and sliding himself, and the blood was still dripping off what was left of his face and the sweat was running into his one eye that still worked, but he lifted and pushed and sure enough the horse started to make some progress except that the horse's bowels suddenly let go and the good sergeant was covered with it. But that didn't stop him, he kept pushing and the horse finally got a good purchase on some dry earth and popped free over the top of the crater as the sergeant slid back down to the bottom. He was standing there in the water again, covered with horse manure, getting his breath back, gathering his strength to climb out of the hole himself, when he looked up and there outlined against the sky were half a dozen German soldiers peering down at him, their guns and bayonets aimed at him, come to find out what all was going on. And Sergeant Riley thought, Okay, this is it, I'm a dead man, and the German soldiers stared at him for a moment, then one of them said something and they all broke out laughing, they doubled over with laughter and clapped each other on the back as if it was the funniest thing in the world, put up their weapons and disappeared, heading back to their own line, he could hear them still laughing, talking about something, saying something over and over as they walked away. Now, Sergeant Riley was angry at this point, and the pain and shock were starting to get to him, the adrenaline was wearing off, but he gathered what strength he had left and made a running start at it and got himself up the wall, threw himself over the edge, and as he lay there panting he could see the German soldiers on their way back to their line—to add insult to injury they had the white horse with them—and then one of the soldiers looked back at him and Sergeant Riley heard clearly what they had been saying: *So ein Misthaufen*. Which started them laughing all over again. It wasn't until Sergeant Riley was convalescing in the hospital, months later, that he found out what *So ein Misthaufen* meant: What a pile of shit. The moral being, I guess, even if it means getting covered with crap, doing a good deed could save your life."

He looked in the rearview mirror and saw that Warren was apparently asleep, his eyes closed, slumped against the car window. John Lincoln adjusted the mirror so he could see Anna; she had her mouth covered, trying to stifle a giggle. She nodded toward the door and they both slipped out of the car, stretching their legs, standing beside the front fender.

"Is he okay?"

"Yes, he's fine. Thank you for telling him a story, I know you didn't want to but you have a very soothing voice and I thought he might get a nap, he needed it after his day."

"Did they tell you what the X-ray showed?"

"They're not supposed to say anything, the results are supposed to come from the doctor, but the technician said they didn't find anything out of the ordinary."

"That's good news."

"Really. After all he's been through, to lose him now to something like pneumonia. . . ."

And he thought, Well, there's your answer, if you still held out any hope for yourself with her, if you wondered if by some miracle she felt something for you. She's never going to leave him, ever, and how could you ever expect her to, she's not that kind of woman, it's part of the reason you think so highly of her. What kind of a person are you anyway, to think she might be capable of such a thing? Not a very good person apparently. You fool, you stupid deluded fool. . . .

Back at her house, he carried Warren inside and helped get him situated again in his bed. But he felt awkward, still being there, watching her fuss over him, calling him "sweetheart," "dear," as if he was intruding on something personal, intimate.

"I guess I should be going," he said, heading toward the front door.

"Would you like me to fix you something to eat?" Anna said, following him down the hallway.

"No, that's okay. I'll get something at the Parlour. Will you be there later?"

"Yes, as soon as the nurse comes here."

She suddenly grabbed his hand and kissed it, holding it to her breasts. "You'll never know. In just these few short weeks you've become as important to me as breath."

He lifted his hand to her cheek, feeling its softness against the back of his fingers. Thinking, This is as close as I'll ever come now to making love to a woman. It's probably a good thing she'd never want me to.

Seventeen

Mal was coming through the curtains surrounding the Zephyr work area as Janet was leaving through the curtains on the opposite side. When Daniel saw him, he whirled around and came at him as if he wanted to hit him.

"How much of that did you hear?" Daniel demanded.

"How much of what?" Mal said.

At that Daniel looked like he actually was going to hit him, he clenched his fist and started to raise his arm but then caught himself—maybe remembering that Mal was the boss' son. He glared at Mal for a couple seconds then turned away, heading back to his tool chest.

"Well, just don't say anything about it."

Mal had had enough. "You know what, Daniel, I'm sick and tired of you trying to boss me around. I don't work for you. If anything, it's more like you work for me, my family's company."

"You better watch it, Mal," Daniel said, though he wasn't looking as sure of himself.

"No, you're the one who better watch it. You're the one on shaky ground. Oh, the hell with all of this."

Mal turned and hacked his way back between the curtains, stormed through the shop, slammed his weight against the panic bar on the side door and popped outside onto the sidewalk. He was only vaguely aware of where he was headed, he was walking for walking's sake, he had to get away from here, get away from the Steam Works, he was fed up with it, with the business, with his father, with the work his father supposedly had him doing, work that amounted to nothing, less than nothing. Fed up with being the owner's son, with having no position or purpose with the company, with everyone treating him with borrowed respect, deferring to him though he had done nothing to earn it on his own, for that matter unable to do anything in the company that *could* earn him purpose or respect. His father said he wanted Mal to do a little bit of everything, had him apprentice to a machinist for a while though not long enough to actually learn the trade; had him work in the engineering department—where he actually showed some talent, not for solving complex mathematical problems, but discovered he had talent as a draftsman, the ability to show in plan and section and perspective the designs and calculations of others—though he was pulled from there as the orders for the company's machines dwindled; had him work in the sales department but then pulled him from there as well when the country's financial condition worsened with the Depression and there was no one to sell to. Mal was left to spend his days aimlessly wandering from one area to another, looking for something to do, occupying himself at times with sweeping floors until his father put an end to that as beneath the dignity of a Lyle. It was while he was doing busywork in the office, helping Janet by copying entries into the ledger, that he happened on the irregularities with Daniel Spalding's billing practices; when he called his father's attention to what he had found, it put an end to Mal's work in the office, his father dismissing what Mal told him as impossible, refusing to consider that his sainted designer could do such a thing. The more Mal thought about it now, the angrier he got, couldn't figure out why he had put up with the situation for so long, kept walking now without plan or destination.

He had been against hiring Spalding in the first place, when his father told him what he intended to do, to completely redesign the Lylemobile, to try to revive consumer interest in the steam car. It wasn't that he was against the idea of the steam car per se, it had been his idea to rename it the Zephyr, though he had heard his father take credit for the name change. Well, so be it. If it was that important to Gus, Mal could live with it. The problem was, as Mal did some research, he was convinced there was no market for a steam car in this day and age, the time when it might have found a market was long past. There was no way that consumers were going to give up the internal combustion engine at this point, it was too entrenched in the modern way of life; besides, the oil industry was too strong, had its tentacles in too many chambers of government, there was no chance that it would let a steam car get a toehold with consumers now. But from his research Mal thought the company could continue to be successful with its large construction equipment, especially in foreign markets; Keystone Steam Works had a good reputation there already for its well drillers and steam shovels, especially in third world countries where a steam engine's ability to use alternate fuels, such as wood, coal, even plant leaves, gave Keystone machinery a real competitive advantage.

Mal's idea was to throw all the company's resources into updating their existing construction machinery; developing new product lines such as road graders, excavators, cranes, front loaders; and target all their advertisement and promotion efforts overseas. After all, the few jobs they still had were all from foreign companies, it only made sense to build on that. But his father wouldn't consider it. Gus' first success with the company, when his own father was still alive and running things, was developing a smaller, quick-starting steam engine, which he further thought would be perfect for a steam automobile, the Lylemobile, and he was never able to get beyond the idea. It was Gus' way that if he just pushed hard enough, he could force things to conform to the way he wanted them. Mal appreciated that about his father, could even admire it in certain circumstances, though he was also aware of how many times his personal philosophy of life had failed his father. For instance, in trying to manipulate his son to be someone he wasn't; and when Gus realized his pushing wasn't going to accomplish making Mal in his own image, simply gave up on him altogether. Let him go any direction Mal cared to in his life, as if Gus had washed his hands of his son, a hopeless case. It was why Gus' hiring Daniel Spalding was so grating; from the beginning Gus gave Spalding carte blanche in the company, treating the young man like his long-lost prodigal son. Which was why when Mal discovered quite by accident Spalding's financial indiscretions, there was a personal satisfaction for Mal, even though his father wouldn't even consider the possibility that Spalding could do such a thing. The memory of his father turning away from him in favor of the designer infuriated Mal all over again. Filled him with a growing rage.

Mal stopped walking. Looked around. His self-awareness slowly returning, his awareness of where he was. Realized that for the past hour or so he must have been walking in a circle. Was right back where he started, across the street from the orange-brick buildings of the Steam Works. At another time he would have laughed at himself, thought it was funny. But not today. Not in the mood he was in. As he watched, the few workers who were still employed at the shop began leaving, the few engineers and secretaries from the office, trickling out the doors like the building had sprung a leak, heading to their cars or starting the long walk up the hill to other areas of town. And he had a thought. He tried to make himself as inconspicuous as possible, standing close to one of the sycamore trees that lined that side of the street, waiting. Daniel was always one of the last to leave, Mal used to think it was from the designer not wanting to mix with the ordinary workers, but now he suspected it had something to do with the billing irregularities. Today it was nearly fifteen minutes after everyone had left that Daniel came out the front door and headed up Twelfth Street. Mal fell in a half a block behind, keeping to the other side of the street.

On the main street, Spalding stopped first in Davidson's Drugstore; Mal took up a position in the doorway of the Monkey Wards down the block. When Daniel reappeared ten minutes later, whatever it was he purchased—cigarettes? aspirin? condoms?—fit into the pocket of his suit coat. From there Spalding continued along the street a couple of blocks to the Blue Room, inside passing the diner at the front and up the three steps into the pool hall at the back. It had been a favorite haunt of Mal's when he was younger, even into his college years, so no one paid attention to him as he followed Daniel into the back room, past the pool tables, taking a seat on a stool in the shadows along the rear wall.

He had been there a few minutes, watching Daniel talking to some of the players, trying to join a game or start a new one, when a guy with a cue sat down on the stool beside him.

"Mal Lyle."

"Bobby Cefalo. How goes it, Bobby?"

"It goes. What're you doing down here, slumming among the common folk?"

"Trying to see how the real people live, Bobby Cephalitis."

"Oh, it's real enough, Malsy Palsy. Don't you worry about that. You looking for a game?"

"Nah. I haven't played in years. You'd take me to the cleaners."

"That's why I'm trying to get you in a game."

They watched the games going on at the half dozen tables.

After a few moments, Mal said, "What's with that guy?" Nodding toward Spalding, alone at a table, setting up a break of balls.

"Who? Swifty?"

"Swifty?"

"It used to be Shifty among the regulars, when he started coming in a couple months ago. He had this shifty look about him and was always trying to hustle a game, but he was so bad at the hustle, giving himself away, they changed it to Swifty. The only ones who will play with him now are the few college students who come in and don't know any better, or the occasional out-of-towner. He's one of yours, isn't he? At the Steam Works?"

"My dad hired him for a special project, I guess. I don't have much to do with him."

"You should tell him he better watch himself. He's a smartass, every once in a while he starts mouthing off at somebody. If he's not careful he's going to find himself lying in an alley somewhere."

"Sorry, not my job to hold his leash."

"Yeah, well," Bobby said, standing up, resting the butt of his pool cue on the toe of his shoe.

"You working?" Mal said.

"Nah. Nothing regular since Screw and Bolt closed. Couple pickup jobs, digging ditches, shit like that. I'd ask you if you got anything at the Steam Works but I hear you're about to shut down, right?"

"It's not quite that bad yet, but seems to be getting there."

"If you do have anything . . . ?"

"Of course."

"If I knock off your friend Swifty, can I have his job?"

"Fine with me, though you'd have to talk to my dad. I'd put in a good word."

Cefalo stood there, looking at the games going on for several long minutes, but neither one said anything, both aware that the topics of conversation were exhausted. In truth they were never friends, barely knew each other in school, revolving in different circles, Cefalo an athlete, football and baseball, his friends the other athletic kids, part of the working-class kids who used to chase Mal home when they were younger, Mal being labeled and

Torn

dismissed as a rich kid, as his father and uncle had been at the same age; the labels between social classes faded somewhat when they got to high school though were never quite forgotten, the nicknames for each other more overheard than ever used at the time. Though Mal never considered his lack of friends or popularity a drawback, rather it seemed the natural order of things; apparently he was meant to be one of those individuals in the world who were designated to be overlooked, taken for granted, always in the background. A self-image that was fostered no doubt by his father's attitude toward him, a figure in Mal's life who was more implied than anything else, reaching critical mass when Mal's mother took him to Kansas and then returned but not to live at Sycamore House, living by themselves on Orchard Hill, his father never coming to see him or as far as he knew even aware that he was still alive. It was only at his mother's insistence that his father gave him a job at the Steam Works and it was painfully obvious that his father didn't know what to do with him, said he was grooming him for the day when the company would be his but never personally gave him direction or insight, leaving that to others. But it didn't matter, or at least that was what Mal always told himself before. But now, since Daniel Spalding came upon the scene and monopolized Gus' attention and interest—to say nothing of the guy taking advantage of his father and the company, as well as rubbing Mal's face in it, or at least that's what it felt like—Mal was beginning to think it mattered a lot.

After several solitary games of eight ball, Spalding put his cue back in the rack and went down the steps into the diner; Mal was ready to follow him but Daniel took a seat at the counter. Mal moved to another stool along the wall, keeping his watch while Daniel ate supper, a fish sandwich and a beer. It reminded Mal that he hadn't eaten himself since breakfast but he wasn't hungry, he was too wound up to eat. When Daniel was finished, Mal followed him back down the main street several blocks, Daniel looking in store windows though it was obvious he was watching his reflection rather than anything on display, turning down the hill at Eleventh Street and letting gravity help drag him back to the hotel. Mal held back, watching through the front window until Daniel was in the elevator and on his way to his floor before entering the lobby and taking a chair in the far corner, close to a pillar, where he could see if Daniel came down again, keep track of the comings and goings in the lobby.

He had been there a half hour or so when John Lincoln came from the restaurant; his uncle probably wouldn't have seen him except John Lincoln was keeping to the side of the lobby, skirting the activity around the front desk and the way to the elevator, obviously trying to avoid contact with anyone. When he saw Mal, John Lincoln pulled up short.

"Mal. What a surprise."

"Hello, John Lincoln."

"What are you doing, tucked away back here?" John Lincoln looked around, as if affirming that it was out of the way. "Keeping an eye on things?"

"Something like that."

"Mind if I join you? Or would you like to go have a drink?"

"No, I'm fine, thanks. But you're welcome to sit down." Mal motioned to the matching wingback chair at an angle to his own. Thinking, *Shit. What the hell does he want? Maybe he won't stay long.*

John Lincoln settled himself in the chair, crossed his legs, appeared ready to stay a while.

"I haven't seen you since I've been back. Been meaning to, but I'm afraid there were some people I needed to see right away. Like your mother."

"She told me you visited her."

"After all, when people think you're dead for twenty years or so, you have some explaining to do after you suddenly turn up again." John Lincoln laughed a little, then caught himself. "I hope the mask doesn't bother you."

"No, not at all. Mother told me about. . . ." He let it trail away, finished the thought with a small wave of his hand. "And I saw you

Torn

at the office, at the Steam Works."

"When your father more or less threw me out. Yes, I remember." Again a laugh, again realizing it was absorbed by the mask. "Not that it probably wasn't deserved. Your father and I never did get along that well—certainly not as I got older. And I can understand that he might wonder if I had come back to try to horn in on the business or something."

"And did you? Come back to horn in on the business?"

"I can assure you: no, I did not. And from what I've seen, there isn't much of a business left to horn in on."

Mal made a face, shrugged. "It could be better."

"Your mother said you had some ideas for the company but that your father wasn't interested in hearing them. I'm sorry to say that sounds like Gus."

What was John Lincoln getting at? Why did he want to talk to him about the company? Or his father? Mal didn't say anything, only gave another little shrug.

"She also said that you thought you had discovered some irregularities in the billing, some possible fraud."

"My mother told you about that?"

"She said it in passing. It was sympathetic to what you were going through at the company, the dealings with your father."

"She shouldn't have said anything about it. I don't have any proof or anything."

"I was interested because I've wondered myself if there wasn't misappropriations with some of the funds. The compensation fund in particular."

"I don't know anything about that. I do know that Dad has done everything possible to fund the work on the prototype for the steam car, the Zephyr. Including moving monies around where he thought it was appropriate."

"I've been trying to get a look at the books to see what's going on, but your father has them under lock and key. And I admit it's unusual for an outsider like me, even though I'm part of the family, to want to see the company's books." Behind his mask he gave a little self-deprecating laugh.

Mal was surprised. John Lincoln was expressing the same suspicions about the finances of the company that he had, and yet the idea of his uncle sniffing around made him protective, of the Steam Works, of his father, of all things. What right did this guy have anyway, family or no, going around asking questions, poking what was left of his nose into things that didn't concern him, things that were literally none of his business? Coming back to town where he wasn't wanted, walking around looking like some weirdo from a sideshow. Mal could feel his anger building all over again.

"I hope you're not suggesting that I do anything to help you get a look at the books...."

"No, no, of course not, I didn't mean that at all. Though it does occur to me, now that you mention it, maybe you could—"

"If you're so interested in what goes on at the Steam Works, there's the person you should be talking to."

John Lincoln looked to where Mal was looking. Janet Santelli was walking through the lobby, heading toward the elevator.

"That's your father secretary, isn't it?" John Lincoln said. "I wonder where she's going. She looks determined."

"Maybe she's here to see you," Mal said. "Maybe you two have something going on, that wouldn't surprise me, sounds like something you'd do, trying to get more information."

John Lincoln looked at him, incredulous. Before he could say anything the bell for the elevator rang and they both watched as Janet got in, watched as the arrow on the dial above the closed doors stopped at three.

"Who do we know on the third floor?" Mal said.

"Well, I know Daniel Spalding's room is there," John Lincoln said. "But maybe there's some other reason completely why...."

"Oh, sure," Mal said, openly derisive of what his uncle said.

John Lincoln regarded him. "Are you mad at me about something? Because you've been less than friendly ever since we started talking. Have I offended you in some way? I thought you and I had a good relationship."

"You did?"

"Well, sure. I remember before you and your mom went off to Kansas, you'd be sitting on the floor of the kitchen playing with that dump truck of yours while your mom and I talked—"

"What I remember is you ignoring me completely when you'd come over to our kitchen, I did everything possible to get you to play with me or at least pay some attention to me, but you always treated me like I was in the way, like you wished I wasn't there. Even as a little kid I knew there was something going on between you and my mom—"

"What? You thought I had something going on with your mother, with Lily?"

"I didn't know what it was at that age, of course, but I knew something wasn't right, that you had no business hanging around her all the time, looking at her like some long-lost puppy, it was sickening, it made me sick then and it makes me sick to think about it now. Is that why you came back to Furnass? To try to start something up with her again? I wouldn't think she'd want anything to do with you now, not with you looking like this, but who knows, lonely people do strange things."

John Lincoln stood up. "I don't know what I did to you, Mal, or what you think I did to you, but I'm really sorry you feel that way about me. I assure you your mother and I were only friends, she helped me a lot during a bad time in my life back then, somebody in the family I could talk to, and I thought maybe I helped her too, someone she could confide in when she was having trouble with Gus. But that was all a long time ago, and I certainly didn't come back to Furnass to try to start some kind of relationship with her. I'm really sorry if I upset you. If you ever want to try to talk about things, I'd be glad to."

"So you can get more information out of me for your vendetta against my father? Oh, sure. Good-bye, Uncle. You take care of yourself."

Eighteen

"I know Mal said something about irregularities with Daniel's billing," Gus said in his mind to Janet, as if she was sitting in the car beside him as he drove away from the college after seeing Lily. "But I guess I never thought he was serious."

"Exactly," Janet says in his imagination, "that's what Lily was telling you: you never took Mal serious when he was younger, and you don't take him serious now."

"I don't know, I guess it's true, you and Lily are right. I guess I never have taken him seriously. I wonder why that is."

"I think that's for you to tell me."

Gus thought for a moment as he continued down Orchard Avenue. "Well, when Mal first came along—"

"That's a strange way to describe your wife having a baby, don't you think? It sounds like Mal just happened along, turned up at the door one morning."

"When Mal was born," Gus continued, making no attempt to hide his petulance, "when he was a little boy, I had just figured out how we could not only reduce the size of our steam engines, but make them easier and quicker to start. It was going to revolutionize steam engines and how they're used in vehicles. And I had the idea for a steam automobile, the Lylemobile, and it was taking up a lot of time at the shop, I didn't get home very often."

"And whose fault was that? That you didn't make time to get home to see your young wife, who was probably having her own problems being a young mother, and to see your bouncing baby boy, spend time with him, get to know him, let him get to know you? It wasn't as if you were working out of town, hundreds of miles away. You were at the Steam Works, what? half a mile down the hill?"

"No, you're right. Looking back at it now, I can see I should have paid more attention to Lily and to Mal during that time."

"And I think you can figure it out why Lily took him and went off to Kansas."

Torn

"Yes. I can see that now about Lily. I guess I certainly wasn't an attentive husband...."

"Not attentive? That's an understatement. How about totally ignored?"

"I didn't *totally* ignore them," Gus protested.

Janet just looks at him, raises her eyebrows as if to say, Oh yeah?

"But why would I do that to a little boy? My son? What kind of monster—"

"I hardly think what you did was in the category of being a monster. I think it was simply a case that you cared more for your work than you did for your wife and son. Particularly your son. That's not monstrous, that's simply selfish. Self-centered. Unloving."

"But I did love Lily, she was the love of my life...." He caught it himself. "I said Lily. But not Mal."

Janet looks at him, makes a regretful face.

"It was an intense time for me. I finally had done something that got my father's attention. He was paying attention to me for the first time that I could remember. When he remarried and he and Missy had the twins, Father paid more attention to them than to me, he was always going on about how special they were. And he more or less overlooked me, didn't even seem to know I was there."

"And why would he, when you think about it? You had witnessed the great error of his life, contributing to the death of his beloved wife in that burning trench. And you made it quite clear that you blamed him for the death of your mother."

"I used to preach it to the twins, what he had done, so they'd know the kind of person their father was."

"What you *thought* he had done. From the perspective of a six-year-old, standing at a window twenty yards away at least, and with his view of what was going on blocked half the time."

Gus kept his eyes straight ahead, two hands on the steering wheel, making the bends into the downtown.

"And you don't think your father knew what you were telling the twins? Knew what you thought of him? Why would he want to be around you? I wouldn't have wanted to be around you, either. But you say with your developments for the steam engine his attitude toward you changed, he started to pay attention to you."

"It was like he was seeing me for the first time. We talked about my design for the engine and the Lylemobile all the time, the two of us working on them. It was the happiest time of my life." He wondered if that was true. What that said about him.

"But the happiness didn't include your wife and your young child."

"I needed Lily at that time more than ever, I wanted to share my happiness with her, all the intense things I was feeling, share my accomplishments. But she was always busy with Mal, taking care of him, he had a number of problems during his early years, it seemed like one thing after another, mumps, measles, chicken pox, bronchitis, ear infections, throat infections, you name it. Every time I went to be with Lily, she'd be called away to take care of Mal, something else Mal needed."

"So to impress your father, you ignored your son. Thus are cycles of neglect born."

"How pathetic," Gus said, pulling into the parking lot at the Steam Works. He stopped the Lylemobile, banked the fire, but continued to sit there, staring at the hills across the river.

"And then Lily took him away," Janet says. "Ran off to Kansas. That should have been a wake-up call. I'll bet Lily meant it to be."

"I suppose."

"And did you pay more attention to him when she brought him back?"

"No, I didn't see him at all after that."

"Even though he was in the same town. Right up the street as it were."

"To have seen Mal would have meant that I had to see Lily. And I figured she didn't want to see me. When she came back she made it quite clear that she didn't want to live with me. So I set her

Torn

up in that house on Orchard Hill and told her I'd pay all her expenses. Which she let me know today that as it turned out she didn't need anyway, that she could get along very well on her own resources, thank you very much."

"So you just went along with it."

"Well, of course, if somebody tells you they don't want to live with you—"

"But she didn't say that, did she? She said she wouldn't live with you at Sycamore House."

"What are you getting at?"

"Did it occur to you that maybe she was waiting for you to reach out to her? That maybe she needed to know that you wanted her back, that you wanted to be with her. Maybe what she was saying wasn't that she didn't want to live with you, she was saying that she didn't want to live with them. With your family in Sycamore House. And who could blame her? From everything I've seen over the years and everything you've told me, your family, pardon my French, is nuts."

"We're eccentric, to be sure—"

"You're nuts. Unqualified bonkers, the whole family. You call yourselves eccentrics to try to justify it, because you all think it makes you sound special, upper-class, learned. But that's all bullshit, again pardon my French. You're snobs and you look down on people and, in everyday language, you're collectively nuts."

"I don't know where you—"

"Well, as I've heard you say many times in other contexts, let's review: There was your father, Malcolm, who spent the latter part of his life punishing himself and everyone around him for what he did to his first wife, Lydia, from all indications the love of his life; who buried himself or tried to in his work of running the Steam Works but knew he never could live up to the standard that his father, Colin, the founder of the company, set for him; who took out his guilt for what he did to Lydia on his son by her, that being you; who went ahead against all good sense and everyone's advice and married the daughter of a college professor, a woman who was feisty and unpleasant and no one else would have because of her bad nature and who had enough emotional baggage to fill a freight train; a woman who gave him two children all at once, twins, your half brother and half sister, who you were able to successfully turn against their father, the daughter, Mary Lydia, who was the apple of her father's eye mainly I suppose because she reminded him of the woman he still truly loved, and the son John Lincoln, who was too smart for his own and everybody's good, who your father tried to groom to take over the company, for a time completely overlooking you, the firstborn, in favor of a second son who though he tended to avoid his father at all costs at least didn't overtly hate him—hate him, that is, until you made your discoveries and improvements on the company's basic steam engine and then you cozied up to your father and did everything you could to be the dutiful son, an act of hypocrisy that certainly wasn't lost on your own wife, who took off for the hills, or rather, to be more exact, the plains of Kansas before whatever craziness was going around in that house infected her too.

"And that's just for starters, as far as the craziness goes. There was your stepmother, your father's second wife, Missy, who once she was ensconced in the house did nothing but lounge around in her collection of frilly peignoirs, propped up on pillows on the sofa in the living room reading fan magazines and eating bonbons; then there was Malcolm's mother, your grandmother, the grande dame of the family in her eighties, Libby, Colin's widow, who everyone was petrified of and who governed the house with just a look here and there, who dressed all in black Victorian clothes, half a century out of fashion, and walked with a cane that made a resounding *thump!* with each step like a bishop's crosier, who haunted the hallways like a dark ghost come to wreak havoc with anyone who dared get in her way; to say nothing of her maid or personal assistant or whatever you want to call her, a Caribbean woman named Perpetual, who actually ran the house and the household, who probably ran your grandmother too, with her room full of potions and medicinal plants and magic spells, the

Torn

actual center of power in the house; and then the twins themselves, in a world of their own, a world within the family's world, which no one could penetrate or even touch, dressing up at times in each other's clothes and running unchecked through the town until Mary Lydia got herself pregnant with no one knew who for certain, maybe even her twin brother, that paragon of manly virtue who appeared to respond to the possibility that he was the father by running off to join a foreign army to oppose the European aggressor and serve the forces of Right and Justice but only ended up getting himself drowned or at least presumed so by falling off the troopship in New York Harbor. Is this all crazy enough for you? And you wondered why Lily might not want to live with you when she came back to town. With the result that you never saw your son for what, a decade or so? until Lily insisted you give him a job at the company after college and even then you paid as little attention to him as possible, a young man who despite the way you treated him was trying to warn you that somebody was taking advantage of you and even then you brushed him aside."

Gus stared straight ahead for several moments, lost in his thoughts, then finally roused himself, climbed out of the car and dragged himself to the door of the Steam Works, saying to himself, out loud this time, "I was so wrong. So wrong."

*

Upstairs, the office area was dark, no one working late in the engineering department, no one in the secretarial pool, all gone for the day. He could remember when at five in the afternoon the day seemed to be just starting, the offices abuzz with phones ringing, the clatter of typewriters and telex machines, engineers and draftsmen bent over their tables. Well, why would anyone stay late these days, there was barely enough work during the day for the few employees who remained, those he hadn't fired yet. He went on to his office, saw that Janet wasn't in hers. Et tu, Janet, though he knew that was unfair, besides being corny.

"You know it's unfair," Janet says. "Remember, I have an aging mother and an invalid aunt to take care of, it's not like I'm running out on you to go somewhere to have fun."

"You're right, I apologize."

She softens. "It's all right, I know you're under a lot of stress, I'm sorry I snapped. . . ."

He went on into his office to see if there were any messages, anything left on his desk that screamed for attention, then went back through the offices, still in his coat and hat, past the empty drawing tables, in the hope Mal was in his office. The light was on, but it was only Old Jake, emptying the wastepaper basket.

"Hello, Jake. You seen Mal?"

"Nope. He usually be gone by this time."

"Yeah, I guess so. Thanks," Gus added, turning away.

"You could probably find him down at the tent," the old man said after him. "That's where he usually be after work."

"The tent?"

"The welfare tent. Down on Seventh Street. They serve food for people out of work."

"What's Mal doing down there?" Gus said. Thinking, Does he eat there at night?

"He volunteers, to help out distributing food. You didn't know?"

Gus was taken back, embarrassed. "No, he never said. . . ."

Yeah, that would be like Mal too. Jake cocked his head at him, went back to his dusting.

Mal volunteers at a welfare tent, Gus thought, heading back to the stairs. Why on earth. . . .

"Maybe he's trying to make up for the sins of the fathers," Janet says. Then titters.

"That's not funny," Mal said.

"No, you're right. It isn't funny. Not at all."

He went back down the side stairs and outside; his first thought was to take his car, but decided it was only a few blocks, the walk would do him good. The early evening was mild, it was dark already at six o'clock, the streetlights flickering like they were just waking up, the checkerboard of lights in the houses up the slope of the town; across the river the valley wall was a looming presence, black on black, the river reflecting the remaining light from the sky, a band of silver—no: lead; quicksilver—trembling toward the end of the valley and its absorption into the larger river. In the flats between the passenger car tracks and the riverbank, a switch engine was backing down the spur from the mill, towing a train of a dozen slag cars, the top of each ladle glowing from the molten metal within; at the end of the spur the train of shimmering cars waited while a brakeman threw the switch, then started slowly toward the river to dump the slag down the embankment.

"I should never have let you talk me into letting that old man sleep at the Steam Works," Gus said in his mind to Janet as he walked along.

"Jake? He's a sweet old man," Janet says. "What's wrong with him?"

"He looks like hell warmed over for starters. He never shaves or cuts his hair, he's always wearing that long coat with the bulging pockets, Lord knows what all he's got in there, and he smells."

"All he asks for is that little space in that unused storage room. And in exchange he does some janitorial work and takes walks around the place a couple of times a night like a watchman."

"Where does he eat, anyhow?"

"At the Grand," Janet says. "Anna feeds him a couple times a day, whenever he shows up. Not just scraps and leftovers, either. The day's specials or anything he wants."

"Anna would," Gus said to himself. Remembering the whole business with the accident of Anna's husband, the refusal to pay any compensation, the look on Anna's face toward him after the judge made his act of God decree regarding responsibility for the accident. He wished now he had simply told her there was no money, if he paid the compensation it threatened to send the Steam Works into bankruptcy, he wanted to pay the money but he couldn't. No help for it. Another failing on his part. Add it to the list.

"Besides," Janet says, touching his arm, "it's great PR, you giving a home to a homeless man. It makes you look like a great humanitarian, a benefactor to the community."

"Just how I want to be remembered," Gus muttered under his breath. "A great humanitarian."

His footsteps crunched along in the stillness; it was more of a path through the grass than a sidewalk on this side of the street closest to the river. From the houses on the other side of the street he heard muffled voices, a woman laughing, though all the houses along the block were dark as if deserted. From somewhere in the black sky overhead came the whistle of a nightjar chasing bugs.

"So, you really never knew Mal, never even saw him when he was a child growing up after he and his mother returned from Kansas," Janet says, in his mind walking beside him. He pictured her in the trim gray suit he liked so much, her spectator pumps. She stumbles slightly on the path; Gus reaches out to steady her, and to keep her close, safe, a rough part of town.

"It's true. I'm not proud of it, looking back on it now. There were reasons, of course, but no excuse. At the time there was so much going on with the company and all."

"Not even at Christmas? What about his birthday, were you even aware that he was having a birthday?"

"Yes. Perpetual, Grandmother's companion, would remind me."

"And did Perpetual go out and get you a present for him?"

"I always put some money in an envelope. . . . As I said, I'm not proud of the way I acted."

"But didn't you ever wonder about him?"

"It was at a time when the company was in transition. Father decided to retire and to leave me in charge. And I was no more prepared to run a company than I was to fly. I was an engineer, not a manager. Not only that, Father had gone along with my idea to concentrate the company's efforts and resources on the Lylemobile. As soon as he made that commitment I realized I never expected him to go along with the idea, not really; when it came right down to it I wasn't even sure I wanted him to. But there

Torn

I was, president of the Keystone Steam Works. We continued to produce our construction machines, the well drillers and steam engines, and they did okay, particularly in foreign markets, but we didn't make any improvements to them, we didn't even outfit them with the smaller quicker-starting engine I had developed. We just—I just more or less went along with what we were doing in the past while we tried to push the Lylemobile. And you know how that turned out. The car never went anywhere while the Fords and the Chevys and the rest of the internal combustion vehicles took over the market."

"Then the Depression came along and finished you off."

"Not completely. But it's certainly looking closer every day."

"All this to support a product, the Lylemobile, now the Zephyr, that once you were given the go-ahead to develop you weren't sure you wanted to do. What's that old saying: Be careful what you want, you might just get it."

"Those whom the gods wish to destroy, first they make mad. But that's too self-aggrandizing, even for me. I'm not mad, at least not yet, I'm just ill-advised."

"Thus spake the madman."

"That's not funny."

Janet pretends to make a sorry face.

"I think I pushed the Lylemobile on my father just to for the sake of pushing him. Oh, I believed in the vehicle all right, I knew it had real possibilities. But I wonder if I didn't push it on Father just to see how far I could push him, just to aggravate him, get under his skin. Something to prod him with."

"And in trying to get back at your father, the one you hurt most was your son. It's a wonder Mal even talks to you at all now that he's older."

The tent, as it was known in town, was erected on a triangular traffic island where Third Avenue angled into Sixth Avenue and Seventh Street. It was actually several tents together, their sides rolled up, with areas for food distribution, cooking, and general services. There was a line of twenty-five people or more, single men, families, women with little ones in tow, waiting to receive bowls of stew that they took to an area with tables. Gus skirted the kitchen area, looking for Mal or someone in charge, when a light-skinned Black man wearing an apron caught his eye and came over to him.

"Can I help you?"

"I was looking for Mal Lyle. I heard he volunteers here in the evenings."

"Indeed he does, indeed he does. But he ain't here this evening, we was wondering if the boy was all right."

"Yes, yes, I'm pretty sure he's fine. He just seems to have disappeared for a couple of hours."

"Not like him to miss a feeding time. We all hope he's okay. You tell him that if you see him, tell him Mr. Cox was inquiring about him."

"I will, I will," Gus said, anxious now to get away from the man, from the area, he felt out of place, conspicuous, exposed in some way. He started to walk away but the man kept talking to him.

"You don't know who I am, do you?"

"You said your name was Cox."

"William Cox. No, I didn't think you recognized me. I was a welder at your Steam Works."

"Oh. Oh, yes. Now I do. Recognize you. How are you?"

"No, you don't recognize me," Cox said without rancor, matter-of-factly. "But why would you? You folks up there in the offices while we're down there on the shop floor. I was a welder for you for twenty-two years. Twenty-two years. Yes sir."

"Well. I hope the company . . . was good to you. We certainly appreciated your service."

"Twenty-two years. Yes sir. I loved that company. But then you let us go, me and a bunch of the welders and fitters. Said there wasn't enough work to keep us on. And you got that right, there be days when we didn't have nothin' to do. We all swept floors to keep busy, that's when I first got to know Mal, he used to help us sweep because he didn't have nothin' to do neither." Cox laughed at the memory.

"Yes. Well. I'm sorry things didn't work out. . . ."

"Me too. I got babies at home. But that's the way things are now-days, with the Depression and all. Nothin' to be done. And don't you worry yourself. We're just fine." Cox looked around at the people lined up for food, the men and women working in the kitchen area, the children playing in a roped-off area. "I'm sure you're hurtin' too with the rest of us. All in your own way. You take care now, mind how you go. And don't forget to give our best to Mal when you see him. Fine boy. Fine boy."

Cox headed back to the kitchen, leaving Gus standing there feeling more awkward than ever. Then he came to himself and turned and walked back the way he had come, back toward the Steam Works.

"Did you see that?" he asked Janet. "I let him go, I fired him, and he's concerned about me, hoping I'm doing all right."

"The best thing is," Janet says, "that he genuinely likes Mal. And it doesn't have a thing to do with him being the boss' son. He just likes him, talks like everybody does."

"I ruined that man's life, and he's worried about me."

"But there you go again. You're making it about you. You haven't changed at all, have you? Learned anything."

"But it is all about me, isn't it? I'm the one who neglected his son for his own selfish reasons. I'm the one mismanaged the company and cost working people their livelihoods. I'm the one who has made all the mistakes, aren't I? What a fool, what a fool."

Gus walked on, through the darkness, passing through the light of one streetlight after another, retracing his steps along Third Avenue. The flats between the street and the river were dark, the train of slag cars gone by this time but in the distance along the river, the slag was being dumped down the embankment, the night illuminated red and orange against the clouds of steam, the valley's hills across the river flickering as if alive. He hoped Mal was back at the office, he wanted to talk to him, let him know that his father did care about him, that Gus would listen to him in the future. If Mal wasn't there, Gus decided to look at the books on his own to see what Mal had been talking about with Spalding's irregularities in the billing. What a fool. What a fool.

When he got back to the office, there was no sign of Mal, no sign that he had been there, but it didn't surprise Gus, he couldn't blame his son for trying to avoid him after the way Gus had treated him. Gus took the ledgers from the safe, and it didn't take long to see what Mal had been trying to tell him, particularly now that he knew where to look, there was no question that Spalding had been siphoning off money for some time.

"That son of a bitch. That son of a bitch. I should—"

"You should what?" Janet says.

"I should beat that little bastard to a pulp, that's what I should do."

"Don't be ridiculous. You should confront him with it, see if there is actually some reasonable explanation for what he did, and whether there is or isn't, fire him and perhaps bring charges."

"That's not good enough. I trusted him. I trusted him like a son."

"And whose fault is that, do you think?"

"I've been so wrong. So wrong." He could feel the anger building in him, now that he had a target, uncontrollable. Daniel had taken advantage of him, had hurt the company, had made a fool out of him. And to think Gus had listened to Daniel rather than his own son. Gus felt overwhelmed with his faults, his neglects. How could he have been so blind?

"How could I have been so blind? Not to see what was right in front of me."

"Be easy on yourself. You can see it now, that's all that's important."

"Oh Janet. Janet." He wished she was there with him, and was glad she wasn't. He had never before felt, or admitted to himself, that he wanted to hold her, take her in his arms. He ached for her now but was aware if he tried something like that it could be disastrous, it would open up a whole new area of their relationship, with the possibility that she might rebuff him, even laugh at him, things would never be the same with her if he tried to push it further. He depended on her, on her good counsel, just seeing her every day meant so much to him, brightened his world, he couldn't chance ruining that. He was afraid.

But there was still Daniel to deal with. He got up from his desk, closed the company's ledgers, and put them back in the safe. Got ready to leave.

"Where are you going now?" Janet says. "You mustn't do anything rash. . . ."

"I want this settled now. Tonight. That little son of a bitch isn't going to get away with this."

"You mustn't—"

"That little bastard almost destroyed my relationship with my son. What there was of it. He's going to pay for this."

"Gus. No." She reaches for him but Gus brushes her aside, hurried out of the office, down the steps and out into the night. Walking quickly to the hotel a block away.

Later, so much of what happened seemed only a blur. He stormed into the Grand, across the lobby, heading for the elevator, brushing aside anyone who was in his way. Eddie the bellman saw him coming and hurried forward to stop him.

"Hello there, Mr. Lyle, how can I—"

"I need the elevator, Eddie. Take me upstairs, third floor."

"Whoa," Eddie said, looking across the lobby as if to find help. "I'm not sure that's a good idea."

"That's where Daniel Spalding's room is, isn't it?

"Yes sir, it is, but I really don't think you should go up there unannounced."

"I'll announce myself, Eddie. Now take me upstairs."

"I'm not going to do that, Mr. Lyle. I'm sorry—"

Gus almost hit him but caught himself, he didn't want anything to get in his way of confronting Daniel. He looked around quickly, then headed for the stairs.

"Okay, Eddie, if that's the way you're going to be about it."

Gus cut across the lobby and started up the stairs two at a

time. That lasted till he reached the first landing and was so out of breath he realized he would never make it at that rate. He continued up, one tread at a time, still barely able to catch his breath, reaching the third floor, puffing away, as the elevator door opened and Eddie hurried out.

"Hold on, Mr. Lyle."

"What room is it, Eddie? Six, isn't it?" He gasped a couple times, sucking air, then gathered himself and headed down the hall toward number six. Eddie beat him to it, standing in front of the door, blocking it.

"I really don't think you want to do this, Mr. Lyle."

Gus did hit him this time, knocking him sideways to the floor. He banged with the side of his fist on the door, then without waiting for an answer stepped back and launched into it with his shoulder. The door burst open, sending him staggering into the room. Across the room Janet was naked on the bed, partially sitting up against the headboard, with Daniel naked facedown between her legs, his head in her crotch, his hands under her buttocks holding her like he was eating a watermelon, the two of them like beasts in the field, in flagrante delicto, like something exposed from under a rock, the look on Janet's face and Daniel's as he rose to see what was happening a mixture of surprise and wonder and fear. Daniel got to his knees, backed away from her, was trying to get up from the bed as Eddie came in and grabbed Gus and threw him back outside the room. Eddie went after him ready for a fight, but there was no fight left in Gus. He stood bent over in the hallway, arms buttressed on his knees, barely able to breathe, something inside him broken.

Nineteen

After he jumped out of bed and hurried into his clothes; after Eddie grabbed Gus and threw him out of the room, then collected him again and more or less carried him into the elevator and headed down to the lobby; after the other people on the floor who had come out of their rooms to see what all the noise was about went back inside; after Janet had scrambled out of bed as well and got into her clothes and took the stairs; after the night manager, all apologies and concern, materialized with another bellhop and they helped him move to another room until the door to his room could be repaired—Daniel sat on the edge of the bed in his new room remembering that, when the door exploded and he saw Gus come charging into the room, he thought he was a dead man. Thinking that was too close for comfort. Thinking this time he had played a game too far.

Because that's what it was to him, his playing around with his billings, a game. He didn't even need the money, the Steam Works—Gus—paid him handsomely for his services, he never even spent the money he made from the fraudulent billings, it all sat untouched in a special bank account. He would be hard-pressed now to explain why he had ever started the fraud in the first place, he guessed it was just something to do, wondering how such frauds were accomplished, wondering if he could get away with such a thing, he always did like to gamble. As it turned out, yes, he could get away with it, no one noticed at all what he was doing, that is until Janet picked up on it. He knew he should have stopped right then and there, but by that time he was too far into it. And he never thought Janet would be a problem. He had taken it as another game, another triumph, when he first suspected she suspected something, that he was able to seduce her; he thought he had brought her under his influence and control, the poor woman too enamored of him to ever pose a threat, he could get her to come to his room whenever he liked and, as he thought of it, service him. The relationship with her lost a lot of its luster and appeal, of course, when she told him that she was not only aware of what he was doing with his billing, but produced the photographs she had taken of the company's ledgers to prove it— when it turned out that she was no longer servicing him, that he was servicing her, sex on demand—but he found there was still an appeal. He was still getting laid a lot.

The truth was he actually owed Gus Lyle and the Keystone

Steam Works a great deal, they had bettered his life, he certainly never meant to do anyone harm. Daniel had grown up in Wilmington, Delaware, and had never set his sights higher than to get a well-paying job after high school, marry one of the girls he knew and dated, get a house and have kids and settle into what was becoming known as the American Dream. He thought he had achieved the first part of the equation, the well-paying job, working as a draftsman in a pottery plant, coming up with designs for pitchers and plates and coffee cups, when the Depression came along and rumors started flying around the shop about layoffs. It was purely by accident that he saw, in the back pages of *Popular Mechanics*—across from a Charles Atlas Dynamic Tension body-building ad with a bully kicking sand in the face of a ninety-seven-pound weakling—a classified ad for a designer with draftsman experience to work on a steam-driven car. He answered the ad, never expecting to qualify for such a position, but after a phone interview with Gus, he learned he got the job. Later he found out that he had been the only respondent to the ad, no one else apparently foolish enough to think a steam-driven car had any future, but by then it didn't matter, he had moved to Furnass and was happily ensconced at the Steam Works. In the beginning the work consisted of making drawings of Gus' ideas, but under Gus' tutelage, Daniel began to develop ideas of his own for the design of the car—he who had never shown much interest in cars of any kind, much less demonstrated any talent for mechanical innovation—found himself working at a level above himself, several levels in fact, making his own contributions to the design of the car reborn as the Zephyr. So, feeling good about himself, cocky in fact, invincible in some way, obviously smarter than average, a cut above the ordinary, it seemed only natural that he'd look around for other ways to spice things up in his life, such as muck around with his billing. You know, take a chance, see what would happen, living on the edge.

    He had always been a wise guy, a smart aleck, a show-off, known among his friends for his tricks and practical jokes; he loved the attention and the reputation, it set him apart from everyone else, made him seem fearless and daring. But this time he had gone too far, he knew that now; on the bigger stage of corporate finance, he had gotten in over his head. The trick now would be to get out of the situation he had made for himself. He kept thinking there must be some way to make things right. Maybe tell Gus how it had all come about, show Gus that he hadn't been serious, it was all sort of a lark, he was ready to make amends, give all of the money back, he had always intended to do so. Get things back to the way they were. If only there was some way to make good on the ledger entries now, reverse the billings or back them out or something, some bookkeeping trick. Susan MacKinnon, the bookkeeper at the company when he first started his finagling, might know. She was always nice to him back then, she was actually the one he was attracted to in the company, not Janet, the one he was attracted to and wanted to try to seduce just to see if he could; they had been friends, more or less, maybe she would know how to fix things. And she worked now right downstairs in the restaurant, was usually the last one to leave in the evenings, he had seen her a couple of times, maybe he could catch her before she left, it was worth a shot, he had to do something to try to make things right.

 He took the steps down to the lobby to avoid running into anyone. Across the lobby, Gus was being helped to the front door by his son Mal—Daniel wondered where he came from. After they were gone, Daniel continued to the restaurant and stepped in the door. The restaurant was dark, closed for the night, though Eddie the bellman was sitting by himself at the bar. Eddie was probably trying to settle down after his run-in with Gus, but Daniel didn't want to talk to him about it. The lights were on in the office at the rear of the restaurant, but there was no way for Daniel to get there without Eddie seeing him. He went back to the lobby and along the passageway to the back door, hoping to catch her on the way to her car, taking up a position in the service entrance among the shadows down the alley. It was a half hour later when a trapezoid of light broke across the darkness of the alley and Susan stepped out, the light from the door closing behind her. Daniel hurried to her.

"Susan, hi, it's me, Daniel."

The woman stopped. "Oh my goodness, Daniel. You scared the life out of me. What are you doing here?" She started to walk on toward the parking lot down the alley.

Daniel hurried after her. "Wait! I need to ask you about my billings at the Steam Works."

Susan hurried on, trying to ignore him. "I don't know anything about that, Daniel. I don't want any part—"

Daniel was frantic, he reached for her, turned her around to face him, gripping her upper arms.

"But you have to help me, there's nobody else—"

Out of the corner of his eye he saw a black shape coming at him at the same time Susan screamed and something came crashing down on his head and then hit him again and then there was nothing.

Twenty

"So, how did you hear about what happened?"

"I heard the sirens and then saw all the flashing lights in the alley. When I went over and could tell that the police and all were going to be there through the night, I opened up the restaurant and made coffee and sandwiches for them."

"That was thoughtful."

"It was also a good way to find out what all was going on." She looked at him knowingly over the rim of her coffee cup before taking a sip and replacing it on the saucer.

John Lincoln grinned and dipped his triangle of toast in the runny egg yolk.

There were days when he never thought about his face, or what remained of it. Whole days would go by, sometimes two or three in a row, when he would realize later that, after his morning ablution, his careful washing and applying of Vaseline and antiseptic, he hadn't thought once about his wounds or what he must look like. It had taken him years to get to that degree of unawareness and self-acceptance, but he was grateful that he had finally reached that point. Then there were other days when he could think of nothing else, was aware of nothing else, but his face, or its lack, that there was no face there. Or none that anyone would want to see. There were days when he was aware of his eyes wrenched out of position, the glob of his nose, the gaping holes in his cheek, the exposed entrances to tunnels and chambers within his skull, when his entire being seemed ready to be sucked into himself, when all that he was or ever would be was on the brink of being drawn into the sinkhole of what had once been the features that had identified John Lincoln Lyle.

"Daniel Spalding. The young guy who works at Keystone. Worked."

Anna nodded. "Somebody beat his head in with a whisky bottle. A whisky bottle from the trash there in the alley. They said it must have been four or five blows. Really brutal, savage. Somebody really wanted to make sure he was dead. They said there wasn't much left of the skull."

"Crime of passion?"

Anna shrugged.

"Sounds like it wasn't premeditated though. Whoever it was just grabbed the first thing they could find. Did Susan get a look at who it was?"

"She said it was dark and happened so fast...."

"Is she all right?"

"Yes. Seemed to be. Shaken up, of course. After the police were done with her I sent her home. I'll give her a call later on. Maybe go over to her house."

"That's weird though. Isn't it? That she didn't really get a look at whoever did it?"

"When it started she said she ran back inside. I would have too."

"I guess." John Lincoln ate the last piece of toast, finished his coffee.

"You want a refill?"

"No, thanks. I'm rattled enough as it is. All that going on right behind the hotel and I slept right through it."

There were days when he could feel the cheek that was no longer there, feel an itch or tickle on the surface of the skin, but when he'd reach to scratch it, he would realize anew that there was nothing there, it was a ghost itch, a phantom tickle, a sensation when there was nothing to give such a sensation. Today was such a day. He could feel the face that wasn't there. It was more pronounced when he took off the mask to eat. The mask was not only a protection to keep from shocking unwary people he encountered; it was a delineation of what was and wasn't there, in addition to being his wall against the world, his protection against flying particles, wayward dust, and bugs, flies, and gnats and even butterflies, inquisitive bees. And as with every wall, he had to be as careful about what was kept out as what might be trapped inside, a wayward insect that might fly right up into his head, get caught there, or trapped between the wounds and the inside of his mask, buzzing away, sending him into fits of trying to extricate it, slapping at himself like a crazy man. At times there seemed as many hazards with the mask as without, though it was certainly a relief to take it off. He wondered, though, didn't it bother Anna to see him this way? All his wounds exposed? It certainly wasn't a pleasant sight. That it didn't seem to disturb her was a marvel to him.

"So, do the police have any idea who might have done it?"

"No one concrete, at least according to what Chief Rocco said this morning when he was having his breakfast. But they have a couple of leads they're following up. For one thing, it seems our Daniel made himself some enemies at the Blue Room because of his pool hustling. But they think it was mostly penny-ante stuff, nothing that would warrant the kind of outburst that got him killed. But Chief Rocco said they're keeping an open mind."

"You never know. A local big shot gets shorted on too many bets...."

"But the really interesting thing is that when they were retracing Spalding's movements last night, Chief Rocco said they came up with a more promising suspect. Mal Lyle. Your nephew."

"Mal?"

"It seems they have a couple of witnesses who saw Mal following Daniel earlier in the evening. He followed Spalding into the Blue Room and kept an eye on him while Daniel was there, and then followed him when he left. No one saw where he went, but Eddie the bellman said Mal was hanging around the lobby later, keeping a watch for somebody, or at least that's the way it looked to Eddie. What? You look like you might know something."

"Mal had found out, or thought he had found out, that Spalding was defrauding the company."

"Do you think that was why he was following Spalding? That he was going to confront him about it or something?"

John Lincoln shrugged. "I don't know. But it's certainly a possibility."

"Another possibility, Chief Rocco said, is Gus. That could have something to do with Gus breaking down Daniel's door last night."

"What? What door? Gus did?"

"Gus went to Daniel's room last night and broke down his door. I thought it must have something to do with Daniel screwing Janet, Gus' secretary, I guess Gus caught them at it, but maybe he also found out what Daniel was up to at the Steam Works. You didn't hear any of that?"

"I heard something around ten thirty or so, but I was listening to the radio in my room and thought it must be something going on outside with the railcars or something. Jesus. I missed everything that was going on last night. What did Gus do when he found them?"

"Nothing. Eddie said after Gus broke down the door and saw what was going on, he sort of collapsed and Eddie could get him down to the lobby. Mal was there and they got him back to the Steam Works."

"Maybe he came back later, after things died down, and went

after Spalding in the alley."

"Would Gus kill somebody over something like that?"

"I wouldn't put it past Gus to do anything. Especially if he thought he was protecting his precious Steam Works. His steam car."

The fact was, for all intents and purposes, the mask *was* his face. His face *was* the mask. Had been that way for more than twenty years now. What the world saw of John Lincoln Lyle. Blank. Opaque. Empty. Impenetrable. Obscure. A white slate on which to project one's own emotions as if they were his, as if they could know what he was thinking and feeling behind his white wall because they thought they could imagine what they might think and feel in his place. Never seeing the turmoil going on behind the square of white cotton cloth, the churnings as well as the moments of peace. The pleasures and angers, the joys and sadnesses, the quandaries, the assurances. The fact being that he found in time he very much liked it that way. Liked it that not just anyone was privy to his thoughts and feelings. He could keep such things to himself. For himself.

He was thinking this as he sat there across from Anna. Neither one of them speaking for several moments. Simply enjoying each other's company. This woman with whom he could drop the mask and not send her running from the room. This woman whom he found he wanted to see behind the mask, see what he might actually be thinking and feeling. He was considering such things on some level of his mind when one of the waitresses started back to their area and Anna rose to meet her while John Lincoln put his mask back in place. After Anna talked to the woman she came back to the table.

"I have to go take care of some things. Without Susan here . . .," she let it trail away.

"No, that's fine. I've got some things I need to take care of."

He got up to leave but Anna put the flat of her hand on his upper arm.

"About Gus . . . you're not going to do anything. . . ."

Torn

He smiled at her, more to put her off than to reassure her, but regardless she didn't see it because of the mask.

Twenty-One

There was no one at the reception desk in the lobby of the Steam Works. The lights were out, the only illumination from the afternoon sunlight coming in the glass panels of the front doors; two phones were ringing incessantly with no one to answer them. There was no one in the adjoining secretarial area either, the lights out there as well, more phones ringing. John Lincoln walked back along the corridor and opened the door to the shop: no one. The place was empty. Deserted. As if everyone had been abducted, evacuated, sucked up, leaving their personal belongings in place, the tools they used for work. John Lincoln felt uneasy, as if he was trespassing, the site of another killing perhaps, some scene of violence or death. He retraced his steps back to the reception area and went up the stairs to the offices on the second floor.

Again, no one. The offices unoccupied, the engineering and drafting tables vacant, the desks in the accounting department, estimating, the mail room, abandoned. Dark at midday. The only light coming from the rear of the floor. He walked down the aisle, his fingers trailing along the edges of the slanted tables, glancing at the half-finished drawings of engine parts, electrical layouts, valves. Janet was in her office, standing at an open filing cabinet, fingering her way through the folders; when she noticed him, she looked at him blankly, without expression, and went back to what she was doing. John Lincoln crossed the room to the door to Gus' office, knocked with a knuckle, and went in.

His brother was sitting at his desk, in his shirtsleeves, his tie askew, looking at the company ledgers in front of him, surrounded by stacks of paper, letters, invoices, bank statements. When Gus saw who it was, he went back to his papers.

"What's going on?" John Lincoln said. "What happened? Where is everyone?"

Gus was obviously trying to ignore him. He continued looking at the papers in front of him, comparing numbers; when it was apparent that John Lincoln wasn't going away, he sighed, put the papers down, and looked at him. Resigned.

"I sent everyone home. The police were here, interviewing everybody about Daniel, nobody was getting anything done, so I figured they might as well go home."

"I see Janet's still here. . . ."

"I told her to go but she insisted on staying. I wish she wouldn't, I have nothing to say to her, nothing for her to do, I don't even want to look at her right now. But there you are."

Gus thought a moment. Braced his head on his hands, then looked at John Lincoln again.

"What I didn't tell them when I sent everyone home is that I'm not having them back."

"You're firing them? Everybody?"

"Everybody. It's done. Kaput. Fini. The Keystone Steam Works is no more."

"When are you planning on telling everybody?"

"I haven't thought that far ahead. I guess I'll put a sign on the door, they can read it when they turn up for work tomorrow."

"Ah, the personal touch. I'm sure they'll appreciate the thoughtfulness."

"You wouldn't understand about these matters. In matters of business, it's better that the message be quick and to the point. Otherwise you get yourself bogged down in explanations."

"No, I'm sure you wouldn't want that. To explain to your loyal employees why, after years of devoted service, you're putting them out on the street." Of course, John Lincoln thought, they can figure it out for themselves when you're arrested for killing your designer. I guess they're lucky you didn't terminate them the same way.

Gus was looking at him. "Is there some reason for this visit? Or did you just stop by to give me grief? As if I didn't have enough already."

John Lincoln ignored him. "What did the police want? Why

Torn

were they questioning everyone?"

Gus tried to go back to what he had been doing but gave up again. "They wanted to know if Daniel had any enemies, if there was anyone who had a grudge against him. They're trying to find a motive."

"And did anyone have a motive?"

"The police didn't share that information with me, if they found anyone who had such a motive." Gus looked at him curiously.

"I imagine they were looking for alibis too."

"Yes. I expect so."

"How about yourself? Do you have an alibi? I'm told the police are very interested in your actions earlier in the evening, knocking down Spalding's door and catching him in the act with Janet. Which was probably tied to what some people apparently have been telling you for some time, that Spalding was stealing from you and the company. If the police were looking for someone with a motive to kill Spalding, I'd say that's a pretty good one."

"Is that what this is about? And is that what you think of me? That I'd kill someone, for whatever reason?"

"From what I've seen of the world and the things that people do to each other, I'd say yes, I would think you're capable of such a thing. Especially from what I know of you."

Gus tilted his head, like a dog trying to hear or see better. "Well, I'm sorry to disappoint you, but I do have an alibi. After I left the hotel I came back here to try to put myself back together. I was here for several hours. Jake, the custodian and night watchman, was working the whole time out in the engineering department, we even talked a couple of times. That seemed to more than satisfy the questions of the police. But I suspect it will do little to change your suspicions of me. Little brother."

Gus was right. That did disappoint him. But it only made Gus' involvement more surreptitious, less direct, though no more commanding. "Then I guess that leaves Mal."

"What about Mal?" That got Gus' attention.

"I'm told he is the other prime suspect. If you have such an airtight alibi...."

"Why would they suspect Mal of anything?"

"Several witnesses saw him following Spalding earlier in the evening. And he was seen staked out in the lobby, apparently waiting for Spalding."

"He was there in the lobby when Eddie the bellman brought me back downstairs, Mal helped me to get back here."

"And didn't you think it was a little strange, for Mal to just turn up like that, to be at the hotel?"

"I didn't think about it...."

"And where did Mal go after he left you here at the Steam Works?"

"I don't know...."

"Evidently no one does. But it's not beyond the realm of possibility that he went back to the hotel to settle the score with Daniel. He saw you really distressed after seeing Spalding in his room with Janet. And then there's the whole business of Spalding's fraud and what it did to you and the company. The loyal and dutiful son, avenging his father." No matter how bad a father he has been, John Lincoln said to himself.

Gus looked stricken. "But he wouldn't, I know Mal."

"Do you? You certainly didn't pay him any heed when he tried to tell you what Spalding was up to. Mal even mentioned your ignoring him to his mother."

"Lily knew." Gus said it as if he just realized it's importance.

John Lincoln shrugged. It was obvious that a lot of things were finally getting through to Gus. It was about time. Welcome to the real world, big brother. The world you made for yourself.

Twenty-Two

Gus remained at his desk a long time after John Lincoln left, staring at the doorway where his brother had walked out. Half brother, he reminded himself. Occasionally, Janet, in the outer office, would cross his line of sight; she tried not to be obvious but would look in at him, her face blotchy from crying. After she passed a half dozen times, Gus got up and went to the doorway.

"Go home, Janet. I told you, just go home."

"Gus, if you'd let me explain—"

"There's nothing to explain, Janet. What's done is done. Now, go home."

"I didn't know—"

"I said, go home! I don't want to hear it! I don't need to hear any of it! None of that matters now. Go home!"

He waited in the doorway until she put on her coat, gathered up her purse, turned off her desk lamp and the overhead, took one last look at him, then made her way through the dark engineering department on her way out. He breathed a sigh of relief and went back to his desk.

He tried to pick up again where he left off analyzing the company ledger, comparing it to the stacks of receipts and invoices, but he had seen enough, he swept his arm across the desk and sent the book and papers flying to the floor. From his desk drawer he took a sheet of company stationary, took his pen from its upright holder, dipped the nib in the bottle of blue-black ink, and wrote, in large sweeping letters: *The Sins of the Fathers*. Underneath it, he signed his name, returned the pen to the holder, took his suit coat from the coat tree, not bothering with his overcoat or hat, turned off the lights, and left.

It was dark already though it was hard to tell whether it was from the late hour of the afternoon or because the smoke from the mill was heavier than usual. His car, Model 3 of the Lylemobile, the only car in the company parking lot, was covered with fine white particles, wisps of ash like a thin layer of snow. He got in and started the engine; when the car was ready to go, he turned on the wipers to clear the windshield. As he headed for the gate, the ash trailed off behind him in a thin white cloud.

He had to talk to Mal, find out what his son knew about what happened to Spalding. He thought he'd try Lily's first, where Mal had been living. When the police interviewed Gus—for the third time—that morning, they said they hadn't been able to locate Mal, that when they went to Lily's that morning she said Mal wasn't at home though maybe she had lied, trying to protect him. As he drove up the hill to the main street and then on up Orchard Avenue to Orchard Hill, his headlights coned through the smoke like driving in a fog. He circled the block with Lily's house, he even cut through the alley to check the garage, but he didn't see Mal's Chevy coupe. When he rang the doorbell, Lily peered out of the sidelight; he wasn't sure when she saw who it was that she wanted to open the door.

"Gus."

"I'm sorry to bother you."

"You look awful. Has something happened? Where's your hat and coat?"

He tried to laugh it off. "It's been a trying day, to say the least. Can I come in?"

"Yes, of course," she said, but he could tell she was hesitant.

"Is Mal here? I guess he's the one I've come to see."

"No, I haven't seen him since he came in last night, he's been gone all day. I supposed he was at work. Is something wrong?"

She motioned for him to follow her into the living room. As he got himself settled in an armchair across from her on the couch, he thought, So this is what my money paid for all these years. But that wasn't the case, was it, she told me she paid for this herself. Comfortable overstuffed furniture; floral prints; plush throw pillows; embroidered samplers on the walls. Definitely Lily's place. Could I have ever fit in here with her? She was still in her clothes from work: straight gray skirt, the bottom half of a suit, unfrilly blouse; a blue at-home cardigan draped cape-like about her shoulders; her feet in medium heels planted firmly on the rug. Seeing her again after seeing her the other day at the college, the first times in twenty years since they had their talks when she returned from Kansas, brought it all back to him, only confirmed to him what he knew in his heart: though he had played with fantasies about Janet, Lily was the only woman he would ever love, could ever love. It was the way he was wired. He sat leaning forward in the chair. Too ill at ease to lean back.

"So, tell me."

"You heard there was a murder last night behind the Grand Hotel?"

"They said something about it on KDKA but I didn't pay attention. Was it somebody we know?"

"Daniel Spalding."

"The designer who worked for you."

Gus nodded. Watching his hands holding each other between his knees.

"The young man Mal thought was defrauding the company."

"He *was* defrauding the company. It's definite."

"That's terrible, Gus. I'm so sorry to hear it. From what Mal said, you were working very closely with him, you must have got to know him very well. I'm sorry that somebody killed him. And sorry . . . that he took advantage of your trust."

Gus gave a small smile, an acknowledgment of her concern. Leave it to Lily to recognize the pain that Daniel's betrayal would have on me. Always attuned to another's feelings. So why didn't she pick up on my feelings when she came back from Kansas?

"Do they have any suspects? Any idea who could have done it?" She suddenly looked stricken. "They don't think . . . you. . . ."

"No, no. I had nothing to do with it, and I can prove I was in the office late. No, but they do want to talk to Mal."

"You know he wouldn't. . . ."

"I wouldn't think so, certainly. But as everyone has been making a point to impress upon me lately, yourself included, apparently I've never known him very well."

"But how could anyone even imagine . . . ?"

"They have several witnesses who saw him following Daniel earlier in the evening, and later Mal was staked out in the lobby of the hotel. And now he's more or less disappeared. It all sounds suspicious."

"I told you I saw him last night, when he came in. Or rather I heard him, I was already in bed reading. . . ."

"What time was that?"

"I don't know, maybe after two. . . ."

"The murder happened sometime before that."

"Gus."

"Do you have any idea where he is today? Because I want to find him before the police do."

Lily looked worried. Well, she should be worried, Gus thought. I would never have thought a son of mine could do such a thing either, but maybe it was as John Lincoln said, Mal thought he was avenging Daniel's wrongs against his father. I should have listened to him earlier, none of this would have happened if I had been a proper father. At least Lily and I can share this, the concern for our son. Something at last that we have in common. How do you like it, my dear? How do you like looking at the world through my eyes for a change? Seeing my concerns from my angle? Quite different, isn't it, from your snug little world here, your ivory tower at the college. He caught himself, surprised at himself, surprised that he would feel such things and with such vehemence, angers and resentments he never knew he harbored. What was happening to him? Who was this guy?

"I think I better be going," he said, getting to his feet. "I want to keep looking for him, there are a couple of other places I've thought of."

"Yes, of course," Lily said, getting up. Dazed.

He got as far as the front door, Lily trailing after him, when he couldn't stop himself from asking.

"I've wondered something. When you came back from Kansas, when you said you wouldn't live at Sycamore House, would you have lived with me if I had offered to get a place of our own, somewhere other than Sycamore House? Somewhere other than with the family?"

She looked at him as if considering whether she wanted to answer. She folded her arms about herself, tucked under the sweater draped around her shoulders, leaned against the wall as if to stop something from crashing through.

Torn

"Yes. I suppose I would have. I would have given it a try, if only for Mal's sake. But I was fairly sure when I came back that you wouldn't leave Sycamore House, you were too locked into the family home. Too locked into your family. Your family's way of thinking. An attitude about the world and about themselves that's endemic to the Lyles. Almost an affliction. Though I could see once I was settled on my own that it never would have worked between you and me, no matter where we were. That it was good that things worked out as they did. It saved a lot of complications and heartache later on to rectify the inevitable. Good night, Gus. Please let me know, or better, have Mal call me when you find him."

She shut the door behind him and at once turned off the hall light inside.

*

He stood on her front steps for several minutes, trying to gather his thoughts. The smoke was as thick as ever, carrying a musty, sulfuric smell, almost dirty, almost like overturned earth. Each light on the street, the streetlamps, the windows of nearby houses, was a globe of light, dissolved into minute particles, swarms, with little illumination. Beyond the college campus, the glow of the mill along the river rose from the cut of the valley, pulsing orange and yellow and red, flaring at times, dying down again. He was shocked at Lily's candor as he was leaving, to say that she might have tried to reconcile with him but was convinced they would never have made it together, irreconcilable as a couple, as parents even. Though he was more shocked at his feelings before that, at his resentment toward her, his anger. Inner rage. He never knew it was there before, never aware that he could, would, feel such things toward anyone, much less Lily. The woman he thought was above reproach, was above all women. He felt empty, drained, unsure of himself now, not a feeling he was familiar with.

He continued down the front steps to his car and sat there behind the wheel though not grasping it, not turning on the engine.

When he did finally start the car, rather than heading down Orchard Avenue toward town, he turned back into the streets of Orchard Hill, leaving the smoke as he got farther from the river, the streets not as blurry here. Overhead the bare branches of the sycamore trees lining the streets interlaced like filagree, like spiny fingers, like patterns of black arteries. The Sarver House, gray stone, in the style of an English country cottage, sat on a corner near the backside of Orchard Hill; every light was on, the windows only slightly flared from what remained of the smoke in the air, looking particularly cozy with their leaded panes, the many glimpses through small thick wavy glass of the life held within.

When he rang the doorbell there was no response for several minutes, then the door was flung open, Missy saying "Come!" as she was already halfway back down the hallway, ducking into the doorway to the dining room. He found her sitting at the table listening to the radio console in the corner, the remains of her dinner in front of her, a casserole of some kind. As he got seated across from her, she held up a finger to her lips to keep him from saying anything, pointed to the radio, then mouthed, Can I get you something? He shook his head but immediately wished he hadn't; he was starving, he hadn't bothered to eat all day, too much going on, but didn't want to be impolite asking for something after he already refused. He pointed to the radio and shrugged to ask what she was listening to. Missy broke her silence to say, "*Mrs. Wiggs of the Cabbage Patch.*" Gus shrugged again, he'd never heard of it. From what he could gather it was the story of a family struggling to make ends meet, a mother and a brood of kids, teenagers and preteens; the current crisis involved one of the boys who was to sing a tenor solo in church the coming week but whose voice had suddenly changed. Missy was enjoying the trials and tribulations immensely, but Gus didn't get it.

When the program was over in a few minutes, she clicked off the radio, turned to him.

"And to what do I owe this august honor? Pardon the pun, I've been wanting to say that for years."

Gus smiled without mirth. "Actually, at one time I wanted to be called August. It would certainly be better than Augustus in this day and age. But August never took. I guess I was fated to be a Gus."

"You certainly do seem to be a Gus, if I may say so."

"And you did."

"You'll understand if I'm surprised to see you. I don't believe you ever went out of your way to see me before in your adult life. Not even when we lived in the same house. Assuming that this visit was out of your way."

"Probably true. But then I never had to go out of my way. You were always there."

"Touché," she said, and scratched an itch under the hairline at the back of her head. "Maybe that's why I left Sycamore House when I did, the way I did. I was always there."

She got up from the table and gathered up her plate and coffee cup and took them into the kitchen; a second trip was to collect the remaining silverware, what was left of the casserole in the baking dish; a third trip was for the bread basket and butter dish; the fourth trip was to refill her water glass. Gus watched her comings and goings, this diminutive older woman, almost like a detailed scale model of a woman, in a shirtwaist housedress and sensible shoes, her white hair as if it cut with a bowl. He remembered when his father first introduced her to him, months before they were married, his father said, "Missy is going to be your new mother." All three of them realized that was the wrong thing to say; though Gus didn't react in any way at the time—didn't scream or holler or cry though he wanted to; no, even as a little boy that wasn't part of his makeup, rather, such things traveled deep inside him to either die there or smolder—it cemented his hatred for this woman, justified or not. Later, after he concluded—incorrectly as he came to understand later on in life—that his father had killed his mother so he could be with Missy, Gus would follow her about the house, watching her, trying to see for himself what his father saw in her, determine what her attraction was, because she never seemed attractive to him, couldn't imagine his father holding her—it would be like a little girl hugging a tree trunk—couldn't imagine his father kissing her—the few times he witnessed it he had to look away—couldn't imagine himself even giving her a motherly kiss and never did. He realized after his father died and it was just the two of them, him and Missy, living in that big house, that in all their time together he had never actually looked at her, just looked in her direction, saw only a dim figure of someone; if he had blinked and focused it could have been anyone standing there, sitting in the living room, walking down the hallway, he never saw an actual person. Much less a woman named Missy.

When she was seated again at the table, he said, "I can understand why you'd feel you wanted to leave. Though I guess I was surprised the way you did it. Just up and left. Without a word. I came home that night and you were gone. Poof. I wouldn't have known anything about it without Nancy to fill me in."

"Yes, I'm sorry about that. Not sorry enough at the time to do anything to make it easier, but sorry enough to know you deserved better than that. The thing was, once I made up mind, I didn't want anything to impede my decision to leave. Such as trying to explain the reasons to anyone."

"Can you explain it to me now? Now that you're settled here?"

"I was talking to John Lincoln and—"

"Ah, I should have guessed it."

"Meaning?"

"Everything seems to have turned topsy-turvy around here since the return of my little brother. He with the mask."

She brushed a few crumbs off the table into her palm and continued, ignoring him. "He got me thinking about accepting the status quo, living with things because that's the way things had always been. And there I was living in that house with you, the two of us who had never liked each other, who had never cared a whit for the other, living there simply because it had been that way for years. Please don't get me wrong, I was grateful that you didn't throw me out on the street after Malcolm died, you would have had every right to, the way I acted in those days. I've tried to make amends for my behavior then, the way I treated people, the way I treated myself for that matter. And I realized from talking to John Lincoln that the only way to really make things right was to completely change my life and that would start by living on my own. Though I have to admit I was also simply sick and tired of being associated with the Lyles and everything your family stands for. I know that's harsh—"

"No, no, I understand, I'm afraid. It's more than warranted. There are times I wish I could stop being a Lyle myself and all that goes with the name in this town. But I'm learning it seems that I'm the most prominent perpetrator of it all."

Rather than go on holding the palmful of crumbs, she decided to dump them back on the table.

"But none of this is why you came to see me this evening."

"No, no, you're right," Gus said, coming back to himself. "I was looking for Mal. I was wondering if you had seen him."

She looked at him quizzically. "Why would I have seen Mal?"

"I was wondering if he had come to see you."

"I repeat, Why would I have seen Mal? What would make you think he'd come to see me? I rarely saw my grandson—my step-grandson—when he was growing up, and I never saw him after he and his mother came back from Kansas. How old is he now, he must be in his twenties or so. I think the last place on earth Mal would turn up is here to see me. Why, what's he done?"

Gus thought a moment, how to put it. "Did you hear that someone got killed last night behind the Grand Hotel?"

"That wasn't Mal—"

"No, it's just . . . the police want to ask him some questions . . . they seem to think he might know something about it . . . and then he seems to have more or less disappeared today, nobody's seen him. I've been trying to find him . . . find out where he's been."

"I think I read it was some young man named Spalding, is that right? He worked for you, didn't he?"

"Yes. I'm surprised when you were talking to John Lincoln that he didn't mention Spalding, my brother's been poking around the business. Mal discovered that Spalding was engaged in some sort of fraud at the company, and John Lincoln seems to be on a private crusade to dig up as much dirt as he can about the company, and my handling of its affairs."

"No, John Lincoln didn't say anything about any fraud with Mal or Spalding. What he seemed concerned with was the possible mishandling of the Mercy Fund that prevented you from paying compensation to the worker of yours who was in that accident a few years ago."

Gus sighed, ran his hand through his hair. This again. Whatever happened to make John Lincoln think he was my self-appointed conscience? I don't need my younger brother to tell me my faults.

"There were extenuating circumstances. . . ."

"Yes, such as you didn't have the money to pay any compensation, you spent it all on your steam car. Things were so bad you even had to borrow money from me, remember? Though you and I both know there's no way now for you to ever pay it back."

Missy looked at him and made a regretful face, as if to say, I'm sorry, but you know it's true.

No, he thought, I was wrong, it's not about the person I've become, it's about the person I must have been all along. I'm just now seeing him, seeing me. And I don't like it. He pushed away from the table, got to his feet. "Regardless, I need to find Mal. . . ."

Missy looked up at him from across the table. "I'll tell you something else too, while we're at it. I don't think you came here tonight looking for Mal, I think you came here looking for Gus. I don't say that unkindly. I'm just at a loss as to how to help you find him."

Twenty-Three

When Mal Lyle arrived at work that morning, his father's car wasn't in the parking lot. That got him worried. Gus' car was

Torn

always in the lot, the first to arrive, the last to leave. It was especially worrisome because there were a couple of police cars parked in front of the administration offices. What was going on? Was his father missing? Gus had been in bad shape the night before, when Mal helped him at the hotel and loaded him in his car—Mal couldn't tell if his father had been drinking or what exactly was the cause of his problem, but it was certain that in his condition there was no way Gus was going to walk anywhere—but nothing that a good night's sleep couldn't rectify. Mal wanted to drive him home but Gus insisted Mal take him to his office, he had some things to do, some things that he needed to take care of, he'd be fine, fine, don't be such a worrywart. Nor did Gus want Mal to come in with him, when they got to the Steam Works Gus piled out of the car and inside, making sure that Mal saw that he locked the door behind him. So what were the police doing at the company this morning? Did it have something to do with Spalding's fraud? Had that come to light? But why wasn't Gus' car there? Had something happened to his father? He had to go looking for him, he couldn't waste any time, he should have stayed with him last night to make sure he was okay, going in the office now would only get him bogged down with the police asking questions, there was no time to lose. He turned his car around and headed uptown.

He was about to turn onto Fifteenth Street Extension, the gravel road that led up the valley's hill to Sycamore House, when Gus in his Lylemobile came roaring down the hill in a cloud of dust, almost hitting him as he flew past, Mal had to brake hard, Gus' eyes straight ahead, gripping the wheel like his life depended on it, never seeing Mal about to turn in the road—or maybe Gus did see him, ignored him on purpose, Get out of my way, coming through. Mal sighed. Either way, that would be Gus. But at least it told him that his father was okay, just running late for some reason. Mal thought of going back to the Steam Works, but whatever was going on, particularly with the police there, sounded like a good place to avoid for a while, let his father sort it out, it was his mess. Though as long as he was here, he decided to go on up the hill and take a look at the old homestead, he hadn't seen it up close since he and his mother came back from Kansas. He drove up the gravel road through the bare sticks of trees, halfway up the hill, and turned into the drive for the house, the circular drive in front of the house, parking where he had a good view of it among the leafless sycamores.

Since he and his mother returned from Kansas when Mal was six, he only knew Sycamore House, the family home, as a place where he couldn't be. Where he didn't belong. Cast out of the garden, as it were. Though not even cast out, it was a place where he wasn't supposed to be in the first place. Before their trip, he had vague memories of living in the house, more impressions than actual images, a grand place, of dark high-ceilinged rooms with shafts of sunlight angling down through the gloom, of motes of dust swirling through the sunlight whenever anyone passed, of slanted lawns on the hillside where he played, and trees, everywhere trees. Then he and his mother went away, he didn't know why, to his grandparents in Kansas, his grandfather a tall burly Scot, a hell-and-brimstone preacher who used to pick him up and rub Mal's cheek against the stubble of a beard on his own, his grandmother an ever-smiling prairie woman in a faded housedress and nothing much to say. Then he and his mother came back to Furnass just as suddenly as they left but they didn't stay at Sycamore House, he wasn't even allowed to go there with her when she went to see his father, he had to stay at the hotel with a hired woman till his mother returned.

He soon enough understood that Sycamore House was no longer home. In a few weeks his mother moved them to Orchard Hill, to a small yellow-brick two-story house with a pillared front porch across the street from Covenant College where she got a job in the registrar's office. He grew up to the accompaniment of the bells of the college, the bells of the library ringing the hours and half hours, the bell in the tower of Old Main marking the changes of classes. Between classes the sidewalk across the street from their house would be crowded with dozens of students grabbing a quick smoke, giving the area the name Tobacco Road, the strict Covenanter code of the college prohibiting smoking on campus as well as most anything else that might be fun. But it was an ideal environment for a boy, the rolling lawns of the campus, the winding walks, everyone nice to him, the coeds thinking he was cute, the son of Mrs. Lyle from the registrar's office. The shopping forays downtown with his mother taught him that the Lyle name held more power in town than just at the college, but that recognition had less to do with his mother than with his father—"Oh, you must be Gus' son." But Mal had no contact with the man, his father never came to see them, he more like a rumor than a presence in Mal's life, and Sycamore House was forgotten with the warm new world on Orchard Hill.

Mal wasn't sure how long he had been sitting there—five minutes? a half hour?—remembering, daydreaming, when a Black woman probably a few years older than himself came out the front door and stood on the porch at the top of the stairs, looking back at him. He got out and went over to the steps, trying his best to look nonthreatening.

"Can I help you?" the woman said. No nonsense.

Mal laughed a little. "You're right, I'm sure I look a little weird. I was looking for Gus, my father, but I saw him leaving."

"Your father? Are you Mr. Mal?"

"Yes. I know I must look suspicious, sitting there in the car like that, but it's been a while since I've seen the house up close like this. It brought back a lot of memories. I'm sorry if I disturbed you."

"You didn't disturb me. Would you like to come in?"

"Well, yes, I guess so."

"Either you would or you wouldn't."

"Yes. Yes, I would. Thank you. Are you sure that would be all right?"

She turned and led the way back into the house. "I can't see why not. You're a part of this family as much as anybody else, as far as I'm concerned. Have you had breakfast? I can fix you something."

"As a matter of fact—"

"Come on."

She led the way down the hallway and into the kitchen and motioned for him to take a place at the table as she tied on an apron. "I'm Nancy."

"When I was a little boy there was a woman here named Margaret."

"That was my mother. I remember you, we used to play together before your mother took you to Kansas. Then I didn't see you again. My mother would bring me over special to play with you though I was a few years older. I guess it was also to help take care of you, your mother didn't do a bad job but she got busy with things. Your father was very demanding and she had to do a lot of things for him, I figured that's why my mother brought me over. We used to have a lot of fun together."

"I was thinking while I was sitting out there in the car, I seemed to have some memory of playing with somebody in a sandbox out back but I couldn't figure out who it might be."

"That would be me. Scrambled eggs and fried ham be all right?"

"It would be wonderful."

Nancy smiled and opened the refrigerator. She kept talking as she worked at the drainboard and the stove.

"You live with your mother up on Orchard Hill. Missus Lily. How is she these days? I haven't seen or heard about her for years."

"She's doing great. She's registrar at the college, seems really happy."

"That's nice. Please say hello to her for me."

"I will." Mal thought a moment. "I'll bet you haven't heard anything about me over these years either."

"I heard something, when you started working at the Steam Works, your father said something about it to Missus Missy while she was here, but it wasn't very much."

"I wouldn't think so."

"Why don't you ever come visit to the house?"

"I guess for the same reason why my father never talks about me."

Nancy looked at him over her shoulder and turned back to the eggs in the pan. "So, why don't you and your father get along?"

"I've often wondered. He seemed to never want to have anything to do with me. I wouldn't be working at the Steam Works now except my mother told him he should hire me."

"That sounds like the Missus Lily I remember. "I know your father is a difficult man at times, but he was always real good to me and my family. One time, when my mother still took care of the house, our house burned down, along with the house next door. Mr. Gus, he not only sent his carpenters from the Steam Works to rebuild it, he had them rebuild the house next door too, and never asked for a penny, not even for the materials. Not only that, he moved our whole family into that back wing here until our house was done, treated us just like family, he did. He even said we could continue to live here if we wanted to, here in the house with him, but we wanted to go back to Blacktown where we belonged, we never would have been comfortable living here, it wouldn't have been right, Sycamore House is for you Lyles, not for us."

She placed a plate in front of him with two dippy eggs, a sliced tomato, slices of ham, and buttered toast. Mal looked at the plate, looked at her, looked back at the plate.

"It won't eat itself, you know," Nancy said, and started cleaning up.

"I had never heard that story about my father."

"I s'pects there are lots of stories you never heard, not being allowed to live with the rest of the family. So, why were you looking for him this morning, if you two don't get along so well?"

"There was some trouble last night and I sort of ended up taking care of him, getting him back to his office afterward. Then when I got to work this morning, his car wasn't there so I wondered if he was all right."

"That was nice of you. It doesn't sound like you have all that much against your father."

Mal thought a moment. "No, I guess I don't. Well, I do and I don't."

"You have trouble making up your mind, don't you?"

Mal ignored the comment. "I get frustrated because he won't listen to my ideas, even though that's supposedly why he hired me, to give him ideas. I even tried to warn him about some bad things I've seen going on in the company but he just ignores me."

"I know he was really upset this morning, that's why he was late, he didn't get back here till dawn this morning with the murder and all. . . ."

"Murder?"

"You didn't know? There was a murder last night, behind the Grand Hotel, another employee at the Steam Works, I think his name was Spalding."

Mal stopped, a corner of bread dipped in egg yolk frozen halfway to his mouth.

"What's wrong?" Nancy said, hurrying over to look at the plate of food.

"No, no, nothing's wrong. I hadn't heard . . . about a murder. . . ."

"Mr. Gus said the young man got his head bashed in with a bottle and the police had a lot of questions for him, they were talking to him about it all night like he had something to do with it."

Gus must have found out about the fraud, Mal said to himself, found some proof of it, that's why he went to see Daniel at the hotel earlier, busted down the door but found him with Janet and couldn't confront him about it right then. I'd never seen my father like that, that angry and broken even. After I left him at his office, he could have gone back to the hotel, found Daniel in the alley for some reason and . . . I knew I should have gone in with him, made sure he was okay. That's why the police were back at the works this morning, looking for him, gathering evidence. It's a good thing I didn't go in with the police there, I would have had to tell them how he was acting, breaking down Daniel's door, his state of mind. I need to talk to Father before I talk to the police or anyone

Torn

else, find out from him what happened.

As he finished up his breakfast, he said to Nancy as she stood at the sink, "Do you suppose it would be all right if I stayed around here today? I'd like to look around, if you don't mind, I promise I won't get in your way...."

She looked at him over her shoulder. "I don't see nothing wrong with that. As I said, I figure it's your house as much as any other Lyle. Was there anything special you were looking to see?"

"No, not really. I just wanted to wander around a bit, bring back some more memories, revisit what I might have known once upon a time."

"You look to your heart's content. Let me know if there's anything I can help you find. I'll be in and out with my dust work. Besides, after Missus Missy left it will be nice to have a real live person in the house for a change. This place has so many noises and spooks around I never know who's coming or going."

After finishing his breakfast he started his tour of the house, visiting each room, the two wings of the house, first the Farther Wing as it was known where he and his mother and father, Lily and Gus, lived before the trip to Kansas, then the Near Wing on the opposite side of the house where his grandfather Malcolm and Missy lived, and the rooms on the second floor in the original central part of the house, the upstairs bedrooms of his great-grandmother Libby, the matriarch of the family, at the front of the house with the balcony overlooking the front as if so she could see who was coming and going, and beside it the connecting room of her attendant, Perpetual, crowded with her magical plants for making ointments and potions, as well as the separate bedrooms of the twins, Malcolm and Missy's children, John Lincoln and Mary Lydia. Rooms full of secrets and mysteries, lives that he never knew beyond the perspective of a six-year-old, only heard of, visiting them as if entering some secret shrines, touching the chairs and dressers and wardrobes, items left on dresser tops and bedstands, sitting on the beds, trying to imagine what their lives had been like here, what it would have felt like then to be a

Lyle, to have belonged. He passed Nancy in his wanderings several times but she only smiled and nodded and went on about her business, content to let him go about his.

    He saved the room he was most inquisitive about till last, the room he wanted most to investigate, the study on the first floor at the front of the house, its French doors opening out onto the veranda and a view of the front lawn, the town below. It had been his great-grandfather's study when Colin Lyle first built the house; later his grandfather Malcolm and then his father Gus inherited it in turn as they took over the company and the role of master of the house. It was a room full of books and history with heavy baronial furniture, the walls covered with pictures of the Keystone Steam Works and photographs of the machines in action in the field, paintings of the town and the valley. Mal sat at the great oak desk for a while before exploring the tall bookshelves, the rows of philosophy and theology and the great works of literature. But the real treasure for him was behind the glass of a row of barrister bookcases: the original drawings and patents for the company's steam engines and various machines, thrashers and tractors, well drillers and steam shovels, rollers and bulldozers. He sat for hours at the desk going through the papers, enthralled. Comparing the dates and whoever drew up the various documents, it became apparent that his grandfather Malcolm, whom he could barely remember, a tall thick tobacco-smelling presence, was a marketing genius who spread the name Keystone Steam Engines across the world, but who was no match as an engineer to Mal's great-grandfather, Colin, the founder of the company who not only developed the basic principles of the Keystone Steam Engines but the farm and construction equipment that they powered; in the same way that Mal's father, Gus, who made a genuine contribution to the company in reducing the size and start-up time for the steam engines, was in the long run no match as either an engineer or marketer or even a businessman compared to his forebears—a gradual degradation of the Lyles' talent and ingenuity and entrepreneurship over the generations that Mal actually found comforting, his own lacks only the latest manifestation of the family's descent and diminishing power; studying the company's history he didn't feel so bad about himself for once, maybe there was a place in the world for a liberal arts major with a modicum of engineering training after all.

When he tired of sitting at the desk, he took several of the latest patent applications over to the daybed and read for a while until he fell asleep. When he woke several hours later the room was dark, the day gone from the French doors, though there was light coming from the hallway. He turned on the lamps in the study and went out into the hall; the lights were on in the rest of the house but Nancy appeared to have left, no one else was around. On the deacon's table in the hall was a note:

Stew in the icebox. Heat 350 for half hour. Rolls in the bread drawer. Beer.

He went to the kitchen, took the Dutch oven from the refrigerator and put it on the stove per Nancy's instructions. While it was heating he made a tour of the rest of the house to make sure his father hadn't returned, then freshened up in the bathroom and went back to the kitchen. Nancy had laid a place for him at the table; he opened a bottle of beer, served up the stew in the bowl provided, and sat himself down. He was midway through the meal—beef stew, lots of carrots and peas—when his father burst through the front door and stomped back to the kitchen.

"There you are. Everybody's been looking for you."

"And I came here looking for you."

"How long have you been here?"

"All day. Just after you left this morning, actually. You drove right by me on your way out and never saw me."

"Do you know the police are looking for you?"

"I thought they might be. That seemed like a pretty good reason to lay low until I had a chance to talk to you. What did they say to you?"

"They wanted to know what happened in the alley, of course."

"I'll bet they do."

"They want to know what you know about it."

"I know Daniel got his head bashed in with a whisky bottle. And I know he had it coming."

"Mal! You can't say that."

I'm having a conversation with my father. A real live conversation where he is actually listening to what I'm saying, and responding to me. "Well, it's the truth, isn't it?"

"They know you were following Daniel last night."

"Somebody at the Blue Room probably told them." A conversation between father and son.

"And that you were lurking about the hotel later."

"I don't know about the lurking part, but I was there, certainly. You know that, I helped you get back to your office."

"We've got to get our stories straight. Do you have an alibi, for later?"

"Do you? You were the one who bashed down Spalding's door."

"This isn't funny, Mal. The police think you had something to do with Daniel's murder. Did you?"

Did I? Wait. He thinks I did it?

"You can't try to hide from them, son. You've got to go talk to them, I'm sure there's a perfectly good explanation for what happened."

That's the first time my father ever called me *son*. "Of course there's a good explanation. I'm sorry he died, but he really did have it coming. He took advantage of you, he hurt you, he hurt the company. There's plenty of people who would call those killing offenses."

Gus looked stricken. He sat down heavily, almost fell, onto one of the kitchen chairs. "It was because of Daniel's. . . ?"

"I'm sure that's the what the police will figure when it comes to a motive. But don't worry, Father. There were obviously no witnesses to what happened in the alley; if there were, the police would be coming to arrest me, not just ask questions. And for the same reason there must not be any evidence pointing to whoever did it. So you don't have anything to be concerned about. If the police find me, fine, I'll talk to them for as long as they want. But I'm not going to go looking for them. If they want me I'll be at home." Look at him sitting there, it's like his whole world has fallen apart. I don't know why he's so upset, I'm the one whose father thinks he's capable of murder. Thanks, Dad, thanks a lot.

Mal got up and left the kitchen, left the house, without saying anything more.

. . . *in the kitchen of Sycamore House, Gus Lyle sits at the table thinking about what his son Mal just told him: He knew about Daniel getting clubbed with a whisky bottle, how would he know a detail like that if he wasn't there, if he hadn't been involved, he wasn't around today to hear something like that from the police or anyone else, he must have been there, and he said Daniel had it coming, he said Daniel took advantage of me, hurt me, hurt the company, Mal must have done it for me, to get even with Daniel because of me, just like John Lincoln said, Oh Mal, Mal, my son, I've been so unfair to you over the years, how could I ignore you like I did and still you would do something like that for me, I was so wrong, so wrong, but maybe it's not too late to do something for him, if the police have only circumstantial evidence I can do something to get him in the clear, I have to do something to make it right, that's the least I can do for all the years I did nothing for him, and why not, I've made a mess of everything anyway, there's no reason to go on, it would be one good thing I've done in my lifetime, ending it with one grand gesture; Gus gets up from the table and goes through the downstairs of the house to his study, sits at the great oak table and takes a sheet of paper from the center drawer, a pen from the holder, dips the nib in the bottle of ink, and writes,*

> *I killed Daniel Spalding, he had it coming for what he did to the company and my family*

signs his full name, Augustus Malcolm Lyle, *looks at the clock for the exact time, 10:01, dates it, folds it, and takes the paper out to his car and puts it under the windshield wiper of the Lylemobile, then goes back to the house, goes to the kitchen and puts a handful of safety matches in his suit coat pocket and goes out the back door, crosses the rear yard, the level area his father made special for lawn croquet and the time he tried to get John Lincoln interested in playing baseball with some of the toughs from down the hill, a fiasco when John Lincoln wanted no part of playing with the very kids who chased him home from school every chance they got—his father never asked Gus to play—a fiasco when the toughs took over the backyard and they had to have his grandmother's companion, Perpetual, scare them off with the threat of putting a hex on them, goes to the stable that once housed the family's surrey and carriages as well as the stalls for the family's matched teams that Gus subsequently converted to a garage for his personal Lylemobiles, takes one of the several ten-gallon cans of kerosene and carries it out and places it on the path back to the house, returns to the stable and takes another of the cans of kerosene, unscrews the lid, and splashes it around the inside of the old wooden structure, empties it and figures that ought to do it, goes to the door and with a safety match from his pocket lights a rag he found on his workbench that he soaked in the kerosene, the rag taking a few seconds to catch fire but when it does it goes up quickly, Gus tossing it into a puddle of kerosene near the several other cans of kerosene and leaves the stable, the whoosh! of the flames igniting coming as he's halfway back to the house with the other can, the yard and the house and the surrounding trees suddenly lit up from the flames behind him, bright as daylight, a sudden sunrise, his shadow preceding him in the back door of the house and into the kitchen where he takes time to stop at the stove, turns off the pilot light and turns on all the taps, opens the oven and turns on the gas for that too, goes into the downstairs hallway, unscrews the lid from the can and*

Torn

begins splashing kerosene on the walls, the rug, the furniture in the living room where his stepmother Missy lounged on the sofa reading magazines and eating bonbons, spending particular time to soak the sofa where she used to lie, then continues into his study, splashing kerosene over the bookcases and leather chairs and the grand oak desk until the can is almost empty, pauses a moment to take one last look around, notices the scale model, one-half inch to one foot, he once had made of the first Lylemobile sitting on top of the barrister bookcases, carries the model along with the ten-gallon can over to his favorite leather chair, empties the can over the drawings and letters and a copy of Clifton Fadiman's *Lifetime Reading Plan* sitting on the end table beside the chair, sits down, gets himself comfortable, the model of the Lylemobile on his lap, then takes a couple of safety matches from his pocket, rubs their heads together until they ignite and drops the flaming matches on the fuel-soaked papers beside him and waits, only a few seconds as it turns out until the papers flame, then the fire follows the trail of kerosene, racing across the room and down the hallway where for the briefest instant Gus could swear he sees the figure of a woman all white and translucent watching him from the doorway as the chair he's sitting in catches fire and from the back of the house comes the explosion of the leaking gas in the kitchen as the house is instantly consumed in flame and he sits there and doesn't care and doesn't move a muscle as the flames take him and all the world and consciousness itself becomes fire . . . as Mal in his Chevy coupe reaches the end of the gravel lane from Sycamore House down the side of the valley and enters the streets of town heading toward the main drag to go home, going over in his mind the conversation he just had with his father—*You think I did it? Don't worry, Father, there's no witnesses or evidence that can tie me to what happened to Daniel*—and realizes he never actually told his father he didn't do it, he was so disturbed and, yes, hurt that his Father would think he was capable of doing such a thing, for whatever reason, that his father didn't know him any better than *that, though it also occurs to him that he was actually no better than his father, he had been afraid it was his father who killed Daniel, a case of mistaken identities between father and son that would be funny except it wasn't, he needs to set it straight so there's no doubt in his father's mind and he needs to do it tonight before there are any more confusions; at the next intersection in the stepped cross streets down the hill he makes a sweeping U-turn, unfortunately right in front of a police car coming up the hill but Mal doesn't see it until it's too late and he doesn't care anyway, he guns it and heads back up Fifteenth Street, saying under his breath, "To hell with you, coppers, I've got more important things to worry about," the police in the car finally getting their wits about them and turning on their flashing lights and siren as they give chase, Mal in his Chevy coupe with a half-block start and gaining distance being decidedly difficult to catch and Mal knows it, his only thought at this point being to set things right with his father, they talked tonight for the first time ever like a father and son should and he doesn't want to lose that now because of some misunderstanding caused by his failure to explain himself fully, gets to the end of the paved city streets and speeds up the gravel lane of the Fifteenth Street Extension but can see already that something is very wrong at Sycamore House: the stable behind the house is on fire, the flames in the already smoky air creating a pulsing red and orange glow up the hillside and the black trees, and he floors it, the car fishtailing in the gravel, the loose stones pinging up against the undercarriage as the police car enters the lane behind him, his rearview mirror all flashing red lights, the siren wailing though the police inside their car are seeing what Mal is seeing, the stable ablaze up the hillside, and have forgotten all about Mal and his U-turn and are racing up the hill behind Mal toward the fire at the same time that one of them is on the radio reporting the fire and calling for the fire trucks and better send an ambulance too, and they'll need backup from whoever is available, Mal almost to the entrance of the drive leading to the house when suddenly the back of the house explodes sending flames shooting up into the night sky and racing through the house until in seconds the entire house is ablaze, the force of the explosion rocking his car and sending him careening off into the brush before he can get it stopped, the police car coming up the lane stopping short right where it is, as Mal gets out of his car and runs toward the house and up the front steps hoping against hope that his father somehow survived the blast and that Mal can get him out of this inferno but the heat and the fire and the smoke pouring out the front door make it impossible to go farther, driving him back, but then on the chance runs along the veranda to the blown-open French doors to the study, calling, "Father! Father!" but there's no possibility of entering the room either with the fire and the smoke and the heat but as he starts to retreat he sees briefly his father sitting in the leather chair, just sitting there, the chair itself in flames, the man in flames, a man on fire, but then the room itself dissolves in fire and Mal is barely able to get off the porch, has to vault over the railing and falls heavily onto the lawn, the two policemen there who pick him up, help him to his feet, the three of them hunched over running down the lawn as the whoosh! of the flames goes up behind them, the trio reaching the edge of the lawn and staggering into the line of bushes as below in the town the fire whistle sounds and the sirens begin and Mal turns back to look at the house, flames burning from every window on every floor, the roof catching fire now, the walls sheets of fire, so that it is a house of fire and flame, to be burning now forever in his thoughts and memories, the Lyle family's, his father's, funeral pyre . . . as below in the town, the whistle and sirens have alerted folks that something is going on, something big and potentially disastrous, the promise of such always enough to attract a crowd, people step from their houses and on first impulse look down the stepped streets of town toward the river and the mill and though the mill tonight with the heavy smoke is in full display of clouds of orange and red and yellow, nothing seems out of the ordinary, nothing unusual in pulsing clouds of orange and red and yellow, and perhaps a bit disappointed, they happen to look up the hill, up the steep streets to the dark hills of the valley above them and lo and behold there is a fire in the woods on the hillside, two fires though close together, a fire at the Lyle place, Sycamore House, Wow, up there on the hill, do you see it, the whole place looks like it's on fire, let's go take a look, a good fire like this doesn't come along very often and certainly not involving a town landmark such as the Lyle house, the people of the town getting in their cars or if they're close enough walking hurriedly up the hilly streets, neighbors greeting neighbors, men who only a few hours ago saw one another on their shifts at work greeting each other now like long-lost friends, mothers who saw each other as they shopped at Kroger's or the A&P or talked over the back fence greeting each other now like sisters, a surprising carnival atmosphere in the air though not without its touch of urgency and Oh isn't it terrible, I wonder if anyone was home at the time, the crowds getting as far as the start of the gravel drive of the Fifteenth Street Extension when the police stop them from going farther, Stand back, stand back, let the emergency vehicles through, the crowds evening out along the last streets at the top of the town jockeying for a good spot, looking up through the bare trees trying to get a glimpse of what is going on, the town not treated to a spectacle of this magnitude since the derailment and subsequent fire and explosions of half a dozen tank cars near the old lock on the river a few years back or the Old Home Days Festival that last took place at the town's quasquicentennial all of ten years ago so everyone feels they are entitled to a little excitement . . . in the parking lot of the Colonel Berry Hotel, across the street from his office below the Masonic Temple, David Laughlin as he approaches his car, one of the few left in the lot at this hour, happens to look up the hill and see on the hillside of the valley the glow of a major fire among the trees, thinks Oh my lord, Sycamore House, can it really be on fire?; thinks, Well, I wonder what that will do for Gus' financial situation?; thinks, I should be alarmed or sad or concerned, but I'm not, why is that?; thinks, That'll teach him, the dumb bastard, I could have helped him if he had only*

Torn

asked, the fitting end to a once worthy family and exemplary company, what happens when you leave things in the hands of the terminally inept—and no more concerned than that gets in his car and drives to his home in Furnass Heights, up the face of the valley by route of Eleventh Street Hill, wondering where Anna is this evening and what she is doing, and, as he often does, wonders if she ever thinks of him . . . while across the face of the valley wall, half a mile along the wooded slope from the burning Sycamore House, in the section of town known as Blacktown, the several streets of small frame houses, some that could almost be called shacks, where a large number of the African Americans in town live, though since the Depression the area has become despite itself more of an integrated neighborhood because of the families of out-of-work Whites moving in, Nancy North hears the commotion outside and steps out on her porch and sees the glow coming from the direction of Sycamore House and takes off running along the path through the woods that leads to the house, the path she takes every morning to the house and every evening back home, the same as her mother before her, running along with her neighbors who are curious about what's going on, Nancy emerging from the woods, stopping at the edge of the clearing to see her beloved Sycamore House in the final throes of burning, the house to which she has devoted her life as her mother and father did before her, gone, that way of life gone, in a way her own family gone, and feels a loss deeper even than when her own home burned, feeling she has no life outside of the Lyles, outside of taking care of this house and the members of this family, and yet, and yet, has a curious sense of relief too, release, a kind of newborn freedom, a burden lifted, some shackles removed, lighter and more herself than she can ever remember, saying to herself, Nancy North, shame on you, you can't feel no such thing, you loved those people and those people loved you, as she finds herself humming, singing to herself as she watches the house burn, wooden embers collapsing in upon themselves, sparks swirling up into the night, *I went down to the valley to pray, studying about those good old ways when you shall wear the starry crown, good Lord, show me the way, O mourner, let's go down . . . as in her second-floor apartment in the remodeled house she grew up in, her aged mother and aunt stowed safely in the first-floor apartment she made for them below her, Janet Santelli is standing at her kitchen sink doing her dishes when she sees in the darkness beyond the window a glow on the hillside of the valley, the flames of Sycamore House burning, and thinks of Gus last evening busting into Daniel's room at the Grand Hotel and catching them in bed, Daniel eating her as they called it, a command performance on her part, what she figured he owed her for keeping quiet about his false billings at the company, and thinks as sad as it is that Daniel was murdered last evening she can't help feeling that it had something to do with Gus and getting even for Daniel's transgressions, thinks of Gus, that lonely portly bumbling man, her boss for how many years, thinks of the way he always watched her, followed her with his eyes, unable apparently not to watch her, unable to do anything about his infatuation and desire such as make a move on her or propose an arrangement, she would have been open to ideas, and then he went and ruined the good thing she had with Daniel, aware that whether Gus had anything to do with Daniel's death or not her relationship with the young man would have been over regardless, her hold on him gone, looks at Sycamore House burning on the hill and thinks of Gus and thinks, I hope that dirty-minded old lech burns with it . . . as in her family's English country-style cottage on the backside of Orchard Hill, Missy Lyle listens as Harlow Wilcox gives the final sign-off for* Fibber McGee and Molly, *repeating the offer of two free spinning tops, one with the picture of Fibber, the other with the picture of Molly, both for just sending in a tracing of the logo from a bottle of Johnson's Wax—"Not available in stores, get yours today!"—then turns off the radio and goes through the downstairs of the house turning off lights, dining room, kitchen, living room, saving her father's study at the rear of house for last as she always does, just happening to look out the French doors,*

Torn

usually only filled with the darkness of the backyard, but tonight with a glow in the distance far to her left, on the hillside down the valley where she knows the Lyle house is, Sycamore House on fire; well, she's not surprised, it almost seems fated to happen, some tragedy, some dramatic end to the house and family, and she opens the doors and steps out into the backyard, into the chill night air, walks down to the edge of the yard overlooking Walnut Bottom Run, able to hear the sirens in the distance now, imagines the flames though with the heavy smoke-tinged air all she can see is a pulsing glow on the dark hillside, thinks of Gus, the last years they lived together in the big house though their lives rarely touched, each keeping to themselves, thinks now that she should have treated him better, his whole life for that matter, she was his stepmother after all, no matter that he obviously hated and resented her, she had been the adult, she should have reached out to him more to try to make his life better, that troubled unpleasant unhappy little boy, and not much better as an adult, she could have reached out to him as they shared Sycamore House, but she realizes that if she had any of it to do over she wouldn't do any part differently, the truth being she simply didn't like him, either as a child or as an adult, if she is brutally honest with herself she didn't much care what happened to him either then or now, why is that, how can we feel such indifference to people we should care about, she doesn't know but she knows it's a fact of living as she turns back and makes her way across the black yard toward the lighted doors, thinking, Rest in peace, Gus, now why did I think a thing like that, almost as if he was dead . . . as in the living room of her yellow-brick house across the street from the college, Lily Lyle has just finished going through the stack of applications for next semester when she hears the sirens of the fire trucks from the Orchard Hill firehouse racing by, down Orchard Avenue toward the main part of town, and thinks, Good heavens, what now, there's been so much trouble of late, thinks about the murder behind the Grand Hotel of that young man Mal was telling her about, the police coming to see her a couple of times on account of it, the first time to make inquiries about her ex-husband Gus, the second time to make inquiries about her son Mal, both times her being unable to tell them anything they wanted to hear, and then all the trouble Gus was having with the Steam Works, he didn't say so in so many words but she got the idea he might have to close the doors, after all he's done over the years to keep the business afloat, after all his dreams have gone bust, and thinks of Gus, thinks of his two visits to her lately, after all this time, admits to herself she was undoubtedly unfair to the man when they were married, she knew what his family was like when she married him, she shouldn't have held the Lyles against him when they tried to reconcile after she fled to Kansas, shouldn't have set as a condition to their getting back together that they not live at Sycamore House even though she found living there intolerable, she should have tried to make it work, that's what love is about, isn't it, she should have let them get established again, acquainted with each other and Gus with Mal, a trial period at the big house and then later broach the idea of living somewhere else, when their marriage and their love were secure, because seeing him again this past week has brought it back to her that she did love him, for whatever reasons, loved him still, loved his dreams and his persistence and his determination to make things happen, it drove her crazy that things never worked out for him, maybe that was what she wanted to get away from in the first place, drove her to run away to Kansas, not to get away from him, but that she simply couldn't stand to see him hurt all the time, couldn't stand to watch him put down by the world only to climb back to his feet again and go on, maybe it was a case that she loved him too much, cared for him too much, could there be such a thing that would drive people in love apart, she guessed so, she was living proof, maybe it wasn't too late for them after all, maybe in a day or so she would call him and invite him to dinner, see if time had given them perspective on their original feelings for each other, Mal could be there too, just like a real family, it was warming to think that maybe they could still get back together . . .

as near the top of Fifteenth Street and the start of the Fifteenth Street Extension leading up to Sycamore House, Susan MacKinnon stands beside a maple tree where Eddie Moon told her to wait as he walked on up the gravel lane toward the burning house, the policeman blocking the lane greeting him as an old friend and letting him pass, Eddie heading up the hill toward the dozen emergency vehicles, fire trucks and ambulances and police cars, all the flashing red lights lined up in front of the burning house, only the burning framework of the walls remaining now like the skeleton of the house, as the upper stories collapse in upon themselves sending sparks and flames swirling up into the sky, then the lower floors as well, nothing left of the house except the flames and the smoke as Eddie appears coming back down the lane, exchanging comments with the policemen on guard again before coming across the street to her, standing with the tree between them, both of them continuing to look up the hill, not at each other.

"He was in there."

"Gus?"

Eddie nods. "Mal saw him in the study just as the fire was starting, but the flames were already too strong, he couldn't get to him."

"That's awful," Susan says, hands clasped to her breast.

"The thing is, Chief Rocco says that Mal told him that it looked like Gus was sitting there in the fire, not even trying to save himself."

"Maybe he was unconscious or passed out or something."

"Not according to Mal, I guess. But there's something else. They found a note on the windshield of Gus' car, written by Gus, saying he was the one who killed Spalding. He even signed it. Mal says it's Gus' hand all right, his signature."

Susan just stares straight ahead.

"So it's over," Eddie says.

"Can we be sure?"

"Chief Rocco says that's that. End of story. As far as anyone will ever know, Gus did it. I have the feeling he wrote the note to keep any suspicion away from Mal, but it doesn't matter."

"And there's no question about you...."

"They got somebody to pin it on, that's all they care about. And they're not going to do anything to jeopardize their best source of information of what's going on in town, now, are they?" Eddie smiles to himself.

"I was worried about the neck of the bottle."

"Funny thing, Chief Rocco told me. One of his guys picked it up and got his own prints all over it before they thought about it, any other prints on it were ruined. Pity, Chief Rocco said."

Susan thinks a moment. "I do feel bad about Daniel...."

"No one touches you. No one. Ever." Eddie tries to soften. "I think we should still wait a couple of years."

"Yes. I need to make sure Matt graduates okay and gets a job and all so he's taken care of."

"Of course. I'm still thinking Canada. Montreal or even Quebec. Someplace where they speak French, I can use what I learned in the war, I know enough words to get us started. Someplace totally new, totally different, I'd say France but Germany looks dangerous again, I think another war is coming."

"Someplace where we can get a fresh start. Someplace where they don't care about mixed couples."

"We'll find it," Eddie says and steps closer. For a moment he looks like he's about to kiss her but remembers where they are, who he is, and looks away, the two of them keeping a respectful distance between them, happy just to be in each other's company this close, the fire giving them a good excuse to be out in public, standing there into the night as the fire finally begins to lessen and burn itself out, becoming only a heap of ash and embers though as fierce in its own way, more persistent, enduring, than when it was all flames . . . as shortly after midnight, in his suite of rooms on the top floor of the Grand Hotel, John Lincoln Lyle, in a burgundy velvet smoking jacket over his street clothes, sitting in the tall-backed brocade-upholstered easy chair that he has

Torn

designated as his chair, *the floor lamp with its tasseled shade shining down over his shoulder as if it is kibitzing, his mask sitting on the end table beside him, in the Victorian-decorated room that he has come to consider as some sort of bizarre cosmic joke, but* his *bizarre cosmic joke,* puts down his well-thumbed copy of Spinoza's The Ethics *and goes to the windows in the corner tower, looking out at the smoke-filled night, the world appearing as if it ends just beyond the windows except in the direction of the mill to his left, the line of coke ovens and the blast furnace and the trio of Bessemer converters, even one of the tall smokestacks, throwing flames up into the night, the heavy particle-filled air capturing the flare of the flames and softening them into a series of radiant orange and yellow plumes, when there is a knock on his door and he crosses the room and opens it, Anna D'Angelis, Anna O'Brien, standing there.*

"I'm sorry if I'm late, there were a few things I had to take care of...."

"You're not late, seems to me you're right on time."

"You're sweet," she says, putting the flat of her hand on his upper arm as she passes into the room. She takes off her coat and hat and places them on the love seat, then sits down beside them. "I usually have more help closing up but Susan took off early, there seems to be something going on, some fire someplace, that she wanted to go have a look at. Seems like half the town was going to take a look but I don't know where it is."

"You're not a fire chaser," John Lincoln says, smiling, sitting in his chair again.

"I saw a fire once," she smiles. "I don't think I need to see another."

"I heard a lot of sirens and all but I'm like you, you've seen one fire—"

"You've seen them all," she laughs.

"Can I get you a drink?"

"I could use one."

John Lincoln gets up and goes to the tray on top of the wood filing cabinet that serves as his bar and pours them each two fingers of bourbon in a rocks glass, no rocks, takes hers to her and sits down again. They lift their glasses to each other: "Salute."

"Salute e cent'anni." After taking a sip, she says, "The smoking jacket looks nice. And it fits okay?"

"Fits perfect." John Lincoln holds out his arms to demonstrate.

"You're not just wearing it because you don't want to hurt my feelings, are you?"

John Lincoln takes a swallow of his drink and stands up, offering his hand. "Silly woman."

Anna takes a swallow of her own drink, stands, and takes his hand, both of them carrying their drinks with them into the bedroom. There are small lamps with black shades on each nightstand, a black-shaded floor lamp in one corner of the room. They each undress on their side of the bed, the arrangement decided without discussion their first time a few nights earlier, John Lincoln on the right, Anna on the left, each laying out their clothes on the straight chairs in the room then the two of them meeting under the covers, though again as decided on their first night, by instinct not discussion, with Anna turned away from him and John Lincoln spooned against her back, his left arm under her, lying that way for a while, each enjoying the feel of flesh on flesh until Anna takes his hand and presses it to her lips and then sucks his fingers and he works his fingers against her lips and tongue, their version of kissing, her one hand reaching behind her and gripping his penis as he begins to work his right hand over her body, cupping her breast, stroking down her abdomen and stomach into her crotch, his left hand continuing to finger the lips of her mouth as his right hand fingers the lips of her pussy until neither one of them can stand it any longer and he removes his left arm and in the process rolls her onto her tummy, taking the pillows from his side of the bed and working them under her pelvis, she lifting up slightly to accommodate them after they discovered the first night that it worked better if he has some leverage with her ass lifted in the air and he kneels between her *legs, looks at her buttocks and the soft soft skin of her back and shoulders and thighs and thinks she is the loveliest thing he could ever imagine in his life, wets the tip of his erection with spit and enters her slowly, gently, beginning their steady practiced motion as she moans softly and he stares straight ahead into the painting above the bed, the image of a cabin on a wooded stream with a bird of some kind arcing across a blue clouded sky, trying to give himself as much time as possible, as much time as she needs, though this time he sees superimposed upon the picturesque scene the image of his own face reflected in the glass covering it, this torn and shattered grotesquerie that he has come to accept as himself and which she has apparently come to accept as well, though by mutual unspoken agreement they both have realized that the closeness of their lips actually touching could in a moment of passion or carelessness cause him real danger and pain while the simple truth is looking at him at a conversational distance is one thing and the spectacle can be grown used to and even forgotten about or at least overlooked but facing it head on, up close, inches away in an act of love would be a little much, more than he could ever ask or expect of her, though desire in their case has found a way—love being a liquid thing, seeking its own level, conforming to what contains it—he is happy beyond measure, happier than he ever thought he could be, and thinks as he is coming to climax, Oh my God, oh my God. . . .*

Twenty-Four

"May he rest in peace."

The Right Reverend William Gavin, pastor of the Ezekiel Tabernacle of the Divine Spirit, closed his Bible, bowed his head, and held his Bible in clasped hands in front of his crotch as if protecting himself. The less than a dozen mourners standing around Gus Lyle's open grave site bowed their heads as well, at the same time as they looked around under their eyebrows to see what they were supposed to do next. Howard G. Griffith, the funeral director, gave a little cough to get their attention and motioned with his head that they could leave. A strong wind was blowing over the hilltop cemetery, small waves of maple and oak leaves tumbling and frolicking over the rough grass, sending a shiver over the bouquets of dead flowers and the plantings on some of the gravestones. Twenty yards away, keeping a respectful distance until they were called upon, four laborers with shovels waited to get on with the business of lowering the casket into the earth and filling it in before lunchtime. As the mourners started to file back to their cars, a noticeable lack of contact between them, a half dozen crows, as if obligatory for a cemetery setting, stacked in the branches of a bare oak tree, complained about the intrusion into their day.

John Lincoln Lyle, standing with Anna D'Angelis, Anna O'Brien, watched the mourners go, the few people from town who bothered or cared enough to come to the funeral and make the trip to Grandview Cemetery. Mal and his mother, Lily; Missy, a standout in a white brocade sheath dress, ankle-length white knit coat, and matching hat; David Laughlin and the woman John Lincoln recognized as his secretary; another woman he recognized as Gus' secretary, Janet something-or-other, looking pissed off rather than sad; and a handful of men he guessed were workers at the Keystone Steam Works. Not the kind of turnout he would have expected on a crisp clear autumn day for the owner of what had been one of the town's leading companies and employers. Though he told himself perhaps that was the problem: had been, wasn't any more. Plus, there was the stigma attached to Gus now: it was generally accepted in town that Gus had been the killer of Daniel Spalding—Chief Rocco said as much, reading the note Gus left on the windshield of his car at the press briefing. Case closed in the collective consciousness of Furnass. As Mal was leaving with his mother, he looked at John Lincoln briefly but turned his attention back to Lily, taking her arm to help steady her in the uneven grass on the way back to his car.

After everyone else had gone and the four workmen with their shovels were approaching the grave, Anna squeezed his arm.

Torn

"You're right," John Lincoln said. "It's time to go. They have a job to do."

They started walking slowly back across the grass, Anna still holding his arm.

"Was there some reason why you wanted to stay?"

"No. I just got to thinking. About Gus and all. Up until recently, if you had asked me why I came back to Furnass, I would have said it was about wanting to see my sister, Mary Lydia, again. I'm not quite sure what I had in mind, but it was like we had some unfinished business between us. We had always said we'd end up together, living together, I don't think it was incestuous, I was too young then to really know what those desires could be. But I don't deny now that they were probably part of it too. Some amorphous undeveloped desire on my part. But I realized that day I saw her that wasn't it at all. She wasn't the reason why I came back. I knew those feelings for her were over long ago. It was something else entirely. Yes, I wanted to see her, to see that she was okay in her life, not that I could do anything to change it for her if she wasn't. But I had a deeper and more devious—more vindictive—reason for coming back. Lily got me thinking about it, raised it as a possibility the day I went to see her. I wanted to get back at Gus for all he did to us as kids, for all he did to me. Filling my head with all his hatred of our father. I have no idea what I thought I was going to do about it once I was back here, what kind of revenge I was after, but I'm sure now it was my intention regardless. That's terrible, that I would hold those hard feelings, that hatred really, all those years. But I have to admit it's true."

They had arrived at Anna's car; they stood facing each other.

"Let's take a walk," Anna said.

John Lincoln nodded. They started along the gravel path circulating among the graves, Anna taking his arm again, huddling into him against the steady wind.

"So. Did you? Get your revenge?"

"That was why I was digging up anything I could find that was amiss with his handling of the company. My talks with Laughlin and Missy and all. I was convinced even before I came back that the Steam Works was failing because of his mismanagement, and I was determined to find out why, even though it was literally none of my business. When I found out he had been tapping into the Mercy Fund to finance the work on the Lylemobile so there was nothing left to pay for your husband's compensation, I thought I'd found it. But the fact is, he didn't do anything wrong, it was perfectly within his rights to move those funds around if he wanted to. It may have been ill-advised as far as the business was concerned, it may have been somehow morally wrong in regard to taking care of the employees as the company had always promised to do. But there was nothing illegal about it. But that didn't stop me pushing at him, pushing and pushing. I was unfair to him. No, he shouldn't have said all those things against our father to Mary Lydia and me, he shouldn't have set us against our father that way. But he had his reasons, I can see that now, he was a tormented guy in so many ways. I should have been more understanding."

"Don't be too hard on yourself," Anna said, watching her feet as they walked along the gravel path. "I doubt that there was anything you could have said to Gus that would have made one whit of difference to him or to the relationship between the two of you. Some relationships are destined to fail, just like some are destined to happen."

"I guess so."

They continued walking for several minutes, the wind sweeping around them, pressing against them, listening to the crunch of their footsteps in the gravel, the crows calling in the trees.

"What I want to know," Anna said, pulling away a little to look at him, a smile on her face, obviously trying to lighten the mood, "is why a Black pastor from a church your brother obviously never set foot in officiated at his funeral?"

John Lincoln laughed. "Mal said that was the only minister he could find who would do it. At least that's what he claimed. I guess he tried a couple of the other churches in town, that big Presbyterian church downtown, the Covenanters, but they all begged off for some reason or another. And then he thought of this guy, he knew Reverend Gavin when they were kids, they went to school together. I think Mal liked the idea of throwing it up in the face of people, portraying his father as truly neglected by the town. Which, of course, he certainly was, witness the small turnout. But still. . . ."

"Have you talked to Mal since the fire?"

"Just briefly. We were never close, so I was surprised he reached out to me at all. As a matter of fact, he asked me if I would consider taking a position in the company. It's left up to him now to run things, and I think he wants as much help as he can get."

"What did you tell him?"

"The last thing I am is a businessman. I told him that I was flattered by the offer, but he would truly be better off without me."

The lane came to an overlook at the edge of the cemetery. Spread below them was the panorama of the valley and the town below. The wind was even stronger here, a continual presence, buffeting them as they stood there, tearing at the tails of his overcoat, threatening to blow away his hat. As they tucked in against each other, John Lincoln put his hand over Anna's hand clasping his arm.

"Which raises the question," Anna said, "what are you planning to do? Are you planning to stay in Furnass?"

"Oh yes. I'm thinking of doing some writing. Maybe a history of the town, or the family, or the company. I'm not sure. Or maybe a novel, I've got a couple of ideas. And I have a lot of other reasons to stay. I'm quite comfortable at the hotel, I think living in a hotel suits me, I like the lifestyle, and it has a wonderful restaurant. And I've found something else I never thought I'd find." He squeezed her hand against his arm.

"John Lincoln, you know, don't you, that I would never leave Warren. He needs me."

"Of course. I know that. I would never ask you to. That's a given.

In time, if the situation would change, perhaps we would change, but that's not even a consideration now."

"Thank you. For understanding."

He took her bottom lip between the sides of two fingers, holding her gently; she in turn kissed his fingers, working her tongue between them. Below in the valley the life of the town went on, the flames rising from the mill, the smoke drifting over the streets stepped up the side of the hill. At the far end of the valley a train was rounding the curve heading toward the station. Beyond the bridge that closed off the end of the valley like a gate, a riverboat on the Ohio pushed a half dozen barges upstream.

"Do you mind if I take off the mask?" he asked. "It will feel good in this wind."

"Of course not."

He took off the mask, enjoying the sensation of the air against the wounds. After a moment Anna giggled.

"What are you doing?"

John Lincoln was lifting his head, lowering it, tilting it this way and that.

"My wounds. Sometimes when the wind hits them just right, it's like they give a little whistle. Can you hear it?"

Anna leaned close. "Maybe you can learn to play a little tune."

They looked at each other and laughed.

"I think we should be getting back," Anna said, hugging his arm.

John Lincoln nodded. He put on the mask again, looked at Anna to make sure she approved, and they headed to the car. The wind now nudging them along.

Acknowledgments

There are three people—friends, actually; dream catchers—without whom I could never have brought these books to publication:

> Kim Francis
> Bob Gelston
> Jack Ritchie

I also thank Eileen Chetti for struggling through my quirks of style and punctuation. For converting all the Books of Furnass to eBook formats, I thank Umesh of Vsprout (umesh@vsprout.in), who works such technical wizardry from half a world away. Kim Francis of Magpie Communications, LLC is invaluable for her work in publicizing the Books of Furnass. Our splendid award-winning website at RichardSnodgrass.com was designed and maintained by Chris Nesci and Crew at My Blue Robot Creative Agency. I particularly thank Jack Ritchie who years ago took on the task of designing the covers of these books so I wouldn't, in his words, embarrass myself, and who has long served as a sounding board, bullshit detector, and all-round good friend. And then, of course, there's my wife Marty....

Because it involved trench warfare to a degree that hadn't been experienced in European warfare before this time, World War I saw a terrible increase in traumatic facial injuries. For more information regarding the attempts to treat these horrific wounds, see "The Birth of Plastic Surgery" on the website of the UK's National Army Museum at https://www.nam.ac.uk/explore/birth-plastic-surgery. To see the heart-wrenching portraits of these victims by one of the participating surgeons and an artist in his own right, Henry Tonks, go to the Tonks Pastels at the Gillies Archives at the Collections of the Royal College of Surgeons, London and the Slade School, UCL: http://www.gilliesarchives.org.uk/Tonks pastels/.

Richard Snodgrass lives in Pittsburgh, Pennsylvania, with his wife Marty and two indomitable female tuxedo cats, raised from feral kittens, named Frankie and Becca.

To read more about the Books of Furnass series, the town of Furnass and its history, and special features for *Torn*, go to www.RichardSnodgrass.com.

Made in the USA
Middletown, DE
15 October 2025